BLOODSHOT

BY

MAC FORTNER

A CAM DERRINGER SERIES

DISCLAIMER

The characters and events portrayed in this book are a work of fiction or are used fictitiously. Any similarity to real persons, living or dead, is coincidental and not intended by the author.

<u>DEDICATION</u>

Thanks to my wife Cindy, who is always there for support and love, just when I need it the most. And to you Cam Derringer's fans. You keep asking for more of Cam and Diane. I'll keep writing as long as you keep reading.

This is book two in the Cam Derringer series. Be sure to pick up book 1–KNEE DEEP.
 KEY WEST: 2 BIRDS 1 STONE – Book 3
 MURDER FEST KEY WEST – Book 4
 HEMINGWAY'S TREASURE – Book 5
 SAME OLD SONG – Book 6

Don't miss the Sunny Ray series:

RUM CITY BAR

BATTLE FOR RUMORA

Bloodshot

Prologue

I **was walking through Central Park**, on my way to our favorite park bench, to meet Robin Anderson, my soul mate.

It was a beautiful spring day. Mothers were watching their children play on the grass while they took advantage of blankets laid under trees. Beauty was the furthest thing from my mind though. Everyone I passed looked as though they had a personal vendetta against me. Paranoid?

A tall, broad-shouldered man in a long overcoat was walking toward me. One hand in his coat pocket and the other clutching a newspaper, he looked ominous. I raised my hand to my waist where I had a nine-millimeter attached to my belt. As we came closer, he looked right at me and nodded his head in a manly greeting. I slightly sidestepped, brushing against a branch, and a flurry of blossom fell onto my suit.

I turned and watched him for a few seconds to make sure he didn't turn back. He sauntered slowly past, not paying any more attention to me than the fish in my uncle's lake did to the many lures I would throw at them.

Stepping off the curb to dodge another cherry tree, I barely missed being hit by a truck. I jumped back to the sidewalk and waved at the driver apologetically.

I took a drink of my coffee and let the robust liquid warm my throat. It relaxed me, and I was lost once more in my world of complacency.

I didn't hear the shot or feel the bullet that hit me as I lifted my cup to my lips once more. I did, however, hear the next shot fly over my head and a return shot wiz back past my head in the other direction. I was caught in a crossfire.

I dove onto the pavement striking my injured arm first. My arm was on fire, and I don't mind telling you, that hurt.

I used my left hand to pull my gun from my belt and glanced up in the direction I was facing. I could see a shooter, a woman, on one knee, arm stretched forward, pointing a large gun over my head in the direction of the sound of the gunfire behind me.

I saw her fire two quick shots and roll to her left. She came back upon her knee and fired two more.

Her shots were answered from behind me in a sporadic volley of explosions from her apparent nemesis.

I rolled to the left toward the curb, trying to get to the pickup truck that had almost hit me, which was haphazardly parked there with one tire on the curb. I thought it might offer some protection.

Every time I rolled onto my injured arm I gritted my teeth harder. If I lived through this, I would be sore for a long time.

Reaching the truck, I rolled under it. Safe, I thought.

I peeked out. I could see the woman, still on one knee, aiming her gun to my left and swinging it slowly toward me, as if she were following someone with her aim. I heard another torrent of gunshots from directly overhead. The woman dove and rolled to her right.

I turned my head to see where the shooter behind me was going. A drop of oil leaked off the truck's undercarriage and hit me between the eyes.

I lost sight of both would-be assassins while wiping my eyes.

I saw the truck I was lying under sink slightly and then heard the door slam. The engine came to life. This wasn't good at all. The heat from the exhaust pipe was now bearing down on me.

I scooted to my right as fast as I could, ignoring the pain in my arm, and barely cleared the undercarriage before the tires started squealing and the truck jumped the curb and sped away.

I fired two shots at the tires but missed. I saw the sparks fly off the back bumper where my bullets had struck. I heard three more shots coming from the direction of the woman. Then there was silence.

"Cam, are you okay?" the woman yelled, running toward me.

It was Robin. I hadn't even recognized her in all the commotion. My soul mate had almost killed me.

Chapter 1

What did I do to you to deserve that?"

"I'm sorry, Cam," she said. "I was waiting for you when I saw him jump out of his truck."

"Are *you* okay?" I asked, gritting my teeth and holding my injured arm.

"Yes, we're both fine, but we need to get you to the hospital," she said.

She pulled a handkerchief from her purse to wrap around my arm.

I heard the sirens in the distance.

I sat up and pulled my sleeve over my elbow. I couldn't look.

"The cops are almost here," she said as she was inspecting my arm. "I have to leave before they get here or I won't get away in time to catch him."

She stopped what she was doing.

"Oh brother," she said, a look of half relief and half derision on her face.

"What's the matter? Is it bad?" I asked, now thinking that I might lose my arm.

She started laughing.

"You're not even hit, you big wuss. The round hit your coffee cup, and the coffee splashed on your arm."

I looked down at my arm.

"Well, it was hot," I said in defense.

"I don't think we'll need an ambulance."

"Are you sure I'm not hit?" I asked, inspecting my arm more carefully and sounding a little disappointed.

Robin is the chief agent of the New York FBI. She was promoted and transferred there four months ago after she broke a case in Key West involving, murder, boat-jacking, and international terrorism. She saved my life and solved the case I had worked on for five years, ever since my wife became a missing person and they discovered her boat abandoned in the Bahamas.

My name is Cam Derringer. I was born in Key West, went to school in New England, and returned to Key West to practice law. Life was good until Melinda disappeared.

I dedicated five years of my life to finding the men responsible for my wife's disappearance. It turned out the sheriff, who was helping me in my investigation, was the one who murdered her. Thanks to Robin, he was held responsible for the act. He was killed in front of me on a boat just as he was about to drop me over the side with a concrete block fastened to my leg. How could I not love her?

And now she had saved me again. I almost wished the bullet would have at least nicked me.

"No, you're not hit, thank God. Would you like another cup of coffee?" she asked and giggled.

"Don't make light of this. That coffee could have scalded me."

"I need to call this in," she said, raising her cell.

Robin walked around trying to relieve tension while she was talking to the dispatcher. She finally hung up and came back to me.

"Can you get up?" she asked.

I was still sitting on the sidewalk. I rolled to the side my good arm was on, pushed myself up to my knees, and then raised to a standing position.

I was a little embarrassed, and my suit was wet. I guess I'd rolled into a puddle of water under the truck. I placed my gun back in its holster.

"Cam, I'm going to have to leave you now. I need to find this man as soon as I can. This is the closest we've been."

"It has to be Bloodshot," I said.

"I think so."

"This was different than his usual MO."

"Yeah, that's what worries me. I think he wanted to kill you."

She kissed me and ran in the direction of the parking lot.

The crowd had returned after quickly dispersing when the gunfight started.

I held my hands in the air and said, "Okay, break it up, folks. Nothing to see here. I have it under control."

That got a few laughs. I hadn't intended it to be funny. I picked up my coffee cup and dropped it in a trashcan.

I walked back to where it all took place searching for a clue. I saw a business card lying in the street where the truck had been sitting. I picked it up and unfolded it. It read, "Cam Derringer–Hand–$25,000"

"What the hell?" I said aloud. "Just like the others."

I looked around the area for another clue. There weren't any.

One thing I knew for sure—someone had a contract on me. It had to be with Bloodshot. The sirens were almost upon me now, so I hailed a taxi.

Chapter 2

One month earlier:

"❝Hi **Diane**," I said, answering the phone after checking the caller ID. "I miss you."

"And I miss you too. There're no strong men way down here in Key West to protect me," she said, mocking a damsel in distress.

"I wish I were there."

"Yeah, me too."

Diane is my daughter, kind of. I took her in when she was fourteen after her father, my partner, was murdered. She is now thirty-three and a highly successful psychiatrist.

"You've already been gone for three months. I thought you'd be back by now," she said.

"I only have nine months to go to get my license back. Time will fly by."

I lost my license to practice law when I made a bad judgment call concerning a drug dealer and serial killer who I happened to be defending. My partner was killed, and the murderer got away. I was disbarred. My old friend Chadwick Kendall—Chad—made a deal with the FBI to get my license back in exchange for me getting out of their way pertaining to a case I was working on. Now I had to live and work in New York, *where the sun doesn't shine*, for a year. It really wasn't so bad, but I do prefer Key West, *where the sun does shine*.

"How is Robin?" Diane asked.

"She is very busy bossing people around."

"Does she boss you around?"

"Yes, in bed that is."

"Enough. I don't want to hear about your sex life."

"Sorry," I said. "That was crude."

"You're not sorry."

"I know."

There was a brief silence.

"What's the matter, Diane?" I asked coaxingly.

"I miss the good old days when you were here to give me a hard time," she said, sadness in her voice.

"I know, but you know I don't have a choice in the matter."

"Yeah, I know."

"Have you repaired my boat yet?"

"There is a crew working on it as we speak, but it needs a lot."

"Yeah, it was blown pretty good."

My houseboat had been the recipient of a bomb three months before. One of the terrorists, whom I was hot on the trail of, decided it would be a good spot to try out a test bomb. It worked very well. It killed the poor soul he paid to deliver it. My boat was blown apart and sank at the dock where I had lived for the past four years in Key West.

"Are you busy this weekend?" I asked.

"No, I'm free."

"I'll have a ticket waiting for you at the airport."

"Great. I'll see you Friday night," Diane said, cheer now in her voice.

"Sounds fantastic. Don't forget my breakfast," I reminded her.

"I don't know what you're talking about," she teased.

"No roll, no ticket."

"You don't think I'd come without one, do you?"

"I love you."

"I love you too," Diane said and hung up.

I put the phone down and thought about Diane. I do love her; I really do, in a father-daughter way.

"Cam," Chad said from the doorway.

"Yes."

"You ready for lunch?"

"What do you have in mind?"

"I was thinking Per Se," he said.

"I was hoping for the 21 Club."

"21 Club it is then."

"I'll get my coat."

"It's a beautiful seventy-two degrees out there."

"Oh yeah, that's right. I'll go as I am then."

"Come on."

~***~

The Bar Room at "21" is one of the world's most charismatic watering holes. It's the hangout of choice for the rich and famous. It's renowned for its whimsical collection of toys suspended from the ceiling. Each of them was donated by sports stars, movie stars, presidents,

9

and business leaders. Evidence of the prohibition era lingers. Even the hidden chute used to dispose of empty liquor bottles is still in use.

There was quite a crowd that day, but Lillian, our favorite hostess and part-owner, waved us to a table situated for privacy but offering a view of the happenings.

"Hello, Cam, Chad. What can I bring you today?" she said, smiling her million-dollar smile.

"Wild Turkey," I replied.

"Shiraz," Chad said.

"Are we drinking our lunch today?" she asked, her tone changing slightly.

"I don't know what I want, and Turkey helps me to think," I said.

"How can I make any money if you don't buy food?" Lillian said, raising her voice and letting her oriental accent slip.

"Come on, Lillian, get us something to drink and we promise we'll eat," Chad said.

She turned and walked away.

"What's with her today?' I asked.

"It was probably a bad idea to come here today," Chad said. "Her brother came to my office yesterday and wants to sue her over their parents' estate."

"Did you take it?"

"No, no way. I told him it would be a conflict of interest."

"Thank God you didn't get in the middle of that."

"Yeah."

Our drinks came. They were delivered by another waitress, who was a little friendlier.

"Thank you," I said. "We'll order after our drinks."

"Take your time, gentlemen. I'll be back in a few."

She left after smiling at both of us.

"I think Lillian told her to be extra friendly," Chad said.

"I think you're right."

We each took a sip of our drinks.

"Wow, potent," I said, setting my glass down on the table.

"Wine is wine, but this one is superb. Don't complain."

"So, why are we here? You didn't even quibble about coming here, even though Per Se is your favorite."

"I'm getting married," Chad said, puffing up and looking a little defensive.

"Married," I said a little too excitedly.

"Yeah, married. Are you surprised?"

"Well, I guess I am. I didn't even know you were dating anyone that steady."

"It was a quick decision. A guy knows when it's right."

"Congratulations, I guess."

"Don't get so excited," he said sarcastically.

I was in shock. I wanted to tell Chad he was crazy. I knew he'd had two dates in the last few weeks, with different women.

"I'm sorry. I'm just a little surprised. Who is the lucky girl?"

"Alexis Arlington."

My jaw dropped.

"Alexis Arlington, as in *the* Alexis Arlington? The one we just defended on the embezzlement case? That Alexis Arlington?"

"She was innocent."

"Thanks to us," I said, my voice rising. "Have you thought this over, Chad? This could have all sorts of complications. Not to mention the conflict of interest thing again."

11

"We're good, ol' boy, quit worrying."

"Just think about it. Don't rush into anything."

"I will, and I have."

The waitress returned to take our order.

"Are you gentlemen ready to order?" she asked in a friendly tone. "I can come back if you're not."

"I'll have the porterhouse, medium-rare," I said, "and the check. My friend here has just announced his engagement."

"Congratulations," she offered.

"Thank you," Chad said. "I'll have the same, only rare."

"I'll bring them right out."

"We'll have another round while we wait," I said.

"When is the big day?" I asked him.

"We plan to be married in August."

"That soon?"

"I don't want to give her a chance to change her mind," he joked.

"Not much time to plan a big wedding."

"We're keeping it on the down-low. Just us, you and Robin. She is going to invite a few family members."

"I'll keep it hush-hush then."

"I would like you to be my best man."

"I'd be honored."

Our drinks came. I downed what was left in my glass and exchanged it for the full one.

Alexis Arlington is the thirty-five-year-old, tall, gorgeous, and well-built daughter of William Arlington the third. William inherited a mass fortune from his father who inherited it from his father. It is traced back several generations to a lucky gold strike. None of the men in the family have done anything to contribute to the wealth. They have all tried to spend as much as possible but can't manage to put a dent in the fortune.

12

Bill Arlington is the only one who has actually increased the fortune but not without innocent people getting hurt—and I mean hurt.

Alexis was indicted on embezzlement charges by the FBI for skimming some of the icing off the cake before it was legally turned over to her in her trust. The Feds didn't have all their ducks in a row. We easily got the charges dropped. We also uncovered evidence of her involvement in the embezzlement in the process. It wasn't our duty to disclose that evidence.

She still denied any involvement in the embezzlement. She said someone set her up.

She was in line to inherit over six hundred million, and the rest after her father's death. It amounted to close to two billion.

Chapter 3

I watched Diane walk through the sliding doors and into the illuminated night from the back seat of our company limo. I noticed a few of the men turn to look at her. She's five-foot-two with long blonde hair that reaches the center of her back and has a very athletic body.

The driver stood at the rear of the car and opened the trunk then hurried to take Diane's suitcase.

"Thank you," she said.

I opened the door and got out to hug her. She hugged me back and kissed me on the cheek.

Before the driver could close the trunk, I stopped him.

Turning to Diane, I asked, "Is there anything in your suitcase I might want to eat?"

"That's for breakfast," she said.

"I have milk in the back seat."

She rolled her eyes. "Okay."

She walked to the back of the car reaching in and opening her case. She retrieved a white sack, which I could smell from where I stood, ten feet away.

I stepped aside, bowed, and gestured for her to enter the back seat.

"Your chariot awaits."

She laughed and got in.

I pulled two plates from a compartment cleverly hidden in a side panel. From another, I retrieved two napkins and laid them on the plates. I then opened a refrigerated compartment and pulled out two bottles of milk.

"You're something else, Cam," Diane said.

She opened the sack and laid a huge chocolate cinnamon honey bun on each plate.

"Bon appétit," she said.

I couldn't answer. I already had a piece of honey bun in my mouth. I just looked at her and nodded my head.

"I guess you're not taking me out to dinner tonight," she stated with a hint of disappointment in her voice.

I swallowed. "Of course I am," I said, neatly folding my napkin around what remained of the roll. "I just wanted a taste. Something to think about while we eat at––" I hesitated, trying to think of a good restaurant I could get into with this late of notice "––Per Se."

"Per Se, I always wanted to go there," Diane said excitedly.

I saw the chauffeur reach for the phone and make a call. After a short pause, he looked in the mirror and slightly shook his head back and forth. He couldn't get us a reservation at Per Se.

I excused myself for a moment from Diane. She was busy looking out the window and hardly noticed. I leaned forward and whispered in the chauffeur's ear, "Try Chad, please."

I leaned back in the seat and Diane looked at me. "Do you think Chad can get us in?" she asked, smiling.

I gestured a surrender. "I hope so."

"It's okay if he can't. Maybe we can go tomorrow night."

Five minutes later, the chauffeur replaced the phone and nodded his head up and down.

"We're in," I said.

"Great. I knew you would own New York in no time," Diane said, looking out the window. "I never get tired of all the glitz and glamour."

"Once around the park," I told the chauffeur. "I always wanted to say that," I said, smiling at Diane.

"You're an old romantic," she said.

"I know."

Chapter 4

The limo stopped in front of the **Time Warner Center** at 10 Columbus Circle in Manhattan. Diane and I exited the limo and entered the building.

"Wow," Diane said with a slight gasp.

"Yeah, pretty impressive, isn't it?"

"Wow."

We took the elevator to the fourth floor to Per Se, where a charming hostess greeted us at the restaurant entrance.

"Mr. Derringer, how are you today?"

"Couldn't be better, Chelsey, and you?"

"Life is good."

I introduced Diane, and we were led to our table.

We started with a bottle of fantastic wine and then ordered our meal.

We chose from the prix-fixe menu, a nine-course vegetable tasting and a nine-course chef tasting menu. Prix-fixe means fixed price, but it still cost around $300 each.

"So, tell me about life in Key West," I said, "and don't leave anything out."

"Not much to tell," Diane said, teasing me.

"Bull, there's got to be something. Give me something."

"Okay," she said, turning in her chair and laying her hand on mine. "But don't get mad."

Oh, oh, what now?

"Of course not," I said.

"I've been dating Jack," she said bluntly.

Jack is my sometime partner in Key West when I'm working as a private eye. Although he is a dear friend, he is also a real rounder with the women.

I just stared at her. I could feel my face turning red.

"Are you okay?" she asked with a slight smile.

"Really?" I managed to say. "I leave you for a few months and you're dating Jack."

"He's a good man," she said defensively.

"I know that, but—"

"Don't worry, Cam; we're just taking it easy. I'm not falling in love."

"Okay, okay, but promise me you'll be careful."

"In bed?"

"No, with your heart."

"I promise."

Changing the subject before I might say something I'd regret later I said, "Okay, give me something else."

"Crazy Wanda ran off with Dave again."

Dave is an old friend who bartends at Schooners down by the marina. He and Crazy Wanda went on a week-long fishing trip a couple of months before. When they arrived

18

home, Dave's wife knocked him out with a frying pan while he slept.

"They're both crazy," I said and chuckled.

"His wife said she would shoot him this time."

"I doubt if she'll do that."

"I don't know; she was pretty ticked off."

I thought on that for a few minutes while I nibbled on some vegetables.

We ate in silence for a while. I thought about Jack and Diane and the song started going through my head. "A little ditty 'bout Jack and Diane…"

"Cam," Diane said, "quit worrying."

"I'm not worried about you," I said. "I'm worried about Jack. He has his hands full."

~***~

The next morning, I woke, showered, and shaved all while trying not to wake Diane.

I tiptoed to the kitchen thinking of the remaining portion of my chocolate cinnamon honey bun. The white sack was in the microwave where we thought it would stay the freshest. I opened the door as quietly as possible and retrieved the bag. It was empty except for a note. It read, "Really, you were going to eat without me?"

I glanced toward Diane's bedroom door. I noticed for the first time that it was ajar.

Standing there with the empty sack in my hand, and a dumbfounded look on my face, I couldn't help but laugh. Then the front door to my apartment opened, startling me, and Diane entered dressed in her running clothes, covered in perspiration.

"Ah-ha!" she said. "I knew you wouldn't wait for me."

"I thought you were asleep. I was going to lay yours out on a plate with a glass of milk before I woke you."

19

"Sure you were."

"Where *is* my honey bun anyway?"

"I ate it before I went running. I thought it might give me some extra energy."

"No. Tell me it ain't so."

"I'm sorry, but it is so."

I couldn't believe it. She brought me a chocolate roll all the way from Key West and then she ate it. I felt nauseous, not to mention disappointed in Diane.

"Why would you do that?"

"Because it was getting stale and most of it was gone anyway from your attack in the limo."

"Yeah, but…"

"Cheer up ol' man, I have reinforcements," she said, smiling.

She went to her room, returned with a plastic food box, and laid it on the table.

"That should hold you for a while."

I opened the lid of the food container and gasped. Lying there neatly in a single layer were six chocolate honey buns. I thought I was going to cry.

"Now, don't you feel sorry for thinking the worst of me?"

"Get the milk."

Chapter 5

That evening, we were joined for supper by my girlfriend Robin and Chad. The four of us had drinks on the rooftop patio of the Chelsea Stratus Building, where my apartment was located.

The grill was fired and warming to five hundred degrees.

I lit the three patio heaters we'd installed for just such an occasion. It was early spring and a little chilly. They warmed the area nicely.

"The view is magnificent from here," Diane said, taking in the jetliner view of Manhattan.

"I never tire of it," I said.

"It's even more magnificent with you two lovely women in it," Chad said, looking at Diane.

He was right. Diane is beautiful, and so is Robin. Her five-foot-six frame and short black hair show off her model-like figure.

"While that is true, Chad," I said, "don't get any ideas. That's my daughter you know."

"Just saying," Chad said, holding his glass up in a mock salute. "You know I'm happily engaged."

Diane said, "I can make my own decisions on men"—then adding quotation marks with her fingers—"Dad."

"Okay, okay, I'll back off," I said.

"Don't worry, Cam," Chad said, "I'm just enjoying all the beauty."

We laughed.

"A father's work is never done."

"It is for now, Cam," Robin said, and, turning to Chad, asked, "Why didn't you bring Alexis with you tonight?"

"She had a prior engagement with her father. Something to do with the family fortune and the embezzlement charges."

The grill was ready. I took orders and cooked the steaks to perfection.

We made small talk while we ate. Chad questioned Diane on her favorite places in Key West.

"Sounds like a fun place," he said.

"It is," we both said in unison then laughed.

After supper, Chad and I lit two Romeo and Julieta 1865 Cuban cigars. Excusing ourselves from the women, we took them to the railing to enjoy.

"Chad, these are marvelous," I said, imitating Billy Crystal, who was imitating Fernando Lamas.

"Fresh from Cuba."

We smoked a few minutes just staring at the beauty that was Manhattan.

"Has Alexis's father decided she is innocent yet? He seemed to be quite angry at the trial," I said.

"I don't think he believes her. That's what tonight's meeting is about."

"I wouldn't want to be in her shoes right now."

"Me neither. I'm going to meet her later for a drink and hopefully sex."

"I'd like to be in your shoes right now," I said, grinning.

We laughed as Chad threw a fake punch at me.

"What's so funny?" Robin asked as she walked up behind us.

"Guy talk," I said and kissed her.

"Never mind, I don't wanna know."

"It's better that way."

"I hate to be a party-pooper, but I just received a message. I have some crime to fight," Robin said apologetically.

"Oh, sorry to hear that. Let me walk you to your car," I said, taking her arm, knowing it would do no good to argue the point. When duty calls, she has no choice.

Chad bid her goodnight, hugged, and kissed her on the cheek.

We excused ourselves. As I opened the door to the stairway, I turned and pointed at Diane and then Chad. I shook my head in a "no" motion.

Chad raised his hands in surrender. Diane just gave me the look.

Chapter 6

The next afternoon, I put Diane on a flight back to Key West.

"I'll miss you," I said.

"I'll miss you too."

We hugged. I held her tight.

"You'll be back in Key West in no time," she said.

"Yeah, only nine months."

"That's not so long."

"Tell Jack I said hi."

"We only had two dates. One was lunch; the other was drinks at the Hog's Breath."

"I thought you were further along than that."

"Nah, just wanted to worry you a little. Thought maybe you'd come home to protect me." She smiled.

"Just be careful with your heart. It's a special one."

I stood at the window watching her plane until it was out of sight. *Hope she comes back soon.*

~***~

I called Robin, hoping she could get away for the day.

"Hi Cam," she answered.

"Hey, sweetie. Ya busy?"

"'Fraid so, but I might be able to get away later. Maybe for a drink or some of that other thing I like so much."

I knew what the other thing was, and it excited me.

"Forget the drink then. I don't want to run short on time."

She laughed. "Okay, I'll call you when I finish here."

"Love ya."

"I know."

~***~

I had some time to kill, so I decided to go back to my apartment to relax a bit. I hailed a taxi and made a stop at a nearby market where I bought cheese and crackers, some veggies, dip, and grapes. Next door, at the wine store I purchased two bottles of Louis Roederer Cristal Brut 2005 Champagne, my favorite. Now that I had a real job, I could afford to drink it again.

I walked the two remaining blocks to my building. As I entered my apartment my cell phone rang.

I hurried to place the sacks on the dining room table and answered the phone.

"Hello," I said, a bit out of breath.

"Sounds like I caught you in the middle of sex," Chad said.

"No, unfortunately, I'm alone."

25

"That never stopped you before."

"Funny, what ya want?"

"I have a date."

"I thought you were engaged."

"No, a wedding date."

"Great. When's the big day?" I asked, shaking my head to myself. I still thought it was a big mistake for him to tie the knot with Alexis.

"June tenth," he said.

"Wow, seven weeks."

"Her idea. I think it has something to do with her dad, but I don't care. There's no sense in putting it off any longer."

"That doesn't leave me much time to plan a bachelor party."

Actually, I had already contacted four of our old college buddies. They said they would love to come to New York for a party. They were going to call a few other friends and get back to me. Then there were the other lawyers in our firm and Chad's brother, Robert.

"I don't need a big party. Maybe just you, me, and twenty or thirty of our best friends."

"Damn, I don't even know if *I* can make it."

"I knew I should have asked Diane to be my best man. She could get it done."

"Where's the wedding going to be?"

"At Alexis's father's mansion and the list is growing."

"You're steppin' in high cotton."

"Don't worry; I won't forget you."

"Well, congratulations again. I wish the two of you the best."

"Thanks, Cam. I'll see ya tomorrow at work."

Chapter 7

I **answered the phone on the first ring.**
"You must be anxious," Robin said.
"I can't wait. Are you coming?"
"Not yet, but I'm on my way to your place."
I laughed. "Hurry."
She knocked on my door ten minutes later. I answered it two seconds later.
"You are in a hurry," she said.
"I was just missing you a bit. Now that you're here I can relax a little. I have Champagne and snacks."
We sat on my private balcony, ate, and drank. The view from the balcony was as good if not better than the one from the rooftop. The chase longue with a pretty girl leaning on me didn't hurt anything either.
"Did you have a rough day at work?" I asked.

"Well, yeah, a little. Looks like trouble brewing."

"Anything serious?"

"Could be. We intercepted a message to a Russian assassin. He's been summoned to New York."

"Do ya think you'll have a chance to get him?"

"It doesn't look good. We've never seen him. He's always in and out before we even know what happened."

"Do you know who his target is?"

"No, but we'll find out soon enough. He always leaves his calling card somewhere where we can find it."

"That's gutsy. What kind of card?"

"Just a calling card that says, 'BLOODSHOT.'"

"Sounds like a nice guy."

"Yeah."

"Well let's just relax for now and enjoy this beautiful warm spring weather."

We kissed softly and then harder.

"Are you ready for some dessert?" I asked.

"What do you have in mind?"

I took my shirt off.

~***~

The next morning, we showered and dressed for work. Robin left clean clothes at my place for just such occasions.

"I'll see you tonight?" I offered, not knowing if she was going to be busy.

"I hope so. I'll have to call you later, but I think I'll get free. Bloodshot isn't coming for a month according to the message."

We kissed and left the apartment. We kissed again as I put her in a cab and then I hailed my own.

~***~

28

Chad was in an extra good mood that morning. I guess he did love her. I hoped they'd be happy.

"Good morning ol' chap," he said, sticking his head in my office.

"Good morning."

"How about lunch today? Your choice."

"Sure. I'm buying," I said.

"Oh-oh, that means the hot dog stand."

"You can have anything you want. Even a soda."

"Okay, sounds good. I've got to go to court this morning for about an hour. I'll see you around noon."

"See ya then."

I had a stack of paperwork on my desk that just seemed to keep growing. I wondered why I wanted my license to practice law back. I didn't really enjoy the work. Not there anyway, just sitting at a desk. However, I did enjoy it in Key West. I guess that's what I have to stay focused on. Just biding my time. I started on the stack.

Chapter 8

S itting in the Bull and Bear restaurant at the Waldorf Astoria Hotel in Manhattan, Andrei Gusarov slowly ate his prime rib as he took in the magnificent sight of the grand bar.

The mahogany bar was one of the top three in the world, and he always enjoyed its splendor when he dined there. He especially enjoyed the view of the young lady sitting at the bar.

His business in New York would not be in and out as it usually was. This time he had an extremely complicated mission. He was looking forward to the challenge. The next three weeks would be consumed by reconnaissance. He had to learn the habits of his targets. Their schedules would be his schedule, one at a time until he was them. Coming to New York four weeks early would throw the Feds off. They wouldn't know when or where these events would take place. That was until afterward, and they found the card which simply said, "BLOODSHOT."

Andrei finished his meal and ordered bourbon on the rocks. He sipped it slowly, letting the fire of the alcohol burn his throat.

He rose and walked to the woman sitting at the bar.

"Beautiful, isn't it?" he said in a slight Russian accent.

The woman turned toward him and smiled as she took in the features of the handsome gentleman.

"Yes," she said. "Yes you are."

Andrei pointed at the stool next to her.

"Please do," she said.

Andrei sat down and said, "The bar, isn't the bar beautiful?"

"Yes, I love it," she said and giggled.

"My name is Demyan Minsky," he said, reaching out to shake her hand.

"I'm Debra," she said, placing her hand softly on his.

"May I buy you another?" he asked, pointing at her almost empty glass.

"Sure, if you'll join me."

Andrei got the bartender's attention and raised two fingers.

"Are you visiting New York or do you live here?" he asked.

"Visiting, and you?"

"Visiting," he said.

Their drinks arrived, and they each took a taste.

"Perhaps you would like to join me in some sightseeing after our drinks," he said.

"Perhaps."

He stared into her eyes. "Green, you have beautiful green eyes."

Debra blushed and said, "Thank you."

They finished their drinks together, each setting the empty glasses down simultaneously.

"Shall we?" Andrei said, taking her hand.

She rose as did he, and they walked out of the restaurant together.

It was dark now, and a slight chill was in the air. He saw her shiver, so he placed his arm around her.

"Is that better?" he asked.

"Much," she said.

They walked a few blocks and Andrei hailed a taxi.

"New York Hilton Midtown, please," Andrei said to the driver.

They arrived; Andrei paid the driver and gave an average tip. He didn't want to stand out in the driver's mind.

Andrei led Debra to the elevator. She followed without protest, not even pretending to be naïve. She knew what he wanted. She wanted the same.

The room was rented to Adrian Boykov, an ID he possessed. One of many.

He opened the door to the room. It was quite magnificent.

"Nice," she said. The first word she had spoken since they entered the hotel.

Andrei turned toward her and pushed her against the wall.

"Not so rough," she said through gritted teeth.

"Fuck you, bitch," he said, letting his Russian accent slip into full dialect.

She tried to break his hold on her. He slapped her and kissed her violently. She squirmed, and a tear came to her eye. This pleased him.

"Are you frightened?" he asked, an evil grin on his face.

"Let me go," she screamed.

He pulled a knife from his pocket, touched the button on its side and let her watch as a six-inch blade snapped open. He placed it beneath her chin.

"Shut up, bitch, or you'll die."

He reached down and pulled her dress up over her waist. Then he pulled her panties out and, with the knife, cut them off.

He spun her around and pushed her against the wall again.

"Put your hands on the wall."

"No," she cried.

He spun her back around and slapped her hard across the face.

She fell to the floor crying. He grabbed her by the hair and pulled her back to her feet. As he spun her back toward the wall, she reached out and placed her hands on it.

"Better," he said, an evil tone slipping into his voice.

He dropped his pants to the floor and roughly entered her from behind.

"You like that?" he asked breathlessly.

"Yes," she cried. Tears had filled her eyes, and she was shaking violently.

Her reaction pleased him even more.

He finished with a hard thrust.

He turned her back around and kissed her long and hard. Then he placed the knife against her throat. He pressed ever so slightly allowing the blade to penetrate until a small stream of blood trickled down her neck into her dress.

He leaned forward and licked the blood.

"You taste wonderful," he said, blood on his lips.

She cried again, and he smiled.

Placing the knife under her eye, he whispered, "If you ever tell a soul about this, I will cut out your eyes and eat them."

He backed away from her, and she fell to the floor sobbing.

"Get up and clean yourself. That is not a good look on you." He laughed.

He walked to her purse, which was lying on the floor where she had dropped it as they entered the room only five minutes before. Pulling her wallet from the purse, he removed her driver's license and placed it in his pocket.

"Now I will always know where to find you. Just in case you decide to talk, or maybe if I want you again."

She pushed her way to her feet trying to move her clothes back into place.

"The bathroom is down the hall on the right. Help yourself, please," he said, pointing in that direction.

When she returned from making herself as presentable as possible, he was sitting on the sofa watching TV.

"Goodnight Debra...." He paused and pulled her driver's license from his pocket and held it up to read. "Sorry, my mistake. Goodnight Donna Wilson. Thank you for a most passionate evening."

She opened the door and left.

Chapter 9

Robin and I entered The Russian Tea Room. Chad and Alexis had arrived first. I told the hostess we were with them, pointing in their direction. She seated us at the table and took our drink order.

"You look lovely tonight," I said to Alexis, and she did. She had cut her long, blonde hair into a very stylish and more sophisticated look.

"Hello Cam, Robin," she said.

"Robin, you also look quite lovely tonight," Chad said, and she also did.

"Well, aren't we just two lucky guys," I said.

"I always said that," Chad said.

"Love the hair," Robin said.

"Thank you; I thought it was time for a change."

"I guess the two of you have been busy preparing for the wedding," Robin said to Alexis.

The wedding was now only five days away.

Alexis gave Chad a look. "I hope he's more help once we're married," she said sarcastically.

"I've been busy at work, honey. Someone has to make some money."

That got a laugh from all of us. Alexis's father forgave her little hiccup, telling her she would inherit her part of the fortune—about five hundred million—after the wedding. I wondered if that was the reason for the rush of the nuptials. The contract also stipulated that she had to stay married and faithful for ten years. Anything short of that would result in the return of the money to the family trust.

"We could always move in with Cam. He's just rattling around in that big old apartment alone," Chad said.

"I keep him from getting lonesome," Robin said.

The waitress took our food order, and we made small talk for a while. Another round of drinks was delivered to our table.

"I didn't know we ordered these," I said.

"They were sent over by the gentleman at the bar," the waitress said, turning to the bar. "Well, he was at the bar. He's gone now."

"What did he look like?" Chad asked.

"Tall, handsome, had a slight Russian accent."

"I guess that makes sense. We are in The Russian Tea Room, but no idea who that was," I said.

"Me neither," said Chad. "Thank you, whoever you are."

We all held our glasses up in a toast and drank.

"So, what are you two young ladies doing tomorrow night while I take Chad out to bid farewell to the single life?" I asked.

"We have plans of our own, to do the same," Alexis said.

"Well, enjoy and be safe."

"Maybe we should just all go out together," Robin said.

This got comments from everyone.

"Just a thought," she said. "I bet I scared you, didn't I?" She laughed.

We ended the evening in Alexis's apartment at The Plaza. Although it was only slightly more extravagant than my own, I knew her apartment went for around $6,500 a square foot.

Robin spent the night at my place again. I wondered if we were getting too serious too fast. A few hours later, I had no qualms about it. We were moving along just right.

Chapter 10

The next day, after work, Chad came to my apartment at five o'clock. We had a drink and talked about the day.

"You get anywhere on the Kindle case?" I asked him.

"The man is as guilty as they come, but I think I can get him off on a technicality."

"Really? The D.A. isn't going to like that."

"Yeah, I know, and neither do I, but they didn't Mirandize him. He robbed a store with a squirt gun. When the cops caught him outside, he gave them the gun. They were laughing so hard they forgot to Mirandize him. They started to but then kept making wisecracks instead and didn't finish."

"Well, you gotta do what you gotta do."

38

"Yeah."

"Are you ready for your big night?" I asked him.

"I guess so. Who's joining us?"

"Can't tell ya. It's a surprise."

"Alright then, let's get this over."

We finished our drinks and stood.

"Are we having strippers?"

"Can't tell ya."

We took the elevator to the lobby.

"Let's go to the bar and see if Robert is waiting for us."

"My brother Robert? You invited him?"

"Of course. What's wrong with that?"

"I haven't heard from him for almost a year."

"He said he'd love to come."

"Well, I'll be damned. It'll be good to see him."

We entered the bar to the deafening sound of **SURPRISE**. It looked as though everyone showed.

Fifteen of his college fraternity brothers, eight colleagues from the firm, and five friends from his apartment building and his brother.

"Shit man, you know how to throw a party," he said, turning to me. "You really got me."

Robert was standing in front of the crowd, holding his drink up in a salute, he said, "Hey bro, congratulations."

"Robert," Chad said and stepped toward him.

They hugged a long brotherly hug. I was glad I had found him and asked him to come.

"Where have you been?" Chad asked.

"Vietnam."

"Vietnam?"

"Yeah. It's a beautiful country. I went with Johnny. You remember him, don't ya?"

"Johnny Craddock?"

"Yeah. Anyway, we went on a vacation. I fell in love with the country and a little lady, so I decided to stay for a while."

"You're going to have to catch me up on that."

"I will, later. Tonight, you just concentrate on partying."

"I'll try."

We rented two limos and hit various bars around New York. When the tour was over, we came back to my building where we had a private room for the evening.

Chad was lost in old stories from his college days. The same stories that had been told numerous times but always seemed to grow in substance every time until they were now actually just lies, with his brother swearing every story was the truth.

I took a headcount near the end of the night, just in case Chad asked how many there were. I came up with thirty. I know there were twenty-nine invited and accepted. I figured one of the guys brought another friend with them. No big deal.

Around two a.m. the party broke up. It was a nice gathering. No trouble, no women, other than the waitress who was a real knock-out. I did see a few men following her around, but this wasn't her first rodeo.

After we had bid the last man goodnight, we went back upstairs to my apartment. Chad decided to spend the night there since it was so late and he was a little inebriated.

"Thanks, Cam. You went above and beyond the call of duty."

"You're welcome. You have a very nice group of friends."

"So do you."

"I know."

"Where did you know the gentleman with the Russian accent from?" he asked me.

40

"I didn't know him. I think one of your friends from the apartment building brought him."

"Probably so."

"Would you like a nightcap?" I offered. "Or do you think you can sleep? You know you only have three days left to party."

"Goodnight," is all he said and went down the hall to the spare room.

Chapter 11

Andrei Gusarov returned to his hotel room around midnight, leaving the party early. He didn't want to be there for the goodnight handshakes. Tomorrow he thought he would drive to Washington DC and leave a card. That would draw Robin Anderson to DC and away from the wedding. They would know he had slipped past them and that he was working in Washington DC, which he wasn't.

"They are so stupid. I love teasing them," he said aloud in his empty room.

~***~

Early the next morning, I left the apartment taking the elevator to the first floor; leaving the building I hailed a taxi. I told the driver to take me to Alfie's Bagel Stand next to the Hilton.

As I was nearing the Hilton, I saw the Russian man from the party the night before walking to the curb carrying a suitcase, hailing a taxi.

As luck would have it, it was my taxi he hailed.

"Hello," I said as I exited the cab.

He turned toward me, and a strange look came over his face. Was it shock or fear or just a surprise to see someone he knew so early in the morning?

I took the brief pause to take in his features. He was tall, maybe six-three, not quite as tall or muscular as my six-foot-four, two-hundred-thirty-pound frame. He had a strong jaw, unusually blue eyes, and short blond hair. His nose had a slight jog in it. Maybe from a fight. I would hate to see the other guy. He was built very solidly.

"Ah Cam, good morning. How did you fare last night?" he said regaining his composure.

"Well, I would have liked to have gone to bed about three hours earlier. I always rise early, even if it's a late night."

"Yes, me too."

"Are you staying at the Hilton?"

"Yes, I was. I didn't want to intrude on the hospitality of an old friend."

"I'm sorry I didn't get your name last night," I said, extending my hand to shake his.

"Adrian Boykov. I am a friend of Tom Carrington's. I was in town visiting and he didn't want to leave me alone for the night. I hope I didn't cause you any inconvenience."

"None at all. The more the merrier. Will you be in town for a while?"

"No. I must leave today for a week. I will return after that."

"Maybe we can get together then."

"I hope so."

"Here, this taxi is waiting for me, but I'll be glad to drop you," I offered.

"No thank you, here is another," he said as a taxi pulled to the curb.

Adrian said, "Goodbye for now," and got in the taxi and left.

~***~

Andrei looked out the back window of the taxi and watched Cam watching him. *That was not a good encounter. We were not supposed to talk. I must change hotels and names.*

"Where to?" the driver asked.

"Hertz car rental please."

Andrei held his case in his lap. He could feel the weight of the rifle inside.

~***~

I bought six bagels, raspberry cream cheese, cinnamons ticks and some biscotti. I returned to the taxi still thinking about the chance encounter with Adrian Boykov. I made a mental note to ask Chad if Tom had mentioned bringing a friend.

When I returned to the apartment, Chad was still asleep, so I changed into my running clothes and headed out for my morning therapy. I grabbed a taxi and went to Central Park.

It was a beautiful morning, and the run through Central Park was rejuvenating. After twenty minutes I realized I should have eaten something. I changed my course and ran to a pastry shop across the street. I bought a donut and a cup of coffee and returned to the park. I sat on a park bench watching the other runners and walkers. I felt a little funny eating a donut while they were working so hard to fight off the very poison I was ingesting, but not so bad that I couldn't enjoy it. We all have our little vices; mine is pastry, among others.

The morning sun was rising higher in the sky now bringing shorter shadows and more brilliant colors to the landscape. I took a deep breath and inhaled the cool air of spring. It seems to sharpen the mind and make the world clearer.

In my heightened state of awareness, I was watching three very shapely young women run by when a voice from my right said, "Busted."

I turned to see Robin standing there in her running clothes.

"Really," she said. "You're sitting on a park bench eating a donut and ogling young coeds."

"Yep," I said. "Would you like some?" I offered, knowing she had too much discipline to indulge.

"Yep," she said, taking the donut from my hand and eating it in one big bite.

"Hey! That was my last bite."

"You shouldn't have offered it."

We laughed. "Have a seat," I said, moving over.

She sat and kissed me.

"I didn't know the morning was going to be this good," I said.

"Neither did I. Now you're going to have to do something nice for me since I caught you girl watching."

"I did. I gave you my donut."

"Hum. That is quite a sacrifice for you, I guess."

"I'll be more than happy to take you out to dinner tonight on top of that."

"It's a deal if I can get away."

"Any more word on the Russian assassin?"

"No, not a word. We have lost all communication with him. We're just waiting for him to send a message back to whoever sent for him."

"Speaking of Russians, there was a Russian at our bachelor party last night."

"Was she the stripper?"

"No, thank God. She was a he, and neither Chad nor I knew him. I ran into him again this morning as he was leaving the Hilton for the airport. He said his name is Adrian Boykov and Tom Carrington invited him."

"So, did you ask Tom?"

"Not yet. I just got that info this morning."

"You sound suspicious."

"Just cautious, I guess. Remember the drink delivered to our table? The waitress said the man had a Russian accent. I suppose that coupled with you talking about a Russian assassin has made me a little leery."

"You have a wild imagination. Of all the people in New York, you think the assassin is after you."

"It wouldn't be the first time."

"True, but he's dead now," Robin said, referring to the case in Key West we went through three months before.

"I'm not worried, just curious."

"Well," Robin said, "I have to get back to my run. I can't let you be a bad influence on me any longer."

"I'll run with you to the other end of the park, and then I need to go home and check on Chad."

"Okay. Let's race."

"Wait, you didn't tell me what you girls did last night."

"I know."

With that, she took off and was way ahead of me by the time I disposed of my coffee cup.

Chapter 1

The day before the wedding, Chad and I had a rather exciting morning in court. Emanuel Barona, allegedly the number two crime boss in New York's western district, vowed to kill us both, even though we got him off for ordering the hit on four Vietnamese soldiers who "hypothetically" invaded his territory. He said we let the prosecutor drag his name through the mud.

Maybe we did just a little, but the creep should have spent the rest of his life in prison anyway. Two hours later, he called me on my private cell number, which I give to no one, and apologized. He said he was still jazzed from the turmoil in court and didn't mean it.

That gave us a little relief, but you just can't trust that guy. He might just be covering himself and allowing us to drop our guard. We reported the threat to Chief McNally of the NYPD anyway.

He said, "Thank you; if you show up dead, it will help us fry the guy."

I don't think he likes lawyers.

Once back at the office I called Robin and told her of the threat.

"I guess you want me to protect you now," she said.

"Well, it wouldn't hurt to at least work under-covers with me tonight."

"I knew you wanted something."

"You can read me like a book."

"I'll be there around seven. Are you ready for the wedding tomorrow?"

"Yep; I've got my tux and speech all ironed out."

"Good boy."

"The wedding has grown a little though. Instead of you and me and four or five others, there'll be somewhere around two hundred attendees."

"Yeah, I know. I've been helping Alexis with the invitations for a month now."

"And you didn't tell me?"

"No, she didn't want it to get back to Chad too soon. She was afraid it would scare him. His family will be there also."

"Great, I hoped they would."

"See ya tonight," she said.

"Okay; love ya."

"I know."

~***~

After hanging up Robin thought about how much she loved Cam, but she vowed never to get too involved with anyone, much less marry. Her job was too dangerous. If she dragged Cam into her world, he could become a target for her enemies. She loved him too much for that. That's why she only told him occasionally that she loved him.

"I hope we can keep our relationship on an even keel for a long time," she said aloud to herself.

~***~

Andrei finished his supper and ordered his usual bourbon on the rocks. He sipped it as he surveyed the restaurant. One young girl caught his attention. She was dining alone at a corner table while reading a novel.

"Hello," Andrei said as he approached her table. "May I join you?"

The girl looked him over briefly and said, "Sure, have a seat."

An hour later, holding her driver's license up, Andrei told her if she ever said a word to anyone, he would kill her family.

She wiped the tears from her eyes, pulled her dress up and left the room.

~***~

The sun was almost down now, and Andrei was ready to choose a victim.

He opened the case holding his rifle and removed a plastic bag, which held a wig and fake mustache.

Looking at himself in the bathroom mirror he was satisfied. Anyone who saw him would never recognize him again without these.

He closed the case, picked it up and surveyed the room one last time. Satisfied that there was no trace of him left behind, he walked out the door. He took the elevator to the 21st floor; he exited and stepped into the stairway leading to the rooftop.

The roof, covered with pea gravel, crunched beneath his step. He made a mental note to clean his shoes good when he left the building.

He found a spot on the south corner of the building that offered a perfect view of the two intersecting streets below.

He opened his case and assembled his father's Dragunov SVD rifle. This Russian-built rifle had been used by their military and his father for over fifty years and was still Andrei's weapon of choice.

Now, he thought, *it's time for some fun. I need to kill someone to get in the mood. I hate to start a job cold.*

He attached the scope and made the necessary adjustments. Looking through the scope now, he surveyed the streets below.

A young lady with her child holding tightly to her mother's hand crossed the street. *No, not them,* he thought. *I am a killer but not a monster.*

Two men in their mid-twenties, one black and one Hispanic, were crossing the street in the opposite direction. As they passed the young mother, one of the men spun around and bashed her jaw. She went down and didn't move. The punks laughed and pointed at the little girl lying next to her mother, still holding her hand.

This made Andrei's mind go back to the beginning.

It all started one morning on the way to school.

~***~

"Come on Annika," Andrei said to his little sister as he was placing his breakfast bowl in the sink, "we're going to be late for school."

Andrei was twelve years old, a year older than his sister. It was his job to protect her and get off to school every morning. A job he didn't mind. He loved her. She was easy to love. She had a great personality and a very caring way about her that made you feel as though she was actually taking care of you.

They picked up their backpacks and filled them with lunch bags and books. Andrei called to their mother on the way out the door. "We're off to school. Love you."

50

"Be careful, love you too," his mother called back.

They walked hand and hand down the sidewalk. The sky was dark. A storm was threatening. They pulled their coats up around their necks tighter.

"Looks like rain," Andrei said.

Annika squeezed his hand tighter. He smiled.

They passed by a tall hedge only two blocks from their house. He didn't see the attackers hiding there. Before he knew it, he was on the ground being kicked. Seeing the boys now for the first time, he recognized one of them as the new kid at school. The other three he had known forever. They were two years older and had been getting into trouble on a regular basis.

The next kick was to the head. His world went dark.

When Andrei awoke, his head was killing him. Feeling his jaw, he was sure it was broken. Searching the area, he saw his sister lying behind the bushes. She was naked and not moving. He got to his hands and knees and crawled to her. "Annika," he said over and over. "Annika, are you okay?" She moved slightly. Her nose looked as though it was broken, and she had blood between her legs.

"No, no," he said.

He found her clothes and laid them over her. Cradling her head in his lap, he said, "Wake up, Annika. Wake up."

She stirred again and opened her eyes.

She would make it, but Andrei knew she would never be the same. Neither would he.

He helped her dress and walked her back home. Their mother burst into tears when she saw them. "I'll call the doctor," she said.

That night, Andrei went to his father's closet and removed a case that held his hunting rifle. He had seen it many times when his parents were gone and he was alone in the house. Andrei liked the feel of it and always wanted to shoot it. Now he would.

He lay waiting in the dark for the boys to appear from the shadows in the park where he knew they hung out. There they were. He placed the crosshairs on the new kid and without hesitating he squeezed the trigger. The gun jumped slightly, but through the scope he saw the boy fall. Working quickly, he turned the scope onto the other three one at a time until they all lay still.

The gun was not as loud as he thought it would be. It didn't draw any attention from the neighboring houses. He walked to the still bodies lying on the ground and peered down at them. He felt nothing but satisfaction.

One of them moved. Andrei pulled his knife from his pocket and raised the boy's head.

"This is for Annika," he said to the kid and slowly sliced through his neck, then faster and more forceful until the head was severed from the body.

He threw the head as far as he could then wiped the blade off on the boy's shirt. "See ya in hell, when I get there," he said and walked away.

The police had made a statement that the ballistics report showed the rifle used was the same one used in ten other assassinations. That was when Andrei realized his father was an assassin. Now he was one too. His father realized at the same time what had happened.

Over the years his father taught him the rules of killing and how best to do it. Now here he was; his own man and still killing.

~***~

"Yes, they are the ones," Andrei said aloud and focused the crosshairs on the one who struck the woman.

It was an easy shot. Andrei squeezed the trigger, and the man's head exploded. His friend, trying to figure out what just happened, only stood there staring at the bloody carnage on the street. Five seconds later his head also exploded.

Andrei disassembled his rifle and set it back in the case. He withdrew a card from his pocket and laid it on the edge of the roof. He placed a handful of gravel on the card so it would not blow away. The card only read, "BLOODSHOT." By the next day the police would have traced the bullets flight and found the card. Andrei would be back in New York City by then.

Andrei returned to his rental car, placed the case in the trunk and sat behind the wheel. It didn't feel right to him. He never just picked a target at random like that. His father had taught him better than that.

The FBI would wonder why an assassin came all the way from Russia just to kill two punks in Washington DC. He wouldn't. They would know it was just a diversion. *What was I thinking? I must retrieve my card.*

He left the case in the trunk of the car and returned to the rooftop. As he opened the door, he saw a man standing at the edge of the roof where he had shot from. He was looking at something in his hand. It was the card. The man must have heard the door open because he turned and looked at Andrei.

"What happened?" Andrei asked. "I thought I heard a shot."

"Yeah, come here and check this out," the man said, holding up the card and pointing to the street below.

Andrei walked to the edge where the man was standing and looked down at the street.

"What the hell?"

"It looks like someone shot those guys from here and left this card," the man said.

"May I see the card?"

The man handed it to Andrei. He held it close and pretended to read it.

"Bloodshot."

"Crazy, huh?"

"Yeah. Can you see who was shot?"

"Yeah, right over there. Two men and a woma…"

The man never got the rest of "woman" out. Andrei pushed him, and he fell twenty-one stories to the sidewalk below.

What a mess, Andrei thought. He turned and exited the roof. As he closed the door, he saw three gang members walking toward him.

They were dressed in blue jeans that were hanging below their ass. They had big silver and gold chains around their necks and their ball caps on backward.

"Whut we got here?" one of them said while holding his crotch.

"Look like a honkey mother fucker wif a nie watch," another said.

The third raised his shirt and showed Andrei a gun.

"Give us your wallet and your watch," he said.

"Yeah, muthafucka. Now."

Andrei wished he had his gun now. It was a long way to the car. *I guess I'll just have to improvise,* he thought.

"Watch first," the one with the gun said, stepping closer.

Andrei removed his watch and extended it toward the man. As the man reached for it, Andrei grabbed his hand and spun him around; at the same time he placed his hand on the man's gun. Andrei pulled the trigger, and the gun fired. The punk screamed in pain. Andrei pulled the gun from the man's pants and kicked him forward towards the other two.

The one who had been shot was still screaming. "Muthafucka, you shot my dick off," he cried.

"Whut the fuck man," the first one said. "We gonna kill you now."

Andrei pointed the gun at him and pulled the trigger.

A hole opened in the man's forehead, and he fell to the floor.

"Woo muthafucka. You un go now. We don what no mo twuble."

Andrei pointed the gun at the other two and one at a time he shot them in the head.

He retrieved his watch and fastened it back onto his wrist. He wiped the gun clean and dropped it on one of the men's chest.

"Fut you muthafucka," Andrei imitated and laughed.

He stood there for a minute thinking.

The FBI would trace his bullets from the street shooting and realize they were from his gun.

He had a thought. If they were going to think it was a diversion, then he would make it look like one. He returned to the roof, pulled his card out and withdrew a pen from his pocket. He wrote on the back of the card. "That's a first," he said aloud.

Now he needed to find a target on the other side of town. An important target. He headed toward the White House.

Chapter 13

Robin buzzed my room just as I was fixing us both a Wild Turkey on the rocks. It just seemed like that kind of night instead of wine.

I pushed the button and said, "Hurry."

When the elevator opened, I was standing there with the two drinks in my hand.

"You're all about partying, aren't you?" she said, taking one of the drinks.

"Yep," I said.

"Good, 'cause I'm in the mood."

We finished our drinks on the balcony and moved the party to the bedroom.

Just as we were starting to pleasure one another, Robin's cell phone rang.

"You're not going to answer that, are you?" I asked, looking up at her.

"I don't want to, but I better."

"This better be good," she said into the phone.

"What, when? Okay, I'll meet you downstairs at the Time Warner Center in fifteen minutes."

She hung up.

"Hurry," she said, "we have five minutes."

We hurried. We had a minute to spare.

"What's up?" I asked.

"Bloodshot. He just shot two guys in the street then threw a man off the top of a building and then he killed three gangbangers as an afterthought."

"Shit, where?"

"Washington DC."

"Damn. Any sign of him?"

"No, but he's not finished. This had to be a diversion. He wouldn't come all the way here to kill these punks."

"Where do you think he's headed?"

"No telling. There are a lot of targets in DC."

We dressed, and I walked Robin to the lobby. "Do you think you'll be back in time for the wedding tomorrow?"

"Don't know. I hope so."

An FBI car rolled to the curb in front of the building.

"I hope I see you tomorrow," I said, opening the door for her.

"Me too."

"Love you," I said.

"I love you too," she said and kissed me softly.

I watched the car roll away with a bad feeling in my gut. That didn't feel like a "goodbye," it felt like a "GOODBYE."

~***~

Andrei sat in his car outside Senator Frasier's house and made a call on his cell phone.

"Is everything on schedule?" he asked.

"Yes, remember, no deaths."

57

"I remember."

"Alright then. Your first deposit will be in your account in the morning."

"Okay, I need to go. Goodbye," Andrei said, watching the figure leaving the house.

"Goodbye."

Chapter 14

I was up early the next morning. I did my usual run through Central Park and returned to the apartment to work out with my free weights.

I wanted to call Robin to see if she was going to make the wedding, but I didn't want to bother her either.

I showered and laid out my tux. It still looked like new. It's not one of those things a guy wears too often.

My cell phone rang. I checked the caller ID; I saw it was Chad.

"Are you still in town?" I asked, answering the phone. "I thought you would be long gone by now."

"No. I'm not running. I'm going to take it like a man."

I laughed. "What's up?"

"Have you talked to my brother lately?"

"No, not since the bachelor party. Why?"

"Well, we kind of got into an argument yesterday, and I haven't heard from him since."

"What about?"

"He said I shouldn't marry Alexis. He told me she was just marrying me so she would get her inheritance and he was worried about my health. I think he's worried that she'll kill me after she gets her money."

"That's ridiculous."

"Yeah, I know, but he's all freaked out about it."

"Wonder why now. He wasn't like that at the party. I'm sure he'll be at the wedding. After he's had time to think about it, he'll come to his senses."

"I hope."

"I'll be by to get you at noon," I said.

"I'll be ready."

My cell rang again. This time it was Robin.

"Hi, Cam. Bad news."

"You're not going to make the wedding, are you?" I said.

"No, I'm sorry. We found Senator Frasier lying in his front yard this morning. He'd been shot. Bloodshot left his card in one of the senator's pockets."

"Be careful. I know you have to do what you have to do."

"I will. Please tell Chad and Alexis I had no choice."

"They'll understand."

"I'll talk to you tomorrow," Robin said.

"Okay, love ya."

"Goodbye."

There it was again. Goodbye.

I didn't like that word. It was quickly becoming my least favorite word in the world.

~***~

I called Diane.

"Hi Daddy," she answered.

"Daddy," I said, "that's a first."

"Yeah, just trying it out."

"Well, I like it," I said proudly.

60

"Me too, but don't get used to it. The girls will think you're old."

"Well, I kind of am."

"No way, Cam, you're hot."

"What is up with you today? Have you been smoking pot again?"

"Not for a long time. I just feel good. You know, a beautiful day, a good run this morning, met a guy on the beach."

"Whoa. What guy?"

Diane laughed. "Just a guy. Tall, dark and handsome."

"Be careful," I said. "I think I need to get back to Key West."

"I'm a big girl."

"Yeah, but—"

"What ya call about, Daddy?"

"I forget."

Diane laughed again. "You're so easy. I didn't meet anyone. Just havin' fun with ya."

"You're mean."

"What's up?"

"Just wanted to talk to someone sensible, but that's not going to happen."

"Sorry. I'm okay now. Talk."

I thought for a minute. Maybe I shouldn't share my thoughts with Diane. She counts on me to be in control.

"Daddy," she said, "talk."

"Okay, I need a psychiatrist and you're the only one I know."

"You mean I'm the only free one you know."

"Same, same."

"Okay, I'm listening."

"Well, first of all, I think Robin is trying to pull away from me. She hardly ever says, 'I love you,' back to me, and her goodbye this morning sounded kind of final."

Silence.

"Are you listening?" I asked.

"Yes, I am. I'm waiting for a question. I can't comment on Robin's feelings because I don't know how your relationship has been moving along."

"Smooth, I'd say. Until now anyway."

"Any recent changes in either of your lives?"

"She's working on a big case. A Russian assassin who is in Washington DC."

"Well that's a little distracting, don't you think?"

"Yes, I know."

"Does she still try to be with you as much as possible?"

"Yes."

"I can't believe I'm going to ask you this, but do you still have sex?"

"Yeah, a lot."

"Maybe she's just preoccupied or worried. Maybe she's protecting you from her life."

"That doesn't make any sense."

"Remember how you always kept your work away from me? You didn't want me involved in any danger. She might feel the same way. Heck, when she was working the case here in Key West, she sent you to New York."

Diane always made sense out of everything. She might have been right. Maybe Robin was being protective.

"You're probably right. I'm just too close to see it."

"Give her time and space. You can't force love anyway."

"I see the college is paying for itself."

"What else is bothering you?"

"Nothing, that's it," I lied.

"No, you started with, 'first of all.' That means there's a second of all."

62

She's good.

"Well, it's probably just me being a P.I., but I've had several encounters with a Russian since this all started. First, one sent drinks to our table, we never saw him, then one came to Chad's party and no one knew him. Then I ran into him again the other morning."

"You're right, Cam; someone sent to Russia for an assassin to bump you off because you're such a hard target no one here could do it."

"Hardy-har-har."

"Just kidding, but do you really think of all the people on the East Coast you're the one they're after?"

"Yeah, that's what Robin said. She's in DC now. The Russian killed a senator there last night."

"He's probably finished with work for a while then. You weren't the target."

"Probably."

"Chill, Cam. Why don't you come to Key West for a little vacation?"

"I'd love to. I really miss it, but I can't. Today is Chad's wedding."

"You better get moving then. You don't want to be late."

"Wish you could have made it."

"Too much work here too."

"Thanks. I'll talk to you in a few days. I love you."

"I love you too, Daddy."

I hung up feeling better knowing that there is someone who will always love me.

Chapter 15

I showered and dressed in my tux. *Not bad,* I thought, looking in the mirror. My mustache was neatly trimmed, and my hair still looked good from my week-old haircut. My gut didn't stick out like most of my friends' did. Working out and jogging had kept my body trim and athletic.

Satisfied that I was perfect, I called for the company limo and took the elevator to the first floor.

I had a few minutes to kill, and the bar was open, so…

I called Chad when we were five minutes out.

"Are you still going through with this?" I asked when he answered the phone.

"Ye of little faith. I made a promise, and I'm going to keep it. I'll be right down."

We rode out of the city to Long Island and past Oyster Bay toward Northport. I'd never been to that part of New York, and I was mesmerized. I could see why it was called the Gold Coast. One mansion after another moved past us in a ballet of majestic splendor. *Must be nice,* I thought.

"Are you going to fit in here?" I asked Chad.

"Of course, I'll be as rich as they are, and I am better looking than most of them."

"Yes, looks are important. I should live here myself."

The driver slowed and turned into a long driveway. Halfway down it, we came to a gate. An apparently armed guard stepped from a small building and asked who we were.

"Mr. Chadwick Kendall and Mr. Cam Derringer," the chauffeur said.

The guard opened the gate without looking at the guest list.

At the entrance of the house, and I use the term *house* loosely, we were met by two men dressed in tuxes of their own. It was easy to tell that they were not a part of the wedding party by the bulges under their coats. Nine millimeters would be my guess.

"Right this way, gentlemen," one of them said.

We were escorted through the front entryway and down a long hall to a library.

"Mr. William Arlington will be right with you. There's a bar over there," he said, pointing to a magnificent mahogany bar about fifteen feet long and flanked by two twenty-foot windows. "Help yourselves. Our servers aren't here yet."

"Thank you," I said. "I think we can manage."

He left the room and closed the door.

"My God Chad, you fell right into it, didn't you?"

"Yeah, think I did. Since I've never been here before, I had no idea."

"Alexis was raised here. You're going to have to up your game a little to make her feel at home elsewhere."

"Shit."

"Yeah, shit."

We made ourselves a drink at the bar, and I toasted to his happiness.

"Thanks, I think I'll need all the luck I can get."

"No, you'll be okay. You're a good man, and Alexis knows it."

"I hope."

"What's her dad like? I didn't get a chance to talk to him at the trial."

"He seemed to be a very nice guy, really down to earth for such a rich man."

"Thank you, Chad," William said from behind us.

"Sorry, sir. We didn't hear you enter," Chad said.

"I am sneaky," he said. "I see you've made yourself at home. That's good because this *is* your home now. Hello Cam," he said, looking at me.

"Hello, it's good to see you again, Mr. Arlington."

"Please, call me Bill. I think I'll make a drink too. Need a freshening up?" he asked, pointing to our drinks.

"I'm good for now," I said.

He looked at Chad.

"I think I could use one," Chad said.

William Arlington is a large man. Maybe six-foot-two, slightly overweight, but still seems to be very fit. He wears a goatee, which is neatly trimmed but makes him look a little like Colonel Sanders. His body language makes him appear larger than he is.

He mixed our drinks and turned back toward us handing Chad his drink. "Well, I guess this is the part where I tell you if you ever harm my little girl, I'll kill you."

Chad turned red and stepped back.

Bill laughed and said, "Don't worry, I won't actually kill you; I have people for that. Besides, you'll have your hands full defending yourself from Alexis. You won't be able to get a punch in."

He had a very subtle way of making a joke out of a threat. If I were Chad, I think I would have excused myself, got back in the limo and left that place and Bill behind.

Chad was still red. He just stared at Bill.

Bill laughed again. "Okay, I've done my job at scaring you, now let's be friends." He raised his glass in a toast. "To you and Alexis, I wish both of you all the happiness in the world. May you go forth and multiply and love your child as much as I do mine."

We all drank, but the mood was much more solemn than it had been five minutes before.

We finished our drinks and set our glasses on the bar.

"I have a lot of directing to do, so you two enjoy yourselves. You may go anywhere inside and out. Alexis is locked away in a room in the east wing, so you won't have to worry about running into her. The guests should be arriving in about an hour."

He shook hands with both of us and left.

When we were alone, I said, "Well, Chad, it's been nice knowing you."

"You don't think he would really have me killed, do you?"

"Yep, I think he would. If he doesn't, Emanuel Barona still wants you dead."

"Aren't you just a bundle of encouragement?"

"I'm here for you, Chad. I'll be right behind you."

"Thanks."

"Isn't Alexis about thirty-five? If she's going to go forth and multiply, you had better get to work."

"I'll do my best."

We left the room with our glasses refilled. We walked through the halls, peeking into several rooms along the way. The home was an endless assortment of collectibles and art.

As we were looking in a second library, a sultry voice behind us said, "Hello gentlemen."

We both jumped. We turned to see a young, extremely attractive woman with long black hair and a slim body and rather large breasts.

"Hello Kailey," Chad said.

"I didn't mean to scare you."

"That's fine. We're just a little on edge."

She laughed. "Did Bill tell you he would kill you?"

"Yes, he did mention that."

"He tried that speech out on me, and I told him not to use it. Don't worry; he's as gentle as a lamb."

"Kailey, I would like for you to meet Cam Derringer. Cam, this is Kailey Arlington, Alexis's stepmother."

I shook hands with her and told her it was nice to meet her, all the while thinking she looked younger than Alexis.

"You have a beautiful house," I said.

"Thank you, but of course I had nothing to do with it. I still get lost occasionally."

"I can see how that could happen."

"I came to show you to your room. You may relax, freshen up or just enjoy the bar. Follow me," she said, turning and looking back over her shoulder at us. She had a very seductive smile.

It was a pleasure following her down the hall. She led us up a grand staircase to an open door.

"Here you are. If you need anything, just press this button," she said, handing me a remote. "The button on the left is for the staff. The one on the right buzzes me. Be sure to press the *right* button," she said, smiling, and left the room.

"Toodles," she said from the doorway.

"I think your mother-in-law is coming on to me," I said when we were alone again.

"It's been nice knowing you, Cam. Thanks for taking some of the attention off me. If Bill has anyone killed, it'll be you."

"I need another drink," I choked out.

Chapter 16

The guests started arriving around two o'clock. The list had definitely grown from the intimate little wedding Chad had agreed to.

His parents, Chesterfield and Addie, arrived and were directed to our room. Hugs and kisses all around. It was good to see them again.

His mother excused herself and went back downstairs to mingle with the guests.

"Dad, have you talked to Robert today?"

"Yes, I just saw him downstairs at the bar."

"Great. Is he doing okay? I mean does he look upset?"

"Seems fine to me. Why?"

"Oh, nothing much. We just had a little disagreement."

"Well, you know Robert; he's probably forgotten about it by now."

"Yeah, I guess."

"Would you care for something to drink, Chester?" I asked.

"Don't mind if I do," he said.

"Follow me," I said.

I led him down the hall to yet another bar.

"My God, this place is fantastic."

"I know. I hope Chad moves in here and brings me with him," I said.

We fixed our drinks and took a small tour of the area before we returned to our room. Chad was hanging up his phone when we entered.

He looked pale.

"What's the matter?" I said.

"That was Robert. He told me why he was so upset. It appears Alexis called him last month and assured him that we would help him financially, and if I died, he would inherit five million dollars."

"Did you know that?"

"No, I had no idea."

"Wonder why he would be mad about that," I said.

"He said it sounded like she was hinting to him that my death would be beneficial to him."

"Do you believe she would insinuate something like that, Son?" Chester asked.

"No. I think Robert misunderstood. I tried to tell him that, but he insisted he understood very well."

"What do you think, Cam?" Chester asked me.

"I agree with Chad, but if it makes everyone more at ease, I'll check into a few things."

"No," Chad said, "I don't want to start this marriage out investigating my wife."

"Very well, Chad," I said, "I'll be here for you if you need me, but I think her father will kill you first anyway."

"Crap, I had almost forgotten about that."

"Shall we refill?" I said, holding up my empty glass.

71

"Might just as well," Chad said.

~***~

Andrei arrived back in New York at two o'clock. He dropped his rental car off at Hertz and took a taxi to the Viceroy New York Hotel. He checked in under the name Demyan Minsky. Demyan means "to kill." He always liked that name. It made him feel charged.

He fixed a bourbon, ran a hot bath and climbed in. Tomorrow was going to be a busy day. The day after would be very hectic.

~***~

The wedding went off without a hitch. I think Alexis was the most beautiful bride I have ever seen, that is after my own wife, Melinda.

I congratulated Chad and kissed Alexis. We danced and drank the night away.

Robert and Chad seemed to get along just fine as if nothing had happened.

Kailey Arlington asked me to dance. I reluctantly accepted. She held me close and pressed her breasts firmly to my chest, and I mean *firmly*.

"Want to see my bedroom?" she whispered.

"I don't think that would be a good idea."

"I do, but I wouldn't want to force you. We'll be around each other often now. I'll get you sooner or later." She kissed me and walked away.

I looked around to see if anyone saw us. Several people, who I didn't know, were looking at me.

"That's all I need," I murmured.

I didn't see her again that night. She must have found a taker.

Around nine thirty, I said my goodnights and took the limo back to my place.

~***~

My apartment door was ajar. That was never good. I drew my gun and entered quietly. I heard someone in the kitchen going through my cabinets, so with my pistol held in front of me, I went in low and fast.

"Where do you keep your wine glasses?" Kailey said.

"Shit, you scared me. I could have shot you."

"How would you explain that to my husband?"

"What are you doing here?"

"Looking for a wine glass."

"Over there in the dry sink," I said, pointing to the corner.

She walked to the dry sink, removed two wine glasses and her dress and walked back to where I was standing, my mouth agape.

"Corkscrew?" she said.

I just stared, still trying to comprehend what was going on. She was a beauty, but she was married, and her husband was deadly.

"Corkscrew?" she said again.

"Look Kailey, you really need to put your clothes back on and leave. You're stunning and a very nice person, but I don't date married women."

"Wow, you're beautiful *and* have morals. There's a lucky girl somewhere. Why isn't she here tonight? I am."

"Please, let's don't make a big deal of this. I'll call my limo to take you home."

"I don't want to go yet," she said. With that, she removed the rest of her clothes.

Christ, this was getting crazy. *What can I do? I can't dress her. If I get that close to her, I'll never get away. I*

73

can't call Chad. I'm sure he has his own hands full by now.

Then my worst nightmare happened. From my front door, which I left open, I heard, "Cam, it's me, Robin."

Chapter 17

"**W**e're in the kitchen," Kailey said as if she were inviting in our best friends.

Oh shit, nowhere to hide. I thought about climbing into a cabinet, but I knew Kailey would give me up. I could lie on the floor and then tell Robin she knocked me unconscious when I came in.

Then, before I could come up with an excellent plan, Robin was in the kitchen.

"Uh, what is this?" Robin asked, looking at Kailey.

I couldn't speak.

"This is Kailey," Kailey said, extending her hand to shake Robin's.

Robin didn't reciprocate.

Kailey withdrew her hand. "Let me get you a glass," she said.

She walked back to the dry sink and removed another wine glass.

I looked at Robin, who was still looking at Kailey. When she looked at me, I just shrugged my shoulders as if this was the first time I noticed Kailey too.

Robin gave me the look.

"May I ask what's going on here?" she asked calmly.

"Well," I said, "this is Chad's mother-in-law, and uh…"

"Is he always this short and sweet with his explanations?" Kailey said and poured three glasses of wine.

She handed me one, which I took, then offered one to Robin, which she took.

"Thank you," Robin said. "Are you chilly?"

"No, I'm fine, thank you," Kailey said.

I turned to Robin, who was looking at me.

"Cheers," Kailey said and downed half her glass.

Then they were both looking at me.

"I wish I could explain, but I don't know where to start," I said.

"Kailey, would you like to explain?" Robin asked curtly.

"Sure. I'll give him a break. I thought he was cute, so I left the wedding before he did and came here. I have ways of getting in anywhere. Money will do that. Anyway, when he came home, about five minutes before you, I took off my clothes and tried to seduce him. He turned me down and told me to leave. Then you came in and, well, you know the rest."

"Cam?" Robin said.

"I couldn't have done better. That's what happened."

"I guess I could still hang around if the two of you could use a third for the night," Kailey said.

"Cam?" Robin said again, her tone sounding a little sharper now.

"No Kailey. I think you had better leave," I said.

76

"How did you get in here?" Robin asked. "This place is supposed to have excellent security."

"My private security guard let me in," she said.

"How did he do that?"

"You ask a lot of questions. What are you, the FBI?"

Robin pulled back her jacket and flashed her FBI badge.

"Well, fuck me," Kailey said. "You are. That's hot."

"I think you should go," Robin said.

Kailey set her empty glass down on the counter and slowly dressed. "I hope we can do this again sometime," she said.

She picked up her handbag, turned and kissed me then turned back around and kissed Robin. "Call me some time," she said to her. "I know my way out. Toodles," she said as she walked out the door.

Robin looked at me.

"How was your night?" I asked.

"Cam, how can one guy get in so much trouble so often?"

"I don't know. Karma I guess," I said, shaking my head.

"What would you have done if I hadn't come in?"

"I don't know. I'm glad you did."

"Well, never mind for now. I need a drink," Robin said, surrendering.

I fixed us both a Wild Turkey on the rocks. I gave her hers and watched her drink half of it down. I kind of wished she would yell at me or something. It was as if she didn't care.

"Why are you back in New York? Did you get your man?"

"No. I just came back to get some clothes. I think it might take a few days. We believe he's still there."

"What makes you think that? He probably killed the senator last night. He could be long gone."

"There was another call intercepted last night. It was to the assassin from a burner phone. The call was traced to DC. He has orders for another hit, but not until he's told to. It sounded like the senator wasn't even a target."

"What about the first killings?"

"He wrote on the back of his card. This is the first time he ever did that."

"What did it say?"

"*This was just for fun.*"

"Cold guy," I said.

"Yeah, he is. They needed killing, but wow."

"When do you have to go back to DC?"

"Tomorrow afternoon."

"Good, you can spend the night here with me."

Robin looked at me. "Do you think I already forgot about Kailey?"

"You know that wasn't my fault."

She thought for a minute. "Okay, but you better be thinking about me."

Chapter 18

The next morning, Andrei rolled out of bed at six thirty, hit the button on the coffee pot and took a hot shower. The room was adequate but not exactly the five-star he was used to. He poured his coffee and pressed the button on his voice recorder. He listened intently. He could hear someone moving around. It sounded as if they were making breakfast.

He drank his coffee, leaving the machine on. The voices began. He smiled at the conversation. "Poor guy," he said aloud.

When he finally heard the part he was waiting for, he changed channels and listened to another conversation. They would all be recorded so he could listen at his leisure.

He opened the case and removed his rifle. He disassembled and cleaned it. The job ahead would call for precise accuracy. *This will be a real challenge.* It might be the most fun he ever had on a hit.

~***~

Chad and Alexis spent most of the day in bed. Around noon Chad went to the market and bought two filet mignons. He was in a fantastic mood. Alexis was the girl of his dreams, the weather was perfect, and he was wealthy. Filthy rich.

Then he thought about what Robert had told him about his suspicions of Alexis. That was crazy. She would never do anything like that. He was sure.

Now, if Alexis died, he would be extraordinarily rich also. Didn't Alexis tell him they had to be married for a year for her to inherit all her money and then ten years for her to keep it? He guessed if he died, though, it would still count.

Why in the hell was he thinking about all of that? Was he trying to ruin a perfect day? *Get a grip and push all those thoughts out of your mind, Chad,* he thought.

Andrei watched as Chad left the market and hailed a taxi. "This will be fun."

~***~

I escorted Robin to the FBI building at one o'clock. We didn't talk much, and I had the feeling she might still be mad about finding a naked woman in my apartment.

"Are we good?" I asked her.

"Yeah, we're good. I could tell by the way she kissed me and you when she left that she didn't care who she fucked as long as she fucked someone. I could see her doing exactly what she said she did."

"Yes, she is a little forward."

We laughed.

"Are you worried about Bloodshot?"

"Yes, he's changed his MO. That worries me. He's up to something big this time. I'm sure of it."

"Be careful. I don't want you getting hurt."

"He probably doesn't know I even exist, but he does know the FBI is looking for him. That's why he left the first card on those gangbangers. He loves teasing us."

The cab pulled to the curb in front of her building. "I love you," I said and kissed her.

"I love you too," she said. "Try to stay out of trouble this time while I'm gone."

"I'll try," I said. "Promise."

~***~

It was Sunday, and I had no plans, so I dressed in my running clothes and went to the park. I ran harder than usual. The more I thought about Kailey and Robin the more I ran. None of it was my fault, but now I had two women I had to tiptoe around. I wished I were back in Key West.

That was when I decided that I was finished with New York. I had a good life as a private investigator in Key West. I didn't need my license to practice law. No one likes lawyers anyway.

I was still running, but I was much lighter. A load had just been taken off my back. I'd stay long enough to tie up the loose ends with my cases for Chad. Then I would be gone.

I finished my run with a big smile on my face.

~***~

Andrei stood across the street and watched Cam return from his run. *He looked happy. He won't be tomorrow.*

Chapter 19

I received a call early the next morning. It was Chad.

"Good morning lover-boy," I said.

"I didn't know it was going to be this good. You should jump in the water yourself," Chad replied.

"No thanks. Not just yet. I think I'll wait a few more years. Maybe I'll find a rich one too."

"There aren't any more."

"There's one. Your mother-in-law paid me a little visit a few nights ago, after the wedding."

"Do tell."

"Later. It's a funny story. I don't want you to have to explain why you're laughing."

"Okay, but don't forget the story."

"Not a chance. What's up?"

"I'm going to be in a little late this morning. Just wanted to give you a heads-up."

"Take the day off. We don't have any court cases today. I can handle it."

"I'll check in sometime today. How's the Bloodshot case going?"

"Haven't heard anything yet. It could take a while," I said, thinking I wished she'd call. I worried about her, in particular in a case like this. He'd outsmarted them before.

"Let me know if you hear anything. I've been thinking about her."

"You've been thinking about Robin while you're in bed with your wife?"

"Sure. Who do you think about when you're in bed with Robin?"

"Robin, of course. She said I had to."

Chad laughed. "I can't wait to hear your story."

"Enjoy your morning. I'll see you later today."

"Goodbye," Chad said and hung up.

~***~

Andrei turned off the listening device. "Good to know," he said.

~***~

I worked in the office until noon. I'd hoped to have lunch with Chad, but since I hadn't heard anything from him yet, I left to get a bite to eat.

I chose the hot dog stand on the corner a block away. "One chilly dog with cheese," I said.

"These things are going to kill you, Cam," Arnie the vendor said.

"You shouldn't tell people that. It could be bad for business."

"I figure it's kind of like puttin' the warning on a cigarette pack. You can't sue me 'cause you've been warned."

"Maybe you've got a point there. Extra cheese, please."

Arnie gave me a look. "You live on the edge, don't ya?"

"That I do."

~***~

Andrei parked the stolen SUV on the third floor of the parking garage. He still had fifteen minutes before the target would arrive. From his vantage point, he had a clear view of the spot where he knew his target would be standing. Removing the rifle from the case, he assembled it, slid in the magazine and inserted a bullet into the chamber. One shot was all it would take, but he always liked having the fifteen extra rounds just as a precaution.

He opened his soft drink and took a big swallow. A little extra caffeine was always good. His father told him to always be sharp before a hit.

He saw the blue limo pull to the curb across the street. Andrei raised his rifle and placed the barrel on a pad he had laid on the wall. His crosshairs were lined up on the door, waiting for it to open.

There it was. It opened, and the man stepped out and closed the door. The profile was perfect. Andrei didn't hesitate. He lined the crosshairs and squeezed the trigger. The bullet found its target.

Andrei watched the commotion across the street. He had made a good shot from the parking garage. He left his card on the wall and placed a brick on it and stowed the rifle back in its case. Taking the elevator down to the first floor, he left the parking garage at the opposite end, away from the carnage on the sidewalk. "One down, three to go," he said.

~***~

My phone rang before I could take my first bite. I didn't recognize the number, but only relevant people have my number.

"Hello," I said, looking at my hot dog and wondering if it really would kill me.

"Cam, it's Alexis."

I didn't like the tone of her voice. She sounded urgent.

"Alexis, what's wrong?"

"It's Chad. He's been shot."

Chapter 20

I **tossed my hot dog into the trash** can and hailed a
taxi. I arrived at Mount Sinai Hospital ten minutes
later.

The receptionist at the front desk directed me to the
waiting area for the ER. Alexis was waiting there.

I put my arms around her. "Is he alright?" I asked.

"I don't know yet. I think he'll be okay. The bullet
sliced his shoulder. They said it didn't seem to hit
anything vital."

"Was it a robbery?"

"No. We were just going to Marko's for lunch. When
he stepped out of the car, someone shot him," she said
and started crying. I held her again.

I held her until she stopped. I sat her down in a chair
and got both of us some coffee.

"Did you see who shot him?" I asked.

"No, I didn't even hear the shot."

"Must have been from some distance."

We waited. Twenty minutes then twenty more.

The door to the waiting room opened, and Chief McNally walked in.

"Hello, Cam. We meet again," he said, removing his cigar from his mouth and sticking it in his coat pocket.

"Yes, we do, but this time Chad has actually been shot. Maybe you'll take us a little more seriously now."

"So, you think Emanuel Barona took a shot at Chad?"

"I don't know, but someone did."

"Any thoughts."

"None you would enjoy hearing."

"Try me."

"Well, to me it looks like the work of a professional hitman. It just so happens that there is one in town from Russia. The FBI is tracking him, but I'm sure you're on top of that."

"Why would I be? The FBI has a bad habit of not sharing with us," he said gruffly.

"Guess they don't want you in the way."

"Ouch. Are you trying to hurt me on purpose?" he asked, feigning insult.

I thought for a minute. This probably wasn't the best way to lobby for help from the NYPD.

"Sorry," I said. "I'm just trying to blame someone."

"No problem. Now, who is this assassin?"

"He goes by Bloodshot," I said. "He's from Russia."

"How do you know this?"

"I've heard," I said, offering no more.

"Okay, I'll check on Emanuel. We have a little birdy close to him. If he ordered this, I'll know."

"Thanks."

"Hope Chad is okay. I'll check back when he's feeling better."

We shook hands, and he left. We waited for another ten minutes.

"I've got to find someone and get some answers," I finally said, rising from my chair. "We should have heard something by now."

As I was about to open the door, it swung open. A doctor was standing there. We startled each other.

"Sorry," I said.

He looked past me and said, "Alexis?"

"Yes, that's me," she said, standing.

"Will you please take this man home? He's been a real pain."

Chad walked from behind the doctor and entered the room.

"Hey everyone, what's up?" he said in a jubilant voice for someone who was just shot.

Alexis started crying again and ran to him.

"Easy," the doctor said. "He won't be quite as happy once the shots wear off."

I was never so relieved in my life. I didn't know how much he meant to me until that moment. Good friends are hard to come by.

Chad hugged Alexis. Then he saw me. "What's the matter, ol' boy? Did you think you were going to get rid of me so you could have Alexis?"

"Well, yeah. That thought did enter my mind."

"No luch suck," he said, twisting his words.

Alexis giggled.

The doctor told us that the police wanted to talk to Chad, but they would wait until he was home.

"They think they already have a good idea of who shot him," he said.

"Really, who?" I said.

"Don't know. They didn't share that with me, but if the shot had been a few inches to the left, he could have lost his arm. A few more inches and he would be dead."

"Well, I guess it's my lucky day," Chad said.

"Doc, how long before the medication wears off?" I asked.

"You have to put up with him for another two hours."

"Thank you. Can we take him home now?"

"He's all yours. My nurse will give you instructions on changing the bandage. She'll be right in."

"Thank you, kind sir," Chad said to the doctor as he was leaving.

"My pleasure," he said back over his shoulder.

~***~

I called for our limo, and the three of us went to Chad's apartment since it was closer than Alexis's parents' house.

My cell phone rang. It was Robin.

"Hello sweetie," I answered.

"Cam, is Chad okay?"

"How did you know about Chad?"

"I got a call from the NYPD. They thought I might be interested."

"Why is that?"

"They found a calling card from where the shot was fired."

"You don't mean…"

"Yes, I do. Was he shot in the arm?"

"Yes."

"On the back of the card, he had written, 'Chad Kendall–right arm–$25,000.'"

I looked at Chad and Alexis. They were staring at me.

"I'm on my way there," Robin said.

"We're going to Alexis's apartment now. We'll see you there."

"So, he's okay?"

"Just a nick," I said.

"That's a first. He never misses, and I don't think he missed this time."

"Lucky for us this time."

We hung up. I didn't know if I should tell Chad or not. This presented all kinds of implications. Someone hired an assassin to kill Chad, or at least wound him. Quickly thinking about who would have done that, two names came to mind. Alexis and Robert. They both had a lot to gain. Well, Robert did. Alexis would get her money either way, but maybe she wanted it for herself.

"What was that about?" Alexis asked.

What the heck. They would know as soon as the police arrived anyway.

"It appears that Bloodshot is the one who shot Chad," I said.

Chad looked at me. I think it sobered him up. "You mean the assassin Bloodshot?" he said.

"Yeah."

"Why would someone want me killed?"

Then another thought came to mind.

"Maybe Emanuel Barona," I said.

"You think?"

"How did Bloodshot know we were going to be at Marko's for lunch? We just decided that this morning and we haven't told anyone," Alexis said.

"Good question. He had to be there before you."

The limo pulled to the curb in front of The Plaza. I told the driver not to wait. "We'll make it home okay. Thanks."

Barry, the driver, said, "I hope you feel better tomorrow, Mister Kendall."

"Thank you, Barry. I hope so too. Thanks for the ride."

We took the elevator to Chad's apartment. I could tell he was already starting to feel the pain a little.

"Anyone for a drink?" Alexis asked. "I think I could use one."

"I'll have one too," I said.

"I could use a big one," Chad said.

We had our drinks and discussed the possibility that Emanuel could have done this.

"Didn't Robin say Bloodshot was summoned here a month ago?" Chad said.

"Yeah, about three weeks."

"He was already coming before Emanuel threatened us."

"You're right. It couldn't be him."

Alexis was quiet, but I could tell something was on her mind.

"What are you thinking, Alexis?" I asked.

"Nothing, just thinking."

Chad was slowly slipping into slumber. We walked him to the bedroom, and he lay down on the bed. I pulled his shoes off, pulled up the covers and turned off the light.

Back out in the living room we made two more drinks and sat on the balcony.

"Do you want to tell me what you were thinking now?" I asked.

"Well, I know I'm probably wrong, but I told Robert, Chad's brother, a month ago that he would inherit five million dollars if Chad died. You don't think he would do something like this, do you?"

I figured it was time to be honest. "Robert told us about that. He thought it sounded as if you said that hoping he would kill Chad. That way you would get your money and still be single."

"No," she said. "You don't believe that, do you?"

91

It was time to be not so honest. "No, I don't, but I could see how that would be strange for someone who doesn't really know you."

"Doesn't know me?" she murmured.

"You mean he does know you?"

"Please don't tell Chad, but Robert and I have met. He came to my father six months ago to offer him a percentage of a venture, if Father would finance it. We went out to supper a few times while the negotiations were going on. They couldn't come to a settlement, so they called it off."

"You haven't told Chad?"

"No, I didn't know they were brothers at first. Then, when I found out, I was afraid I'd lose Chad, so I didn't say anything."

"Robert told us he was in Vietnam six months ago," I said.

"No, he was here."

"What did he want the loan for?"

"I'm not sure. I didn't have anything to do with that deal."

"Okay. Keep this to yourself for now. I'll do some checking."

"I will. Thank you so much for all you've done for us."

Chapter 21

Robin **arrived two hours later.** I filled her in on what was discussed. She questioned Alexis about Robert.

"I want you to let me check on him first," I said.

"I don't know if I can do that," Robin said.

"Please, give me twenty-four hours."

She thought it over. I could tell her instincts said no, but her loyalty said maybe.

"Okay, but that's all I can do," she said.

"Why were you going to give Robert the five million?" Robin asked Alexis.

"It was the amount he asked Father for. I thought Chad and I would back him. I told him that, but I wanted him to know if something happened to Chad, he would still get it."

"How are you going to tell Chad that his brother wants you to back him and that the two of you already know each other?" I asked.

"I haven't figured that out yet," she said.

"You need to figure it out soon. Like tomorrow."

"I will."

Robin put her arm around Alexis. "I'll help any way I can."

"Thank you," Alexis said.

I hadn't told Robin about Robert's thoughts on Alexis wanting Chad dead. I wanted to check it out myself first.

Robin and I said our goodnights to Alexis and went to my apartment.

We fixed a drink and sat on the sofa.

"I'm trying to figure out how Bloodshot knew where Chad was going to be before he arrived," Robin said.

"I know. Alexis asked the same question. She and Chad were the only ones who knew."

"Do you think he placed a bug somewhere in their room?"

"I don't know how," I answered.

"It can be done."

"You know, there is the chance Alexis could have something to do with this," I said.

"I know. She was my first thought."

"She was?"

"Yep. I always look at the wife or husband first. And one more thing."

"What's that?"

"How did the NYPD know we were working on a case called Bloodshot?"

"I might have slipped a little in the heat of an argument."

"You shouldn't do that."

"I know. Sorry."

"Well, this time it was a good thing. We were informed right away, but I did get a little ass-chewing from McNally."

"Sorry again."

"Forgiven."

"Why would someone hire an assassin just to wound someone?"

"That's a good question. It doesn't make any sense."

"This is going to be a tough one. I don't want anyone to be guilty," I said.

"I know the feeling. When friends are involved, sometimes you have to back off and let someone else do the dirty work."

I took a drink of my Wild Turkey and held it in my mouth. The warm liquid perked my senses.

"No, I can't do that. What if I would have backed off in Key West when I was told to? I might never have found Melinda's killers," I said and instantly tried to push the thought from my mind.

"I had you covered on that," she said.

"Are you forgetting I also saved your life?"

"And I saved yours."

"Well, aren't we just a couple of heroes?"

"Yeah, superheroes."

~***~

The next morning, when I woke, Robin was in the shower. I made my famous omelets and fried some bacon.

"Smells good," she said from the kitchen entry.

"Thought it might be a big day. We need our energy."

"You only have sixteen hours left to find the goods on Robert. You shouldn't waste your time cooking."

"I'm already working on it. I have a call into Johnny Craddock."

"Who's Johnny Craddock?"

"Robert's friend. Supposedly they were in Vietnam together last year. Johnny came home, and Robert chose to stay. He just returned last month, and Alexis said

Robert visited her father then. I'm just a little concerned about the timeline. Why did he come home just in time for the wedding, and why Alexis's dad? Not to mention, Chad and I were defending her at the same time, and Robert never contacted Chad."

"You sure don't sound like someone trying to defend a friend."

"It's just that I have to find a logical explanation for all of this. I know there has to be one," I said.

"Good luck, I hope you're right."

We dug into our bacon and eggs.

"This is good," Robin said. "I could get used to this. Why don't you just quit work and take care of me?"

"Is that a proposal?" I said.

She got a funny look on her face. "I don't know."

"I was just kidding. You can relax," I said.

"What if it was a proposal?"

"I think you would make an excellent partner in life, but we would have a lot to discuss before making any permanent commitment."

We just stared at each other.

"Wow, that was intense," she said.

"Yeah, but think about it and I will too."

I was confused now. I already had my mind made up to return to Key West.

She finished her eggs and said, "Thank you, it was awesome. I'll call you tonight, and you can fill me in on Robert."

"I'm working on it," I said.

"How long will Robert be in New York?"

"He said he'd be here for another two weeks."

"Okay, it doesn't sound like he's running."

I walked her to the door and kissed her softly. "I love you."

"I love you too."

Chapter 22

I decided to take the day off and concentrate on Robert. My first stop was at The Barclay, where Chad lives. I wanted to talk to Tom Carrington, Chad's friend and neighbor. Adrian Boykov told me that Tom invited him to the bachelor party. I thought this was a good place to start since I hadn't heard from Johnny yet.

I found his apartment on the sixth floor. No one answered my knock. I knew it was a chance anyway. People do have to work.

As I was leaving, a neighbor opened his door. "Excuse me, sir. Are you looking for Tom?" he asked.

He was a young man, around thirty-five, dressed in a well-tailored blue suit.

"Yes, I am. Have you seen him?"

"No. Not for a couple of days. We had an appointment with a broker this morning, but he hasn't shown up. I'm a little worried."

"Do you have a key to his apartment?" I inquired.

"No, but the concierge does."

I introduced myself to the man who said his name was Jerald Banks. I gave him my card and asked if he might contact the concierge and try Tom's room. Would he please call me and let me know if it gave any clue as to where he might be.

"Sure. I've been thinking the same thing myself," he said.

I left the building and hailed another taxi. "The Hilton, please," I said.

I thought I would check there to see if Adrian had returned. The desk clerk said he had checked out. Another dead end.

My cell phone rang. "Hello."

Mister Derringer?" It was a question.

"Yes, this is he."

"This is Johnny Craddock returning your call."

"Johnny, thanks for getting back to me. I'm a good friend and associate of Chad Kendall's. I was calling regarding his brother Robert."

"Is he okay?" There was panic in his voice.

"Should I worry that he isn't?" I asked.

"No, I guess not. I just haven't heard from him for a while."

"He's fine. He was telling me about your adventure in Vietnam. You haven't seen him since he returned?"

"Well, after we got back, he hung around here for about a week and then said he had somewhere he had to go. I haven't seen him since."

"So, he came back from Vietnam with you?" I asked, puzzled.

"Sure."

"He didn't stay there after you left?"

"No. Are you sure he's okay?"

"He's alright. I think. At least he was a few days ago. I'm just trying to contact him."

"Sorry, I can't help you. If you see Robert, will you tell him I miss him?"

I could tell by his tone that he was worried and that they were more than just friends.

"I'll tell him."

"Thanks."

After we had hung up, I sat on a street bench and contemplated the information. Where had Robert been if he wasn't in Vietnam?

I called my office and asked Susan, my assistant, to try to find any activity on a credit card belonging to Robert Kendall. She said she would call me back in a bit.

The thought went through my head again. *Why would someone want to just wound Chad?*

I didn't see any gain in that for Robert.

My next call was to William Arlington. Maybe he'd tell me why Robert needed the money.

"Cam. To what do I owe the pleasure?"

That really made me feel bad since I just saw his wife naked in my apartment.

"I was hoping to get a little information from you."

"I'll try to help. Is this about Chad?"

"In part."

"Is he okay?"

"He'll be fine."

"Good to hear. What can I help you with?"

"Robert Kendall came to see you about a month ago. I was curious as to what he wanted the loan for."

"Does this have anything to do with Chad?"

"Maybe. I'm not sure. Just trying to eliminate acquaintances."

"He wanted me to invest in a venture down in Florida. I can't talk about what it was since he's still working on it. Let me say that it just wasn't my cup of tea. Nothing illegal, mind you. It just wasn't for me."

"Fair enough," I said. "Can you tell me what amount Robert needed?"

"Five million."

"That checks out with what we heard."

"I guess Alexis has told you about her knowing Robert," he said.

"Yes, I knew about that. Now she's trying to find a way to tell Chad before Robert does."

"What a tangled web we weave."

"How true."

"Keep me updated on all this if you don't mind," he said.

"I will. Thanks for the information."

My phone rang just as I hung up.

"Cam, it's Susan. I have some activity on Robert's card. Most of it from the last year is in Florida at the Sunny Lake Nudist Colony."

"Really, just where is that?"

"Near Kissimmee."

"That's where he's been living?"

"It sure seems like it. He's been buying groceries and gas and paying rent. All on credit."

"For how long?"

"About eight months as far as I can tell."

"Thanks, Susan."

"Anytime, Cam."

Chapter 23

I called Robert's cell phone. He answered on the first ring.

"Hello."

"Robert, it's Cam."

"Oh, hi Cam," he said, sounding disappointed.

"Sorry, were you expecting someone?"

"Yeah, Chad. I haven't talked to him since the wedding."

I dreaded telling him that his brother had been shot. It's something I should have done immediately.

"That's why I was calling you. First of all, Chad's fine."

"Something happen to him?" he asked, now with concern in his voice.

"He was shot in the arm, but he's fine."

"SHOT?" he said, his voice now turning to panic. "Did Alexis shoot him?"

"No, she was with him. Actually, he was shot by an assassin from Russia."

"What?"

"Yeah, the FBI has been tracking him. They knew he was here for a hit, but it seems he just wounded him on purpose."

"What hospital is he in?"

"He's home sleeping it off."

"Home? When did this happen?"

"About noon yesterday."

"And you just now called me?"

"It's complicated. Can we meet? I'll fill you in on everything."

There was a brief silence on his end.

"Okay. Where?"

"How about my place around one?"

"Fine," he said, sounding a little mad.

I gave my address and told him we would have lunch in the restaurant at my apartment.

I had about an hour to kill so I went to my apartment and got out a good book that I had been reading. It was a young adult book but recommended to me by Diane, who found it fascinating. It was mainly located in the Florida Keys. The name is *Rum City Bar*. I was very engrossed in the book when my cell rang again.

"Hello."

"Mister Derringer?"

"Yes."

"This is Jerald Banks, Tom Carrington's friend."

"Oh, yes, Jerald. Did you find anything?"

"It looks as though Tom has packed a suitcase and gone on a trip."

"And he didn't say anything to you about going somewhere?"

"No, he didn't. Even though it looks like he went on vacation, I don't believe he would go without telling me."

"So, you think something else happened to him?"

"I don't know what to think, but I know he didn't just leave without telling me."

"Thanks for calling, Jerald. If you hear anything from him will you call me?"

"Sure. Will you do the same?"

"I will."

He gave me his phone number and we hung up.

I thought about Tom and Adrian. Funny how Tom disappeared when I was just about to question him about Adrian.

Did Tom disappear because he didn't want to answer any questions or because someone made him disappear? My gut told me it was the latter.

I was just getting into the kidnapping of a beautiful redhead in my book when my doorbell rang.

I opened the door.

Robert came in without saying a word. He walked to the bar, which was openly located in the corner of the living room. He opened a bottle and poured a generous shot of Knob Creek.

"Help yourself," I said.

"I can't believe you didn't call me immediately when Chad was shot."

"Like I said, it's complicated."

"How so?"

"Sit, please," I said, pointing to a chair as I sat on the sofa.

He hesitated and then took the seat.

"Okay, here's the deal. Don't say anything until I'm finished."

"Maybe," he said curtly.

"Anyway, I didn't tell you because the FBI considers you a suspect."

He stood. "WHAT THE HELL YOU MEAN, A SUSPECT?"

"Calm down and sit back down," I said sternly, pointing at the chair.

He stared at me for a moment then sat back down.

"It appears that if Chad dies, you receive five million dollars."

"I told you that," he interrupted.

"I know you did, but that doesn't change anything. I talked the FBI into giving me twenty-four hours to prove you are innocent before they question you."

"It's Robin, isn't it?" he asked accusingly.

"She is the one who gave me twenty-four hours. You're lucky she is on your side."

He calmed down again, slightly.

I went on. "I retraced your steps for the last eight months and found that you weren't in Vietnam."

He turned red and looked away.

"I also talked to William Arlington who told me you came to him for five million dollars. While you were with him, you took Alexis out to dinner a few times."

"Nothing ever happened between Alexis and me," he said sharply.

"I know," I said. "You're gay."

Robert turned red again and swallowed hard.

"Why would you say that?"

"I googled the Sunny Lake Nudist Colony. It's a gay organization."

He just looked stunned.

"That's nothing to be ashamed of, Robert, but I take it you haven't told Chad."

"How can I?"

"I think he would understand."

"I don't think he or Mom and Dad would. I've never let on to them. That's why I moved to Florida, and the reason I've been trying to raise the money is Sunny Lakes is for sale. Two other investors and I want to buy it and develop it into the biggest adult gay and lesbian resort in the world. We'll have our own grocery store, theaters, medical center and restaurants."

"That's a very ambitious plan."

"We're ambitious people."

"Nothing wrong with that, as long as you have your ducks in a row."

"We do."

"Good. Now for the business at hand. Do you have any idea why someone would want to hurt Chad?"

"Not a clue. Other than Alexis. She would have her money and still be single."

"You're really stuck on the idea that Alexis is behind all this. Why? What makes you think it was her?"

"Look at her. Sure, Chad is handsome, but she's one of the most beautiful women I've ever seen. The only reason she got married was to get her money."

"Maybe, although I don't think so. Anyone else?"

"No, not really."

"Okay, give it some thought. If you think of anything, call me."

"I will."

"Alright, let's go get some food. The fare downstairs is one of the best in town," I said, getting up from the sofa.

"Mind if I take a rain check? I don't feel like eating."

"Sure. I understand."

"Thanks."

"Robert, I think you can tell Chad. He's a good man and he loves you."

"Yeah, I guess we'll see."

"What are your plans now?" I asked.

"I'm going to see Chad at his apartment. Then at five, I have an appointment with William Arlington, at his house. He called and said he wanted to talk to me again about the investment."

"Maybe he had a change of heart, now that you're family."

"I hope so."

I walked him to the door. We shook hands and I told him, "Good luck."

~***~

Andrei turned off his monitor. "Five o'clock," he said. "See you then."

Chapter 24

Robert took a taxi to The Barclay. The doorman greeted him and opened the door directing him to the front desk.

"Please check in at the counter, sir."

"Thank you," Robert said.

He walked to the desk where he was greeted by the concierge, a man in his mid-fifties, seemingly in decent physical condition and dressed very sharply in a three-piece gray suit.

"May I help you, sir?" the concierge asked.

"Yes. I'm Robert Kendall, and I'm here to see my brother Chadwick," Robert said.

"One moment please," he said and raised the phone.

Robert took in the lobby and what he could see of the restaurant from where he was standing. He thought Chad

had done very well for himself. With a little luck, he'd be able to do as well someday.

"You may go up, sir. Room eight thirty-five."

"Thank you," Robert said and walked to the elevator.

~***~

Robert tapped the door with his knuckles three times then twice then once. That was their secret knock from childhood. From the other side, Robert heard Chad knock three times; then he opened the door.

They laughed. "You remembered," Robert said.

"Hard to forget a secret code we used until after college, just in case one of us had a girl visitor."

Alexis appeared from the kitchen. "He has one now," she said.

"Good thing I knocked," Robert said.

"I don't think I'm in any shape for hanky-panky right now, so it would have been safe just to walk in."

Alexis hugged Robert and said, "I'm glad you're here. I need to get away from Chad for a while. He's so needy. He's milking that little scratch for all it's worth."

"Yes, I remember he's like that," Robert agreed.

"Hey, you guys know I'm standing right here and I can hear everything you say."

"Robert, will you stay for supper? I'm going to the market now to get some steaks to grill."

"I would love to, but I can't. I have an appointment in a few hours."

"Oh, that's a shame. Maybe next time."

"Will the two of you excuse me for a moment? Nature calls," Chad said and left the room.

When Robert heard the bathroom door close, he said, "Alexis, can you stay for a few minutes? I have something to tell Chad, and it concerns you and me."

109

"I haven't told him about knowing you before," she said, worry and panic in her eyes.

"I think it's time. My appointment is with your father. I believe he's going to give me a second chance."

"Are you going to tell Chad that you're gay?" Alexis said.

"Yes, but how did you know?"

"Women can tell those things, and Father told me what you wanted the money for."

"Yeah, I'm planning on telling him."

"I'll stay. You're right, it's time."

"Time for what?" Chad said as he walked back into the room.

"Let's all sit and have a drink, and I'll fill you in on life, bro," Robert said.

"I'll get the drinks," Alexis said.

She walked to the kitchen while Chad and Robert took a seat on the sofa.

"How's the arm?" Robert asked.

"Burns a little, but, all in all, I feel good."

"I wish someone would have told me right away. I would have been at the hospital to help Alexis."

"We did fine. I was looped, and Cam was there, but thanks, I know you would have been there."

"Well, you're going to want to be looped for this too, so I'll wait for Alexis," Robert said.

Chad just looked at Robert for a minute. Their eyes were stuck on each other's.

"Robert, did I ever tell you that I backed numerous organizations?"

"No. I figured you probably gave to charities. You're a good person."

"Yeah, I do that too, but I also give to the LGBT. I have for years, ever since you joined it. I got a call from Skip Collins, remember him?"

Robert sat still, staring at Chad in disbelief. "Yes, I remember him."

"He told me he saw you at a meeting. That was about six years ago. I have known since then. I've just been waiting for you to tell me first. And now that you were about to, I thought I would make it easier for you. Did I?"

Robert was still speechless but found his tongue. A tear came to his eye and he said, "I'm sorry I haven't told you. I was ashamed at first, and then later I was just scared."

"Well, it's out now, and we don't have to worry about it any longer. I still love you and I always will," Chad said and hugged Robert.

Alexis came into the room with a tray of drinks. "Looks like I missed something," she said cautiously.

"The drinks are for celebration now," Robert said, "not courage."

"Great," Alexis said. "So you told him about us."

Robert and Chad looked at each other. "I'll take that drink now," Robert said.

"Oh no, you didn't tell him."

"No, just the gay part."

"What's the rest of the story?" Chad asked.

"I came to William Arlington a few months ago, while you were defending Alexis, and offered him an investment opportunity. I didn't tell Alexis I was your brother. We went out to eat a few times. Very innocent, as you might imagine, I'm not even bi. Then I left again. When I heard the two of you were serious and going to be married, I wanted to tell you. Instead, I called Alexis and told her that I was your brother. We decided to keep it to ourselves until we could find a good way to tell you. Part of my wanting to keep it quiet was because the investment was for the expansion of an adult-only gay resort."

Chad sat for a minute drinking his bourbon. "So, the two of you have been sweating over that too? Do you guys worry about everything?"

"Kind of," Alexis said, unconsciously wringing her hands.

"Yeah, me too," Robert said.

"That's no big deal, but in the future, will you both be upfront with me?"

"I promise," Robert said. "I don't have anything else."

"Me neither," Alexis said.

Chapter 25

Alexis finished her drink almost instantly. "I still
need to go to the market. I'll be back in about an
hour. I wish you could stay, Robert, but I know
you want to see Father."

"Thank you for the invite, maybe next time."

"You gentlemen enjoy, and I'll see you later," she said,
kissing Chad and leaving, closing the door behind her.

"I love that woman," Chad said.

"I know you do, but I want you to know that I still
don't trust her one hundred percent."

"I know, but you will."

~***~

Andrei's phone rang. "Yes?" he said.

"Andrei, I've got a tip for you. Robert is on his way to
the Arlington estate at five o'clock."

"I know. Will you be there?"

"No, I have things to do. I'd rather be far away. Your money will be in the box."

"I'll talk to you tomorrow," Andrei said and hung up.

~***~

Robert finished his drink and asked Chad if there was anything he could do for him before he left.

"No, I'm good," he said. "Keep an open mind about Alexis though."

"I'll give her every benefit of the doubt."

"You know, if William won't give you the loan, or invest I mean, I'll be glad to."

"Can't do that, bro, but I appreciate the offer. Family and all, you know."

"Yeah, I know, but the offer stands. I have hundreds of millions now."

"Are you bragging?"

"Yeah, I think I am."

"See ya. Take care."

"I will, you too."

Chapter 26

I was still at my apartment going over my notes when my phone rang. It was Chief McNally

"Hi, Cam."

"Hi, chief."

"Did you get in trouble for ratting out the FBI?"

"Yep. Thanks for that," I said.

"You're welcome. Anyway, I've got a report for you. Emanuel didn't have anything to do with this. Whoever hired that assassin, it wasn't him."

"Too bad. I was hoping it was."

"Yeah, me too. I'd like to put that bum away. And I might have if you wouldn't have got him off."

"You had a weak case. Next time, get it right."

"Next time, don't look for loopholes."

"Thanks for the call, chief."

I hung up and thought about Tom Carrington again. If he left of his own accord, he would have told Jerald Banks, so what if he didn't leave on his own? The first time I visited Chad there, I had to jump through hoops just to get to his apartment. Security there is top-notch. I had a thought. I called the front desk at The Barclay.

"The Barclay," the concierge answered. "How may I help you?"

"Hello Ben, this is Cam Derringer."

"Yes, hello Mister Derringer. How are you today?"

"I'm well, thank you. I have a question for you, though."

"Alright, I'll try to help you."

"Do you have security cameras inside showing the hallways on each floor?"

"Yes, we do."

"I wonder if I could have a look at the tapes from the last few days."

"May I ask why?"

"I'm working on a missing person case, and I think he was last seen in your building," I lied.

"Who might that be?"

"Tom Carrington."

"I didn't know he was missing. I'll be glad to show you."

"Thank you."

"You're welcome. How is Mister Chadwick?"

"He's doing well. I'll visit him while I'm there today. Is it alright if I come over now?"

"I'll have the tapes ready for you. I'll set them up on a monitor in our office."

"Thank you. I'll be there in a few minutes."

I took a taxi to The Barclay. By the time I arrived the office had been set up for me. I started reviewing the tapes from two days before. I was able to fast-forward through all the impertinent action. I stopped when I saw Tom arrive in the lobby. I paused the screen and checked the time. It was five sixteen p.m. the day before yesterday.

I started the action again slowing down the speed a little. I didn't see anything again until eight twelve p.m. It was Adrian Boykov. He went to the desk and talked to the night manager. The manager picked up the phone and dialed. I stopped the film and called for the concierge.

"Yes?" he said as he entered the office.

"Do you have a record of visitors?"

"Yes."

"Can you tell me who this gentleman visited the night before last at eight twelve p.m.?

He looked at the screen.

"Let me check," he said, going to the computer on his desk.

"Yes. Mister Boykov visited Mister Carrington at that time."

"Thanks. Is there a film of the hallway in front of Tom's room?

"Yes. Press R and 652."

I did. The screen changed to the sixth floor. I started the movement again. Adrian appeared from the elevator a minute later. He walked to Tom's apartment, 652, and knocked. The door was opened, and Adrian entered.

I hit fast forward again. At nine twenty-three the door opened, and Adrian stepped into the hallway. He was carrying a backpack. He didn't have one when he entered. I picked him up again in the lobby and watched him exit the building.

I guessed he really did know Tom, but I wondered what was in the backpack. It sure wasn't big enough for a body.

I thanked the concierge and asked him if I might come back and review the film again later.

"Any time, Mister Derringer. Just let me know."

I asked Ben to call Chad and let him know I was on my way up.

~***~

Andrei pressed the combination on the rear gate of the estate to turn off the alarm. Next, he pressed the numbers to unlock the gate. It opened, and he walked in. He walked toward the front lawn and stopped at the spot he was told would have the perfect view of the driveway. She was right. He had just enough room to kneel behind the bushes and lay his case on the ground.

He waited. A taxi pulled into the drive and circled to a point in front of the mansion entry. Andrei raised the rifle and watched Robert open the door through his site. With the crosshairs perfectly lined he squeezed the trigger and watched Robert fall. He replaced the rifle in its case, retraced his route and left the estate grounds. When he closed the back gate, he placed his card behind the keypad.

Chapter 27

C had was sitting on the sofa in tennis shorts watching TV when I entered.

"I see you're living the good life," I said.

"I'm sick of this damn TV. You want to go get a drink?"

"I'm game if you are."

"Let's do it."

"Would Alexis like to join us?"

"She's at the market. She must have stopped to shop along the way."

Chad changed into khakis and a golf shirt.

We went down to the bar and ordered two Pinot Noirs.

We sipped our wine in silence for a few minutes. I could tell something was bothering Chad.

"Is something on your mind, Chad?"

"Yes. I had a visit from Robert today. He told me something I already knew, but I want to tell you."

"Alright, but I might already know."

"I doubt it. Robert is gay."

"Yep, knew it."

"You did? How?

I told him about having twenty-four hours to prove Robert innocent and what I found in the process.

"You mean they think Robert might have something to do with me getting shot?"

"They're trying to cover all the bases. I think this pretty well proves that he did not."

"And what about Emanuel? Could he have had anything to do with it?"

"I don't know. I talked to McNally, who assured me he would know if it were Emanuel who ordered the hit."

We paused and took another drink of our wine.

"Is the FBI any closer to finding Bloodshot, or are they just looking at Robert and Alexis?" Chad said.

"They've never been close to finding Bloodshot. He's good. He comes into the country, makes his kill and leaves. Never leaves a trace, other than his card. He just taunts them."

"I wonder if he's going to take another go at me."

"He hit you where he was aiming. I think he's done with you. The question is who's next?"

Chad's phone rang. He checked the caller ID. "It's William," he said. "Hello."

"Chad, you need to go to the Mount Sinai Hospital. Robert has been shot in the leg. He's conscious, and the wound isn't life-threatening, but he's in some pain."

"I'm on the way."

"What is it?" I asked.

"We know who's next."

~***~

120

When we arrived at the hospital, we were directed right to his room. We were glad to see that he was sitting up in his bed and he smiled at us as we entered.

"He got me," Robert said. "That damn Russian got me."

"How ya feeling?" Chad asked.

"I'm good. Just a nick."

"I'm sorry I got you into this," Chad said.

"How do you know I didn't get you into this?"

"How?"

"Maybe it's something to do with the Sunny Lake property."

"I don't know. Really, no one does."

"We need to find this guy before someone gets killed," Robert said.

"I'm working on something that might be of use to us," I said. "It's a long shot, but I might know who Bloodshot is."

They both looked at me. "You mean you might have figured out what the FBI has been trying to reckon for years?" Chad said.

"Maybe. As I said, it's a long shot."

"Tell us, maybe we can help," Robert said.

"Do you remember that Russian from the bachelor party that no one seemed to know?"

"Yeah, I remember him," Chad said.

"I ran into him again, quite by accident, in front of the Hilton downtown. He said his name was Adrian Boykov. We talked a little about the party. He said that Tom Carrington invited him since he was in town to see Tom. Supposedly they were old friends. Later, I went to The Barclay to see Tom, but it seems he has disappeared."

"I haven't seen him in a few days, but then I've kind of been laid up," Chad said.

"Well, I watched some security tapes and saw Adrian enter Tom's apartment. He left with a backpack he didn't have when he entered."

"Was Tom with him?" Robert asked.

"No. he was alone."

"Did you see Tom leave later?"

"No. I quit watching the tape after Adrian left."

"So, where's Tom?"

"Don't know."

I thought about that for a while. Maybe I should go watch the rest of those tapes.

"Any ideas why this guy is just wounding people? He could easily have killed us instead," Chad said.

"That's the big question. It doesn't make any sense," I said.

Robin entered the room. "Robert, are you okay?"

"I'll live."

"Thank God," she said. "We found his card again. This time on the back gate, where he knew the combo and just strolled right in."

Robert looked at Chad. "That doesn't mean anything," Chad said.

"He could have gotten it from anyone."

"Yeah, maybe, but why would anyone there give it to him?" Robert said.

"I don't know, but that's what we're going to find out," Chad said.

"I'm sorry guys," Robin said, "but this proves that Robert didn't hire him, so I'm going to have to look at everyone. Alexis included."

"Fine," Chad said, "but look at her father too. Maybe he didn't want me to marry her. He'll lose a lot of money."

"I'll look at everyone," Robin stated.

Chad's phone rang again. It was Alexis.

"Where are you?" she asked. "I have steaks marinating."

"I'm at the hospital. Robert's been shot."

"Oh no. Is he okay?

"Yeah, just a little nick in the leg. It was Bloodshot again."

"Hey, it was a big nick," Robert said, "bigger than yours."

"As you can tell, he's medicated," Chad said into the phone.

"I'll be right there," Alexis said.

"I don't think that's necessary. He'll be out before you get here."

"Bring him here, and we'll take care of him."

"Okay, put on an extra steak."

They hung up, and Chad told Robert he was coming to supper.

Robert was silent. "Come on, Robert. I'll protect you from her. I'll taste your food before you eat it," Chad said.

"Yeah, okay, what the hell. I like living on the edge."

"Any more questions for Robert right now?" I asked Robin.

"No, not now. We'll let him rest."

"I'll see you guys later, I have a few things to look into," I said. "Come on, Robin. I'll walk you out."

On the way, I filled her in on my thoughts about the Russian from the party.

"To me, it sounds as if you have an overactive imagination. The man evidently knew Tom or he wouldn't have let him in."

"Yeah, maybe, but it doesn't feel right."

"Leave the investigating to me, Cam. You can defend him when we catch him."

"What's that supposed to mean?"

"Nothing, just a little frustration coming out," she said apologetically.

"I have a few things to do," I said. "Will I see you for supper tonight?"

"I'll have to take a rain check. I have a few things of my own to check on."

"Okay, I'll talk to you tomorrow," I said then kissed her on the cheek, turned and walked away.

I was a little mad about her comment. I knew I shouldn't let it get to me. Coming from anyone else, I wouldn't have given it a thought, but I thought my job bothered her.

Chapter 28

I went back to my apartment, fixed a stiff drink and ran a bath in my spa. I had finished the drink before the tub was filled, so I fixed another.

I was listening to some good ol' down home Key West music and singing along. I opened my eyes. Kailey was standing in my bathroom watching me. She was naked again.

"What ya' doin'?" she said, giggling.

I sat up and pushed some bubbles over my private parts.

"How did you get in here?"

"Same way as the last time," she said, stepping into the bath.

She sat down and raised her own drink, which I hadn't noticed before. How could I? "To good music," she toasted and drank.

So did I.

"Kailey, what do you think your husband would say if he knew you were here?"

She said in a deep voice, "Come on Kailey, not again," and laughed.

I couldn't help but laugh too. It was funny. This girl came off so gentle and loving, but I bet she could take your head off if she wanted to.

"Is Robin here?"

"No, not today."

"Too bad. She's hot."

"Yes, she is."

"Is Chad okay? That was terrible."

"Yeah, he's fine. Did you hear about Robert?"

"No, what happened to him?"

"He was shot in the leg today by the same guy."

She got a frightened look on her face. "The same guy?"

"Yep."

"Why? Who is this guy and what's he want?"

"We don't know, but we'll find out."

"I hope so."

"Kailey, why are you here? This is kind of weird having a conversation with a naked girl in my tub."

"Just thought I would drop by to see if you have changed your mind. I would still like to fuck you," she said.

"I haven't changed my mind. You're married, and I don't sleep with married women."

She looked disappointed. "Well, can I stay and finish my drink?"

"Why not," I said in surrender. There was a time when I would have killed for that opportunity, but now I felt as if I was cheating on Robin and I really wanted that to work.

"Cool," she said.

She was sitting up, and her breasts were higher than the waterline. It was an amazing sight.

We made small talk. She said she was from Biloxi, Mississippi. She was born Kailey Parker. Her father wasn't around much, and he died a few years ago, an accident, and her mother left with a coworker when she was seventeen. She was left on her own to survive. She got a job at Walmart and finished high school. She moved to New York and got a job waiting tables. That was where she met William. We talked about William and all his money.

"You know, I just married him for his money," she said.

"Really?" I acted surprised.

"Yeah, but I told him upfront. He said it was okay as long as I would sleep with him and walk around the house naked."

"How very understanding of him," I said.

"Yes, he is. He's a good man, and I do love him. I'm just not *in love* with him."

"I see."

We finished our drinks. I was a little sad that we did. The more we talked the more I liked this girl. She was overly honest and quite a free spirit. Really, just the way everyone would like to be. You couldn't help but like her.

"Well, I guess I'll go now," she said, standing.

"Let me get you a towel," I said, standing also.

She looked down at me. "Nice," she said, smiling.

I looked down at her. "Likewise," I said and smiled also.

We dried off and dressed. I walked her to the door.

"I'll see you around," she said and kissed me.

This time I didn't break it off as fast.

"I'm going shopping the day after tomorrow at Osterman Boutique. There is a nice hotel across the street if you change your mind—eleven," she said.

"Goodbye," I said and opened the door.

"Toodles."

It was late, so I decided to call it a night. I would go back to The Barclay the following day and review the rest of the tape.

I was lying in bed reading the next chapter in my book when I heard my door open. *Oh no,* I thought, *not Kailey again.*

I stood and walked to the bedroom door and peeked out.

"Robin," I said. "This is a surprise."

"Hi, Cam. Hope I didn't wake you."

"Not at all, I was just reading."

"I felt sorry about today and I want to apologize. I know your job is just as important as mine. I'm just frustrated. Sometimes you hurt the ones you love because no one else is around."

"Apology accepted."

"Thank you. Are you sleepy?"

"No, I'm not. What do you have in mind?"

"I'll fix a couple of drinks if you'll fill the spa," she said.

I would be wrinkled as a prune by morning.

Chapter 29

The next morning, I made Robin breakfast again. She came to the table showered and dressed for work.

"You look lovely this morning," I said.

In a Southern accent I hadn't heard her use since we were in Key West, she said, "Why thank you. You are such a gentleman."

"Jenny, it's you," I said. She used that name undercover in Key West.

"Who were you expecting for breakfast?"

We laughed, but deep inside I missed Jenny. A carefree well-to-do that only wanted to be with me.

After breakfast, she cleared the table while I took my shower and dressed.

"Well, I guess I'll see you tonight if our busy schedules will allow," she said.

"Works for me. I can always find time for you."

"Why don't you meet me in the park today for lunch? Say about twelve thirty," she said.

"I'll be there. Shall I bring some hot dogs?"

"No thanks. Let me take care of the food," she said.

She left; I sat down and went over my notes. I hoped to have time to review the rest of the tapes that day, but I needed to go to the office. I'd been neglecting my work, and with Chad out we needed to catch up.

~***~

Andrei turned off the recorder and cleaned his rifle again. This was a good game. *Just like Canada seven years ago when I only shot to draw blood, not to kill.*

Andrei thought back to that time and how he took his name—Bloodshot—from the game. *I didn't leave calling cards then. I wish I could have. I wanted everyone to know who shot the eight people in Ontario.*

He poured a vodka neat. He drank it down in one long, smooth motion and poured another.

"I am Bloodshot," he said aloud. "I am the victor."

He ran the game through his mind again, as he often did.

Two very wealthy men were making a friendly wager. One man, Nathaniel Barton, said he was a much better hunter than the other, Eric Meninx. Nathaniel said he bet he could draw more human blood without killing anyone than Eric could. Eric took him up on the bet. If anyone died, the shooter would lose the bet—one million dollars.

Eric let the alcohol make the wager in the first place. He was not really that good of a shot, so, unbeknownst to Nathaniel, Eric contacted a friend of mine. My friend said he would run it by me.

130

The game sounded challenging. I wasn't really doing anything better. I would receive twenty-five thousand for each target I hit. Nathaniel would choose Eric's targets and vice versa. The game became known as Bloodshot by the locals.

With me secretly shooting for Eric, I hit eight targets. Nathaniel hit seven before killing the eighth. That made Eric the victor by default.

The Royal Canadian Mounted Police captured Nathaniel, thanks to an eyewitness who happened to disappear afterward.

He tried to tell them of the friendly bet between him and Eric, but Eric denied everything, coming up with multiple alibis as to his whereabouts at the times of the shootings.

No charges were brought against him.

Nathaniel died in prison shortly afterward. Not by natural causes. I am sure Eric had a hand in Nathaniel's death.

I've missed that game, and when I received the offer for this job, I suggested the game would be a good way to disguise the goal—with an added twist. They were more than eager to take me up on it.

Now I'm pleased to be back in the game. I've wanted to do it again ever since. This time I will get the credit for the shootings, and I will reveal myself as the one who started the game—Bloodshot—in Canada.

Andrei downed the second glass of vodka.

~***~

Chad was at the office when I walked in. "So, you're feeling better today I see," I greeted.

"No, not really, but Robert is driving me crazy. Get this; get that. He's too needy."

131

I laughed. "Where have I heard that before?"

"I couldn't have been that bad," Chad said.

We worked at our desks for a few hours. The work was really piling up, but with the help of the staff, we were seeing daylight by noon.

Chad stuck his head in my doorway. "Lunch?"

I looked at my watch. "No, not today. I'm meeting Robin in the park at twelve thirty. I better get going."

"Take your time. The work will get done."

"Alright, see you this afternoon."

I left the building and walked toward the park. The crisp weather opened my senses and made me more alert. To cap it off I stopped at the bagel stand and ordered a cup of coffee. I thought about Chad and Robert getting shot and began to worry about getting shot myself. Everyone I passed looked ominous. As I was nearing our favorite park bench, I raised my cup to take a drink. That's when it exploded, and I felt a burning in my right hand. I heard the shot at the same time. Then I heard shots from in front of me. I was caught in a crossfire.

I dove to the ground, my hand on fire; I'd been hit. As the volley of gunfire continued, I rolled beneath a truck, which was half parked on the curb. The truck door closed, and the engine started. Bad for me. I rolled back out just as the truck jumped the curb and roared away.

I managed to get two shots off but missed my target.

"Cam, are you okay?"

It was Robin.

"Yeah, I'll live, but my arm is on fire."

If I hadn't moved my arm to take a drink of coffee, I would have been hit in the hand, possibly injuring it forever. It was just a slight coffee burn.

"This is the closest we've been," Robin said. "I have to go."

"Go, I'm all right," I said.

"Did you get a look at him?" Robin said.

"No. I was a little busy."

"Neither did I. He had a hat pulled down over his eyes."

I found Bloodshot's card where the truck was parked. It was on the street. I think he dropped it accidentally. It said, "Cam Derringer–hand–$25,000."

This is one he shouldn't get paid for, I thought.

~***~

That's where the story began. We've had multiple murders and two of my friends wounded by Bloodshot, not to mention me almost getting killed, and we're no closer to closing in on him than we ever were. We can only hope he makes a mistake before he kills any of us.

~***~

Andrei sped away, barely missing people who were walking and running in the park. He turned onto East Seventy-Second Street and exited the park. Pulling his hat off, he almost hit a taxi head-on. At the first cross street, he turned right, pulled over to the curb and abandoned the stolen truck. He walked one block and hailed a taxi.

How could I be so careless? he thought. *Now I will have to wait to shoot him again. I already have two more lined up.*

~***~

I found a taxi in the park. "Chelsea Stratus Building, please," I said.

"Did you see the shoot'n in the park?" the driver asked.

133

"Yeah, I did. Did you?"

"Not the shoot'n, but the guy almost hit me coming out of the park."

"Did you get a good look at him?"

"Yeah, I did. We were face-to-face."

"What did he look like?"

"Hey, are you a cop?"

"No, just curious. I've never seen anything like that before."

"He was a big man, short blond hair. Scary eyes."

"Blue by any chance?" I asked.

"Maybe, kind of steely."

It had to be Adrian.

"If I hadn't swerved," he said, "I would have hit him head-on, I tell ya."

~***~

The FBI and the NYPD quickly threw a net over a one-mile circle. They found the truck only ten minutes after the shooting.

Robin personally searched the truck. She found nothing. She ordered that the vehicle be swept for fingerprints, although she knew none of his would be found.

By six o'clock they gave up the search of the area. Robin contacted the major taxi companies and asked for a report of passenger pickups in the vicinity of the truck from twelve thirty to twelve forty-five.

She received sixty-three hits.

"Christ," she said. "We don't even know if he took a taxi."

She put five agents on it. "If you see anything that might raise a flag, try to contact the driver. Especially

134

look for one man within a one-block area carrying a case."

"Really?" one of them said.

"Yeah, I know, but what else do we have?"

~***~

I took the elevator to my apartment and called Chad after a stiff drink.

"Have you finished with lunch already?" he asked.

"Yeah, I lost my appetite."

"What's wrong?"

I told him the story.

"Shit," he said.

"Yeah, shit."

"Are you okay?"

"Yeah, but I think I'll get in the shower and change into something more comfortable and go check those tapes at your apartments."

"Sure, go ahead. I'll be home around three. Maybe I'll see you in the office."

"Good, see you then."

Chapter 30

I **arrived at The Barclay around two o'clock.** The office was ready for me, and I went right to work. Ben had the film stopped where I had left off. I watched the sixth floor in fast forward. It went through the night and into the next day. Finally, I saw movement. I slowed the tape. It was Jerald knocking on Tom's door. He waited a moment and left. Four hours later, I saw myself knocking on the door. Then I saw Jerald talking to me. A few minutes later, the door was opened by a maintenance man. He and Jerald entered the room. They left and locked the door.

Where was Tom? He never left, but he wasn't there either. He wasn't in the backpack. What was?

"Ben," I said.

"Yes, sir?"

"Can we go into Tom's apartment again?"

"I guess that would be okay."

He retrieved the key, and we went to Tom's apartment. We opened the door cautiously and stepped inside. It was clear that no one was home.

"On the tape, I saw Adrian enter this room. The door was opened from the inside. Adrian left, but Tom never did. He had a backpack when he left but not when he entered."

"I guess we should search the place," Ben said.

We did. There was no trace of Tom.

I found a suitcase under the bed. I slid it out and opened it. It was packed as if he were going on a vacation. I thought that strange.

"Do you see anything out of place? Something missing maybe that could have been in the backpack?" I asked.

We searched again. Nothing seemed to be missing. I decided to look in the refrigerator. "Maybe he stole some food," I joked.

I opened it. There was Tom. The fridge was empty except for him. I surmised that Adrian took the food to make room. If he had left the food out, we would have found him right away.

"Oh my," Ben said.

"Yeah, oh my."

I called Robin first and told her of my discovery. While we waited, I asked Ben if he had ever seen Adrian before. He said, "No."

He glanced down at my hand. "Is your hand okay? It's awful red."

I told him of the happenings of the last few days.

"Really, just like in Ontario, huh?" he said.

"What do you mean?"

"Bloodshot, the game, about seven or eight years ago. I was working in the Kingston hotel downtown when it happened. Two men made a bet about who could shoot the most people without killing them. Fifteen people were wounded before one was finally killed. The game was nicknamed Bloodshot, although I think that was by locals. Never saw it in the papers."

"Did they get the men?"

"One of them. He suggested another man was involved, but he had alibis."

"Do you know the man's name? We might want to talk to him."

"He was sent to a luxury prison where he was killed in three weeks. The other man, who he accused, is still alive, as far as I know."

"I'll tell Robin, thanks."

"I had best take my place at the desk. I'll send the FBI up when they arrive."

"Thanks, Ben. They'll probably want those tapes."

"That's not a problem."

Robin showed up with a team in thirty minutes. I was waiting at the door.

"He's in the fridge," I said as they reached me. They went in without saying anything to me.

I heard one of the men throwing up. He came back out. He was a little pale.

Robin came out where I was waiting in the hall. "Good job, Cam. Are you okay?"

"I'm fine, but I don't think Tom is doing too well."

"No, I don't either. How did you know?"

"The tapes I told you about. I never saw Tom leave, but he was gone. It looks like Adrian, or whatever his real name is, put the food in a backpack and took it away."

"We need to see those tapes."

"I told Ben, the concierge, you would. He has them on a thumb drive for you."

"Thanks, but you know there still isn't any proof that this has anything to do with Bloodshot. This could be unrelated."

"Could be, but it's not. I found a taxi driver who saw him leaving the park. His description of the man matched Adrian."

"You found a witness?"

"Yes."

"Where is he?"

"Driving a taxi would be my guess."

"You just let him go?"

"Not my job," I said.

She paused for a minute.

"Now we have a picture of him," she said.

"Not one that will help. You can't see his face in any of the shots. I knew who it was because I've met him."

"Great. You're the only one who knows what he looks like."

"I guess. The others at the party say they didn't really get a good look at him. He didn't talk to very many of the guys."

"Shit."

"Yeah, shit."

"He's probably changed his name again by now," Robin said.

"I think I know where he got his name."

"You do?"

I told her about the games in Ontario and my feeling that he was the other shooter.

"Thanks, I'll check on that, but the name Bloodshot should have come up on the scan."

"It wasn't in the papers. It was the locals that named the game. Ask Ben about it. He was there."

"Okay. Cam, I'm sorry I doubted you. If this guy is Bloodshot, we owe you a lot."

"You've been doing a lot of apologizing lately. Maybe you should start trusting my judgment."

She didn't say anything.

"Well, I guess you can handle it from here," I said. "I have other fish to fry."

"I want to put a guard on you. He's tried once, and he failed. He probably doesn't take that lightly."

"No, it wouldn't do any good anyway. He knows where his targets are going to be and waits for them. I was lucky I took a drink just as he pulled the trigger. And I was lucky you were there to keep him from taking another shot at me."

I kissed her on the forehead and left. I was starting to get tired of being taken lightly. Robin was upset about something and she was taking it out on me. I'd wait for her to tell me. For a while anyway.

Chapter 31

As **I was leaving the building**, I ran into Chad.
"Leaving already?" he said.
"Yeah, I think my work here is finished."
I filled him in on all the happenings.

"That's terrible. Tom was a good friend."

I could tell Chad was upset. It hurts when you lose a friend.

"You want me to hang around for a while?" I asked.

"Would you mind having a drink at the bar before you go?"

"Not at all; in fact, I insist."

We ordered and took a table close to the window.

I told him about the games in Ontario and my suspicion that Bloodshot was the other shooter.

"You mean you think this might be a game?"

"Could be. At this point, it's hard to tell."

"Who would do that?" Chad said. It was more a statement than a question.

"Someone rich. According to the cards, he's getting paid twenty-five thousand for each bloodshot."

"Bloodshot. Now it has a whole different meaning," Chad said.

"Yeah."

"Let's keep this conversation between us. Okay?"

"Okay," I said, knowing we were about to get into a territory we wouldn't be comfortable in.

"First of all," Chad said, "who do we know who has the money to do something like that?"

"William, Alexis, Emanuel, you, although I don't think it's you."

"Thanks."

"For what it's worth I don't think it's Alexis either."

"Thanks again."

"I definitely wouldn't put it past Emanuel, but McNally says no."

"That kind of leaves us with William," Chad said.

"Yes, it does. Why would he do something like that now? Supposedly Alexis has her money already because you married her. If you died, she would keep her inheritance."

"Yes, but if we divorce, she'll lose it," Chad said thoughtfully.

"So, maybe he's trying to scare you away."

"Maybe."

"How are we going to prove that?" I asked.

"Maybe we should ask him," Chad said.

"If we're wrong, you have just broken any friendship chance you had between you and your father-in-law."

"If we're right, he wouldn't confess anyway," Chad said.

142

"Is there a way we could bring him in on the investigation?" I asked.

We thought it over for a bit while we drank our bourbon and ordered another.

"We could ask for his help. Tell him it's over our head but he might have some connections that would be able to get information," Chad said.

"I guess it's worth a try. At least we could see his reaction when we ask."

"I can tell you right now, the reaction won't be good."

Our conversation was brought to a halt when Robin entered the bar.

"Hi Chad," she said.

"Hello, Robin. Will you join us?"

"Can't right now. Just wanted to tell you I'm leaving and that I ran a trace on Adrian Boykov. We found him in the Novodevichy Cemetery in Moscow. He was murdered two years ago."

"Well, it was a long shot anyway," I said.

"Yes, but if this man is the one who murdered him, it seems he can freely move in and out of Moscow anytime he wishes," Robin said.

"So, he could easily be Bloodshot," I added.

"Yes, he could."

Chapter 32

C had and I spent the next day at the office. We had two cases to prepare for. Author Hicks shot his girlfriend through their closet door. He was inside, and she was trying to talk him out. He swore he thought she was an intruder trying to kill him.

She didn't die from the shot. She said they were sitting on the sofa watching an old rerun of *True Detective* about a man hiding in his closet to kill his wife when he jumped up, grabbed his gun from the drawer and locked himself in the closet.

She didn't connect the two events and tried to talk him out. He shot through the door, hitting her in the arm.

The other case was much worse. A woman, Iris Stetson, supposedly came home from work on her lunch break, found her husband and another man in bed together and shot and killed them both. She then cut off their private parts and sewed each in the other's mouth. She

144

returned to work, finished her shift, went home and rediscovered them. Then she called the police and frantically told them what she found.

A neighbor said she saw her come home around eleven thirty and leave around twelve thirty. Iris said it wasn't her that came home and had a witness that saw her at Denny's at that time. No gun was found.

I was trying to find the other man's wife, who had disappeared. From a picture, I could see a resemblance between the two women.

These cases wouldn't come to trial for about a month if at all, but we needed to set the wheels in motion and have our team investigate.

Around four o'clock we called it a day. Chad said he and Alexis were going to Per Se at seven and wanted Robin and me to join them. I told him I would check with her schedule and let him know.

I caught a taxi and went home. I debated whether to call Robin. Things weren't going too well with us just then, and I thought we needed a day off.

I was standing on my balcony having a drink when my cell rang. It was Robin.

"Hello," I said.

"Hello," she sounded a little sheepish. "What are ya doing?"

"I just walked in from work and fixed a drink."

"I had lunch with Alexis today. She wanted to know if we wanted to meet them for supper at Per Se."

"Yes, I was just about to call you. Chad said something as we were leaving work. You wanna?"

"Sounds good to me," she said.

"Alright, I'll pick you up around six thirty."

"Come a little early if you can, and we'll have a drink before we go."

"Alright. See you about six."

"Bye."

"Bye."

Well, I guess I'm going out to supper.

I picked up my guitar and returned to the balcony. Writing songs relieves my mind for a while. I started playing a country tune and threw in some words I had been thinking about. I decided to call it "Where the Sun Don't Shine."

The streets are crowded in New York City

I'm all alone, and it's just a pity

That I'm not home, breathing fresh air

Out on my boat, without a care

This might be your home, but it's not mine

I'm stuck here where the sun don't shine

Gotta get back where my soul can rest

Back home–to old Key West

I was writing another verse when I looked at the clock. I was running late. I hurried to the shower and then dressed.

Lucky for me a cab was letting someone off just as I exited the building.

I rang Robin's apartment precisely at six. She told the concierge to send me up.

When I entered, she kissed me and handed me a drink.

"Service with a smile," I said.

We laughed.

"Let's don't talk about work tonight," she said. "Okay?"

"I couldn't agree more."

We stood on her balcony and stared at the city lights. She slipped her arm around my waist. I leaned around and kissed her. It was nice. I was glad I came.

We stood in silence. Finally, I said, "What do we talk about if we don't talk about work?"

"I don't know. That's all we've been talking about lately."

"Where did you and Alexis have lunch?"

"Hot dogs in the park."

"No, not you. You're always preaching to me how they'll kill me."

"I felt like living dangerously."

Silence again.

"How's Robert?" she asked.

"He's okay. He's still at Chad's. They have a visiting nurse stop by twice a day to scratch his back, or whatever he needs."

"Good."

We finished our drinks. "Another?" she said.

I looked at my watch. "Sure, we have about fifteen minutes before we have to leave."

She fixed two more drinks, and we took a seat at the kitchen island. I sipped my drink in silence as did she.

"Okay," I said, "if we need to talk about work, we can. We seem to be having a hard time getting this conversation going."

"You're right. But only good stuff. No arguing."

"Fair enough," I said, "you first."

"Well, I showed the tapes of The Barclay to my staff. You were right, we can't see his face. I told them that you identified him as the man who attended the bachelor party. They would like for you to go through a book of suspects and try to pick him out."

"On one condition," I said, "they go through it first and pick out the ones that fit the description I give them."

"Fair enough," she said.

I held my glass up, and she clinked it with hers. "Here's to agreeing," I said.

"Yeah, that wasn't so hard," she said and kissed me.

147

We held the kiss too long. We were breathing heavily and moving closer together. Finally, she broke it off.

"Not if we're going to make it to Per Se," she said.

"I'm not hungry," I said.

"Save it for dessert."

"Can't wait."

~***~

Per Se was packed as usual. The hostess, who knows me, escorted us to Chad's table next to a window.

"Looks like we beat them here," I said as I pulled Robin's chair back for her to sit.

Before I could sit Chad and Alexis walked in.

I remained standing until Alexis sat. "How are you two tonight?" I asked, kissing Alexis on the cheek.

Chad did the same to Robin.

"Tired, but ready to party," Alexis said.

"She's always ready to party," Chad said.

"Oh, to be young again," I said.

We ordered drinks and made small talk. We had a spectacular view of Central Park from our table. We laughed and joked as if we didn't have a care in the world.

Our drinks were refilled, and we ordered our food. The women excused themselves and headed for the restroom.

When they were gone, Chad asked me if I was caught up enough to take the next day off and go with him to see William. I said no, but I would go anyway. We decided on ten a.m.

"No one was shot today as far as I know," I said. "Do you think he's taking a break or do you think he's trying to decide if he should come after me again?"

"I *hope* he doesn't come after you again."

148

"If this is a game, as it was in Ontario, why is he just shooting our little group? In Ontario, it was a random thing."

"I know, I thought about that. Even the more reason to believe it's someone we know."

The women returned. They were laughing.

"What's so funny?" Chad asked.

"You wouldn't want to know," Alexis answered.

"Alright then."

Our food arrived, and we spent a seemingly calm night. We said our farewells around ten thirty and went our separate ways.

Robin and I didn't waste any time picking up where we left off.

Chapter 33

William Arlington was sitting in his office, drinking coffee and reading the *Wall Street Journal* when his phone rang. Since his secretary wasn't in yet, he answered it himself.

"Hello," he barked, in a gruff, morning, coffee voice.

"Mr. Arlington," Chad said.

"Chad, is that you?"

"Yes, sir."

"I told you to call me Bill," he puffed.

"Sorry Bill. I'll try to get used to that."

"What do you want on this beautiful morning so early?" His voice calmed back down.

"I was hoping Cam and I could come by around ten thirty and have a talk with you. It won't take long."

Bill looked at his schedule book.

"I don't have anything until one o'clock. We'll do brunch out on the veranda."

"Sounds great. Thank you. See you then."
"Are you going to bring my little girl with you?"
    "No, sir. Not this time."
"Too bad. I'll see you around ten thirty."
"Goodbye," Chad said, but Bill had already hung up.

~***~

The limo stopped at my apartment at nine thirty. It was a cloudy morning, which made me dread the business at hand all that much more. William would see right through our little plan. But I guessed there wasn't any other way to do it. If we didn't confront all our suspects, we'd never get to the end of this.

We picked Chad up at nine fifty-five. He was ready and waiting on the sidewalk.

"Good morning," he said, "are you ready for this?"

"Good morning to you. And no."

The drive to the Arlington estate was as remarkable as I remembered. The sky was starting to clear, and by the time we arrived, it was a beautiful sunny morning.

"Mister Arlington is waiting for you on the veranda," the butler said as we stepped in.

"Thank you," I said.

As we were making our way to the veranda, we saw Kailey coming toward us. She looked magnificent in a short black dress with a plunging neckline. She hugged Chad and kissed him on the cheek. She then turned to me and said, "Mister Derringer, so sweet to see you again." She hugged me and kissed me right on the lips.

I turned and looked at Chad. He was trying to hold back a laugh.

"I'm sorry I can't join you for brunch, but I have plans this morning. Enjoy your meeting," she said and kissed me again. "Toodles," she said and left.

"You old hound," Chad said and slapped me on the back.

"I hope no one else saw that. I could get into real trouble."

"Yes, you could," he said and laughed again.

Bill was sitting at a table on the veranda talking on his cell. He was dressed in blue jeans and a T-shirt. I never realized how athletic he was. His biceps were stretching the cotton sleeves.

"I have to go now," he said and hung up.

"Good morning, gentlemen," he said.

"Good morning," we said.

We sat and a buffet was started immediately on a side table.

"Brunch will be ready in a moment," he said.

"How is Robert this morning?" he asked.

"Not bad for getting shot by an assassin," Chad said.

"What are we going to do about that?" Bill asked.

"Well, that's why we are here," I said, to take a little pressure off Chad. "We were hoping you might be able to help us."

Bill laughed. "I wondered how long it would take you to come to me to try to find out if I was behind this."

"No sir," Chad said, "we don't suspect you."

"You would have to be stupid not to," Bill said. "I already threatened your life."

Chad was silent.

"Bill," I said, "we thought maybe you might be able to help us. We don't have the connections you have, and the FBI only knows what we've told them. I would really like to stop this before someone gets killed."

I told him about the game in Ontario and how we suspected that Bloodshot was the other shooter there.

"Sounds plausible," he said, "but if it's a game, where's his adversary's shots? He's the only one racking up points."

"Good thought," I said.

"Anyone else bidding on the resort?" Bill asked.

"I don't know of anyone," Chad said. "I can ask Robert."

"Could be someone doesn't want Robert buying it."

"Why would they shoot us?" I asked.

"Maybe the message will come. They might be setting the stage for a warning."

"Maybe."

"Gentlemen, I can assure you it's not me. I have no need to bring in outside help for something like this. As I said before, I have people for that," Bill said. "Understood?"

"Understood," I said.

"Chad?" Bill said.

"Understood," Chad said.

"Good, it looks like brunch is served."

We filled our plates and sat back down at the table. There was enough food to feed an army.

"You know what this man looks like?"

"Yes," I said. "We both do."

"I'm not sure I would recognize him," Chad said, "I only got a glimpse of him at the party. He didn't really talk to me."

"But he killed your friend I understand," Bill said.

"Yes, he did."

"Do you think they were actually friends?"

"Not now I don't," Chad said.

"You need to find their connection. There might not even be one. Maybe they just got to be friends at the party."

"That's what I think," I said. "He just needed someone to fall back on if he were questioned, which he was, by me."

We were interrupted by the butler. "Sir, a Detective McNally on line one for you," he said.

Bill thought for a second.

"I think you should take it, Bill. He's the one working with us on this case," I said.

Bill picked up the phone. "Hello, William here."

He listened. He turned white and said, "We'll be right there."

He laid the phone back down and looked at us, a look of shock on his face. "It's Kailey, she's been shot in the arm."

Chapter 34

Andrei left the hotel where only the day before he had rented a room. He had his case in hand and could hear the sirens as the patrol cars approached.

I hated to shoot that beautiful young lady, he thought, *but those were my instructions. She seemed like such a nice person. I would have rather had a few hours with her than shoot her. Cam Derringer is crazy for turning her down. Whoever it is that hired me is as ruthless as I am, but, all in all, it is fun.*

He covered his face with his hands and faked a sneeze, pulling off his mustache and slipping it into his pocket.

Cam is becoming a thorn in my side. I really need to get him out of the picture. My contract says no killing of my targets though.

Andrei entered the post office and went to box 408, slipped in the key and removed an envelope. He placed the envelope in his pocket and left.

Eric Meninx, in disguise filling out a mailing slip, watched as Andrei left. *He would be an easy target if I chose to kill him,* he thought.

~***~

We arrived at the hospital again. Three times in four days. Kailey was being attended to by Doctor Rivers, the same one who treated Chad only four days before.

We waited in the waiting room. The doctor appeared five minutes later. "Mister Arlington," he said. Then he saw Chad and me. "I should have known," he said. "Anyway, Kailey is fine, just a scratch. The police will be here shortly to talk to her."

McNally entered the waiting room. "I see you beat me here, Bill. I'm sorry this happened."

"Not your fault, George," Bill said.

"Hello Cam, Chad," he said.

"Hello chief," I said. "I wasn't aware you two knew each other."

"We've met," Bill said.

"We'll find this guy, Bill. I promise."

"If you don't, I will."

"Leave it to us. We don't need a war, and you know how quickly this could turn into one if you go around accusing people."

"You have three days to find him; then I'm going to start looking," Bill said sternly.

Kailey appeared at the door in a wheelchair being pushed by a nurse.

"Kailey, are you okay, honey?" Bill said.

"I'm fine, just a little weak. I think it's just from being scared. Why would someone shoot me?"

"I don't know, sweetie, but I'll find out."

"Kailey," McNally said, "did you get a look at this guy?"

"No, I had just gotten out of the limo at the Osterman Boutique. I dropped my sunglasses. When I bent down to pick them up, I felt a sting on my arm. First, I thought it was a bee; then, when I looked, I saw a long gash. That's when I knew I'd been shot. The first thing I thought of was Chad and Robert being wounded."

"It's a good thing you bent down when he shot you," Bill said. "If you wouldn't have, it might have been worse."

McNally's cell rang. He answered and talked a few seconds then disconnected. "We found his calling card in the hotel across the street. He rented the room last night."

"How did he know a day ahead of time that she would be at the Osterman Boutique at eleven o'clock?" Bill said.

"I don't know," McNally said.

"Kailey, did you tell anyone you were going there?" Bill asked.

My stomach got weak. She had told me she was going there and that there was a hotel across the street.

"No, not a soul," she lied.

Bill turned to McNally to speak. Kailey looked at me. I looked away.

"Find this man now," he said. "And search my house for bugs. Someone has been reading our mail."

McNally's cell rang again. He listened intently. "Are you sure?" he said. He listened again. "I'll be there in twenty-five minutes," he said.

He turned to us, a puzzled look on his face. "There's been another shooting on the other side of town," he said. "They found a card that read, 'Bloodshot.'"

"When did that happen?" I asked.

"About the same time as Kailey's."

"A copycat?" Bill said.

"Can't be. No one knows about Bloodshot."

I told McNally about the games in Ontario. "There were two shooters. They nicknamed the game Bloodshot.

"Who was shot this time?" I asked.

"James Osborn. Do any of you know him?"

We all shook our heads no.

"It looks like a new game," McNally said.

"If the shooter here is only shooting people in our circle, so to speak, I wonder if the other group will be acquainted," I said.

"We'll check if it happens again."

We left the hospital. Bill and Kailey returned to their home and Chad and I went to my apartment. On the limo ride there, I told him about Kailey coming to my apartment again. He enjoyed the details too much. I explained to him about her telling me she was going shopping.

"What do you think?" he said.

"I think my apartment is bugged," I said. "I think that's how he has found out everything. I was going back over the other shootings. All three shootings occurred after someone standing in my apartment said where they were going to be."

"I have a team that can check your place out. Just be careful about what you say until then. I'll send them over tonight," Chad said.

"Thanks."

Chad dropped me off and went to the office.

~***~

Bill and Kailey arrived at their home, and Bill walked her to the bedroom.

"You lie down for a while," he said. "If you need anything, ring the bell, I'll come check on you."

"Thanks, honey, I'll be okay."

Bill went to his office and made a phone call. It was answered with, "Hello Bill."

Bill said, "Osborn has surfaced. His brother has been shot, just nicked."

"You want me to check it out?"

"Yeah, take care of it."

"As good as done."

"First meet me at John's Grill. I want to give you a calling card to leave on the body."

~***~

I decided I needed to talk to Diane. I sat down at the bar, not wanting my conversation listened to by Bloodshot.

I ordered a drink and dialed her number.

"Hi Daddy," she answered.

I felt better already.

"Hey, Diane. I miss ya," I said.

"Miss you too."

"How's life?"

"Not bad actually. My practice is going great guns. I might have to hire more help."

"Great."

"How are things in the Big Apple?"

"Crazy," I said, dreading having to tell her about all that had happened.

"What's up?"

"Well," I said, "remember me telling you about the Russian I met at the party?"

"Yeah."

Then I told her the whole story.

"Oh Cam," she said when I finished. "Are you okay?"

"Yeah, I'm okay. So are Chad, Robert, and Kailey."

"If he missed you, do you think he'll be back to get you?"

"Actually, I don't know. Maybe."

"Please come home. You can live with me until your boat is ready."

"Can't do that. I'm the only one who really knows what he looks like. It seems no one else at the party talked to him, so they don't really know what he looks like. They don't remember him."

She was silent.

"I would like to tell you not to worry, but I know that wouldn't do any good. I'll be fine."

"That doesn't mean shit. He could accidentally kill you. You have to come home."

"You know me better than that. I'm going to help finish this. Robin needs me."

Silence again. "I love you," she said weakly.

"I love you too. I've decided that, when this is over, I'm coming back to Key West. I don't need to be a lawyer. I liked being a private eye."

"Please do."

"I promise."

Then I told her about Kailey and my two encounters with her in my apartment.

"Jesus Cam, the women just can't keep their hands off you."

"I know. Great, huh?"

We laughed.

"Watch out for her husband. He sounds a little … let's say connected."

"I'm keeping an eye on him."

"Call me every day and let me know you're okay."

"I'll call you if anything happens."

"Love you."

"Love you too."

Chapter 35

That night, Chad called me and said his team would be over around nine o'clock.

They arrived on time. It took them an hour to find two bugs, one in the kitchen and one in the bedroom.

I told them to leave them in place. I would deal with them. We were very careful not to talk in the apartment.

How did they get there? Did someone break in and plant them? Kailey got in, so someone else could too. I don't think she planted them since she was shot too.

I thought about Alexis. She had several opportunities to plant them, but I still didn't think she would.

Back to Kailey. She said her bodyguard let her in. If he let her in, he could get in any time he wanted. He could plant the bugs for Bill.

I decided the best thing to do was fix a drink. I did.

~***~

The next morning, Andrei stepped off the airplane in Key West. It was a muggy ninety-five degrees.

162

The stewardess, who had been talking to him and giving him free drinks on the flight from Miami, slipped him a piece of paper as he disembarked the aircraft.

He smiled at her and said, "I hope to see you again soon."

"I hope you do, Demyan," she said.

Andrei checked into the Galleon Resort in Key West's old town. The room had a beautiful view of the marina.

A bottle of Premium Russian Vodka was sitting on the table. There was a note on it. *I hope you save some for me, Julie.*

The stewardess, Andrei thought. *That's why she wanted to know where I was staying.* Andrei called her and thanked her for the vodka. "I hope you will consider joining me tonight for a little celebration," he said.

"I would love to. I'll be there around eight thirty."

"I'll see you then," he said and hung up.

Andrei showered and changed into some more casual clothes. Shorts and a T-shirt would not draw any attention. He would blend in with the thousands of tourists that lined the streets.

He walked four blocks into the old town, turned on Eaton Street and rented a bicycle. A little wobbly at first, he soon caught on. This was the first time he had ridden in over thirty years.

Andrei followed his GPS to William Street and then to Southard Street. He passed a row of Key West style homes. They were very colorful and well kept. Some, which were in need of repair, had scaffolding and dumpsters in the yards. They were trying hard to preserve the heritage of the Keys here.

He took note of a beautiful blue home with a full front porch. Diane's house. He held his phone up and snapped a shot of it as he rode past. He would return later to meet Cam's daughter.

~***~

Diane returned home around two thirty. A short day at work, only three patients. She showered, changed clothes and called Jack Stiller, Cam's friend and partner when he was working an investigation.

"Hey, Jack. Doing anything important?"

"Nothing could be more important than you," Jack said.

"Then why don't you take me to a late lunch?"

"Give me a half-hour and we'll make it an early supper," he said.

"Sounds great; I'll meet you at Kelly's around four thirty," Diane said.

"Be there or be square."

They hung up, so Diane poured a glass of wine, picked up her new book, *Knee Deep*, and took a seat on the front porch swing.

It wasn't such a bad day for Key West. A rainstorm early that morning had cooled the temperature down a few degrees. Several tourists walked by just wanting to look at the neighborhood. A man on a bicycle with a ball hat pulled low raised his phone and snapped a shot as he passed, nearly falling in the process. He caught himself but not before hitting the curb. He fell slowly to the sidewalk.

"Are you okay?" Diane yelled. She jumped up and ran to the man lying in her yard.

"Yes, I'm good," the man said in a slight Russian accent, "just a little embarrassed."

Diane offered her hand and helped him up. "It's been a while since I've ridden," he said.

"They say you never forget, but that doesn't mean you're as good as you once were," Diane said.

164

They laughed.

"I'm Demyan Minsky," he said, offering his hand now.

"Diane," she said, shaking his hand.

Now that she could see him better, he was quite handsome and not as old as she had first thought.

"Sorry to crash in your yard. Hope I didn't hurt your landscape."

"It doesn't look like you did," she said, glancing at the flowerbed he only missed by inches.

"Do you live near here?" she asked.

"I live in New York at the moment," he said. "I came here to see the Keys. I think it would be a beautiful place to live. I have already met the prettiest girl in town, and quite by accident."

Diane blushed. "You're a fast mover, aren't you?" she said.

"I am an opportunist," he said.

She laughed.

"Maybe I could take you to supper tonight. I don't like eating alone. People look at you as if you don't have any friends," he said.

"I'm sorry, but I already have a date with a friend for supper," Diane said.

"Okay, what about dessert then? There must be a good dessert house around here."

"There are plenty of those," she said and looked at him thoughtfully for a second. He had beautiful blue eyes.

"Okay," she said. "I'll meet you at a little place called Better Than Sex. It's a dessert-only restaurant and excellent. How about six thirty?"

"I will be counting the moments," he said.

Andrei picked up his bicycle and mounted it.

"Be careful," Diane said. "There's a lot of traffic."

Andrei smiled and waved, nearly falling again.

Diane just laughed.

165

Chapter 36

I woke, not knowing that the assassin was stepping off the plane in Key West.

I was even more confused than the day before. The first thing on my mind was that there seemed to be two shooters now. If someone created a game, maybe no one we knew was even involved with the planning. It could be that Bill and Alexis were both just future victims like the rest of us.

I dressed in my running clothes and went out the door. It was another cloudy day and looked as though it could rain at any minute. I stayed close to home running in a five-block area. When I was as far from home as I was planning to be, it started pouring rain. I ran into a coffee shop. I had to squeeze through the door as the place was packed with men and women in business suits who had also gotten caught in the sudden rain.

I took a seat at a small table by the window and watched it rain. It was a beautiful sight—the world getting a bath. God knows, it needed one.

A young, full-faced waitress came to my table and asked if I wanted anything or if I was just seeking shelter.

"Both," I said. "I'll have a cup of coffee, black, and one of those donuts I saw in the case when I entered."

"Coming right up," she said and disappeared into the crowd.

My cell rang. It was Robin.

"Good morning," I answered.

"Not here, it isn't," she said.

"What's the matter now?"

"Another shooting. Brady Osborn, James's brother from yesterday.

"Same MO?"

"We found the card, which read Bloodshot."

"Which shooter was it?"

"Neither, different caliber and MO."

"What was different?"

"He was shot in the head. He's dead."

"This is getting crazy."

"Why didn't you call me last night and tell me about a second shooter?" Robin said.

"Me? Why should I? I thought you and McNally were keeping up on that stuff."

"Evidently not."

"It's not my job, and don't rely on me to keep you informed," I said.

"I was just hoping you would pass anything on to me that came across your desk."

"What's the matter, Robin?" I asked.

"Nothing."

"Something is. You're trying to push me away. You keep trying to pick fights with me."

"I'm sorry. I think I might be trying to pick a fight with myself." She hesitated. "I received another job offer—in LA."

"Really? Doing what?" I said calmly.

"Executive assistant for National Security," she said. "It's a big promotion."

"It sounds big. We should be talking about this in person though," I said. "Don't you think?"

"Yes, I'm sorry. You're right, we should," she said.

"Can we get together tonight?" Robin asked.

"I insist. Why don't you come over around six? I'll have a couple of steaks ready to grill, and we'll pop a cork."

"Sounds fantastic," she said, a little cheerier.

I hung up and gave the conversation some thought. It would be a relief to her and me when I told her that I was returning to Key West anyway.

The waitress brought my coffee and donut. I thanked her, tore my donut in half and dunked one half in my coffee.

It's a good thing I work out every day because I love my sweets.

I finished my coffee and donut while reading the morning paper. There was mention of two brothers being shot, one fatally, two days apart, but no mention of Bloodshot.

Finding cards at both assassins' shootings led me to believe that Bloodshot was not a man but a game. Or maybe both, and now a copycat.

The rain eased, so I decided to make a run for it. I paid the bill, left a tip and walked toward the door. A man was standing in the doorway. He wore a suit and hat. He glanced at me and turned his head away.

"Excuse me," I said as I accidentally bumped him.

"Sorry," he said, in a thick Russian accent and moved over a bit.

I looked at him again, and he turned away again.

I stepped out into the light rain and began running. I thought about the man in the coffee house. It seemed to me that he didn't want me to see his face, but I did. I got a good look. Might not mean anything, but I'm quite paranoid nowadays. I stored his face in my memory bank. I reached my building. I was soaked, my running suit clinging to my body.

The doorman opened the door, and I stepped in. Once inside I turned and surveyed the sidewalks. I didn't see anyone in a suit and hat.

~***~

Eric Meninx watched from his taxi as Cam entered the building. He looked at his watch and made a note of the time.

"Excuse me, Mister Derringer," the concierge said.

"Yes Paul," I said.

"A young lady is waiting to see you in the bar area."

"Thanks," I said and walked to the bar.

I saw Kailey sitting at a table drinking iced tea.

"Hello Kailey," I said, approaching her table.

She looked at me. She didn't smile. "What's going on, Cam?"

"I don't know what you mean. About what?"

"You were the only one, other than Bill, who knew I was going to the Osterman Boutique, and he didn't know until that morning."

"My apartment was bugged. We found two bugs last night. Someone has been spying on us. They knew where everyone was going to be. Chad, Robert, you and me."

170

Kailey looked at me wide-eyed. "Someone? You mean like a spy?"

"Kind of. They were spying on us anyway."

"Did you get rid of the bugs?"

"Yes," I lied. I thought it better not to tell anyone that we left one bug in place.

"I'm sorry, Cam. I better not come to your apartment again until you're sure the bugs are gone," she said apologetically.

Really, I thought. *Does she think I want her to come to my place?*

"That's alright, Kailey, I understand. It would probably be better for all if you never came again."

"That's a shame," she said sadly. "I really enjoyed our conversation in the tub."

"Yes, so did I."

She stood and put her arms around me. "I'm sorry I was mad at you," she whispered.

"That's okay, Kailey. I understand." Looking down at her I said, "Now you're soaked from hugging me."

She kissed me again on the lips. "That's okay," she said. "And I'll find a way to be with you."

She turned and gathered her purse and umbrella. She gave me another light peck on the lips. "Toodles," she said as she left the bar.

What am I going to do about her? I have enough drama in my life right now without this sideshow. But she is a sweetheart.

Chapter 37

Diane walked into Kelly's and saw Jack waiting at a table close to the open patio doors. He waved at her and stood.

She went to his table.

"Hey, girl," he said and kissed her on the cheek.

They sat and turned in their drink order.

"What's new in your world today?" he asked.

"Found a man lying in my front yard."

"Really? Was he drunk?"

"No, he was just a bad bicycle rider. I helped him up, and he asked me out to supper tonight."

"Fast mover. What did you say?"

"I told him I was having supper with a friend," she answered.

"A friend. I thought you were in love with me."

"I am, but you know Cam said I can't date you," she teased.

"I'm gonna have a talk with him."

"It won't do any good."

"So, are you going to see this guy again?"

"Tonight. We're meeting at Better Than Sex."

"That's an awfully romantic place for a first date," he said.

"Yeah, I know. He asked about a dessert place, and that's the first one that came to mind."

"I'm going with you," Jack said.

"Thanks, but no thanks. I'll be okay. The place is well lit, and the streets are crowded. If I yell, someone will rescue me."

"I don't like it. But I can't stop you. What's he like?"

"He's funny. About six foot three, short blond hair, blue eyes, and a slight Russian accent. His name is Demyan Minsky. Is that a good enough description?"

"Russian, huh? Watch out for him. They can be mean."

"Quit worrying about me," Diane said.

The waitress came with their drinks, and they ordered their meal.

"I talked to Cam today," Diane said.

"What's new in the big apple?"

"That's what I asked and wished I hadn't."

"What's wrong?"

Diane relayed the whole story to Jack.

"Oh shit. Do you think I should go help him?"

"No, I guess not, but I do wish you were there. You two make a good team."

"I'm going to call him tonight," Jack said.

"Good. I think he needs to talk to someone. You know what else he told me?"

"After that, I haven't the slightest."

"He's going to move back here after they catch the guy. He said he would rather be a P.I."

"Well, that's the best news I've heard all day," Jack said.

Their food came, and they busied themselves eating.

From a hidden vantage point outside the restaurant, Andrei watched as they ate.

After their meal, Jack ordered each of them a pina colada.

"Umm, these are great," Diane said.

"Yeah, if you don't get a brain freeze."

"The trick is to hold it in your mouth for a little bit. That will warm it up," Diane said. "Cam taught me that."

Jack tried it. "Ooh, it didn't work. My head," he said, holding his head.

"Yeah, I could never get that to work either," Diane said.

"Now you tell me."

At five thirty they were finished and ready to leave. The waitress brought the bill, and Jack reached for it.

"I've got this one," Diane said.

"No, let me get it," Jack said.

"No, remember I do the books for you and Cam. I know how much money you have."

"I have plenty stashed I don't tell you about."

"Even so, I called you for the date," Diane said.

"I hope we get married someday," Jack said. "I would be the luckiest man in the world."

"You'll never get married, Jack. You have commitment issues."

"There you go being a shrink again."

"I am a shrink. That's what I do."

They left the restaurant, and Jack walked Diane to her car.

"Thanks for supper," he said.

"You're welcome. Next time, you can buy. We'll go somewhere more expensive."

"You're on," Jack said.

He bent over and kissed Diane on the lips. She kissed back.

"That's a first," she said.

"I hope not a last," Jack said.

Diane got in her car. Jack said, "Are you sure you don't want me to go with you?"

"Thanks, but I don't think taking a date to my date would go over to good."

"Be careful and call me when you get home."

"Really? I finally get Cam off my back, and now I have you."

"Yep."

"Goodbye," she said and drove away.

One of these days I'm going to convince her and Cam that I'm the right man for her.

Diane thought about their kiss. It felt right to her. All that time she thought Jack was just teasing with her, but now the kiss. This was going to take some thought. She had to be careful. They were too good of friends to rush into anything. *We don't want to end up enemies.*

She stopped by her house and freshened up. Better Than Sex was within walking distance from her house, so she decided to take advantage of the good weather. The streets were crowded with tourists, something you eventually get used to if you live here. As she reached for the door to go inside a hand beat her to it and pulled it open.

"Thank you," she said.

Turning to the gentleman, she saw it was Demyan. They laughed.

"That is good timing," he said.

They were shown to a cozy table with a white tablecloth and a candle. He pulled her chair out, and she sat.

"This place is charming," he said.

"Wait until you taste the food."

175

They made their choices for dessert and ordered a bottle of wine.

"So, Diane, what do you do here in Key West?"

"I'm a psychiatrist. I have a practice here," she said.

"Impressive," he said. "Smart and beautiful."

"You don't have to keep flattering me. I already said yes to this date."

"I can't help it. You pull the best out of me."

"So, what do you do in New York?" Diane asked.

"I'm an attorney," he said.

"My father is an attorney there also," she said.

"Really? What is his name?"

"Cam Derringer," she said.

"Cam is your father?" he said, acting surprised.

"Do you know him?"

"Yes, I've worked with him on a few cases. He's with the Kendall group."

"That's right," Diane said. "What a small world."

"Yes, it is."

"I guess you've heard about the trouble they're having with the assassin. He's shot three people and almost hit Cam."

"Yes. He's a very dangerous man," Andrei said.

"It sounds like it."

"They call him Bloodshot. He is Russian, like me. I hope they catch him before he kills someone."

"Me too. I have faith in Cam."

"Diane, are you dating anyone?"

"Not seriously. I go out with a friend once in a while. He was Dad's partner here. They're still good friends, and Cam doesn't want me to date him. He has a checkered past with the women."

"What is his name? Maybe Cam has mentioned him."

"Jack Steller, a really nice guy and a good friend."

"Maybe one day Cam will come to his senses and allow you to date him," Andrei said.

"Maybe, but we've been through so much together, I don't know if dating would be a good idea."

"The better for me if you don't. Maybe the next time I come to Key West we can have a real date," Andrei said.

"Call me, and we'll see," Diane said.

Their dessert came. It was delicious. They washed it down with the wine. A good combination.

"I'm sad that I have to leave tomorrow, but my short stay here couldn't have been better. I was blessed to have dessert with the prettiest girl in all of the Keys," he said. "And now people think I have friends too."

Diane laughed. "You do have a friend here," she said.

"Thank you so much."

They left the restaurant and talked a while on the sidewalk.

"May I walk you home?" Demyan asked.

"Sure," Diane said. "It's not very far, and we shouldn't waste such a beautiful night."

They walked and talked. Demyan took her hand and held it. When they got to her house, he turned to her and said, "Thank you for the lovely night. I hope I see you again soon."

"You were a perfect gentleman. If you come back to Key West, be sure to call me," Diane said.

"I will," he said. "Tell Cam I was a gentleman when you talk to him."

"I will. I'll be talking to him tomorrow."

They stared at each other for a few seconds; then Demyan leaned down and kissed her. His kiss was very tender and passionate at the same time.

"Goodnight," he said.

"Goodnight," Diane whispered.

Chapter 38

I **opened my computer and googled** Ontario serial shootings.

I went back eight years and scanned the pages. I finally found it seven years back. A Mr. Nathaniel Barton was arrested, prosecuted and sent to prison where he died shortly afterward.

A second man was accused by Mr. Barton but wasn't arrested. His alibis checked out. His name was Eric Meninx.

So, it seemed that Eric Meninx hired Bloodshot to do the shooting for him, allowing him to establish an alibi, I thought.

Next, I googled Eric Meninx. His picture popped up on the society page. My blood ran cold. Staring back at me was the same man I had encountered at the coffee shop that morning.

Could they be playing the game again? I looked up a more detailed summary of the shootings. It seemed Barton spilled his guts after he was found guilty. He said the rules of the game were that no one could be killed. If someone were, the game was over, and the killer would lose. If someone missed a shot and the other one found the target and shot him, the game was over, and the second shooter would win if their scores were the same at the time.

Oh shit. That meant, since Bloodshot missed me, Eric could find me and shoot me and maybe win if he had shot as many as Bloodshot.

I needed to locate the money person. Someone wanted us shot for some reason. These guys wouldn't just come here and choose us. Someone called for them.

I had enough time to shower and marinate the steaks. I chose a wine from the cooler, popped the cork and let it breathe. While I was waiting, I fixed a Wild Turkey and sat on the balcony.

My phone rang. I looked at the caller ID and smiled, it was Jack.

"Hey ya, Jack. What's up?"

"Hi, Cam. Thought I would call and see how the other half is living."

"Never a dull moment."

"That's what I hear. I had supper with Diane today. She told me about your troubles. Good and bad."

"You must be referring to Kailey and Bloodshot," I said.

"Yeah, too bad that something bad has to happen every time something good happens."

"I know. It just isn't fair."

"The reason I called was to see if you wanted me to come to New York and give you a hand."

"No. I'm afraid if you come here, you'll just be another target."

"Well, is there anything I can do from here?"

I thought for a moment. "Maybe," I said. "Could you try to find some information on Eric Meninx from Ontario? I just saw him here. I think he's following me. He was involved in a game with Bloodshot, seven years ago. I believe that they're playing the same game now."

I'll check it out and get back to you," Jack said.

"Thanks. Now, what is this about taking Diane out to eat?"

"Actually, she called me and paid for the meal, so technically she took me out."

"How is she?"

"As beautiful as ever."

"Yeah, I bet she is."

"She even had another date for dessert with some guy that fell off his bicycle in her front yard. Demyan Minsky, a Russian," Jack said.

"And you let her go?"

"I tried to stop her, but you know Diane."

"I'll call her and check on her," I said.

"No need to. I've got that covered. She promised she would call me when she got home. It should be any time now."

"Okay, let me know if I need to come home and off anyone," I said.

"I will, I have his description and name," Jack said.

"Good. We might need it.

"Do you have a pen and paper handy?" I asked.

"Yeah. What do ya have?"

"I want to give you these names. They're related to the case."

"Go," Jack said.

"Chad Kendall, you know him. His brother Robert, Alexis Arlington Kendall, Chad's new wife. Kailey and William Arlington."

"Yeah, your girlfriend and her husband," Jack said.

"Funny," I said. "Anyway, there is also an Eric Meninx, the one I told you about, and Nathaniel Barton. He was in the game with Eric. Adrian Boykov, I'm sure it is an alias. He's the one we think is Bloodshot. Then there was another man shot by a different shooter. I now think the shooter might be Eric Meninx. The man shot was James Osborn. Then Brady Osborn, his brother, was killed by what we believe was a copycat killer. That's all for now."

"Really, that's all? I'll look up all the names. If anything pops up, I'll call you right away."

"Thanks again," I said. "Keep an eye on Diane."

"I'll be happy to," Jack said.

"Yeah, well, I'll talk to ya later."

"Bye."

My phone rang again as soon as I hung up.

"Hello."

"Cam, McNally. I've got something for you. I figure you're in this as far as anyone."

"You had better be relaying it all to Robin also. I got an ass-chewing because you didn't tell her about the second Osborn shooting."

"Oops, it must have slipped through the cracks. Sorry."

"What do you have?" I asked.

"A young girl just came into my office and said she was raped last week. The man was a Russian. He took her ID and said if she ever told anyone he would kill her and her family. It happened at the Hilton downtown. He said his name was Demyan Minsky. I checked the hotel, and there was no one registered in that name. But here's the kicker, he dropped a calling card in her purse. Want to guess what it said?"

"Bloodshot," I said in shock, running Demyan Minsky's name through my mind.

"Right."

"Check the Hilton again. This time ask about Adrian Boykov."

"The guy from the Tom Carrington murder?" McNally said.

"Yeah, one and the same."

"Okay, thanks," he said.

Silence.

"Cam, you alright?"

"Did you say Demyan Minsky?"

"Yeah. You know him?"

"He's in Key West with my daughter," I choked out.

Chapter 39

I **called Diane**.
"Hello Cam," she said.
I was never so happy to hear her voice.
"Diane, are you alright?"
"Sure. Why shouldn't I be?"
"Did you have a date with Demyan Minsky?"
"Boy, Jack didn't waste any time, did he?"
"Never mind that. Describe him to me."
"He says you know each other. He told me to tell you hi."
"Describe him."
"Why?"
"Please."
"Okay. Six foot three or four, short blond hair, beautiful blue eyes and—"

"Lock your doors," I said.

"What? Why?"

"It's him. Demyan is Bloodshot," I tried to say calmly.

"He can't be. He's in New York."

"Lock your doors."

"Okay, okay, I'm locking my doors," Diane said, walking to the front door and then the rear.

"Demyan Minsky is an alias he used here when he raped a girl. She just came forward today. He left a calling card in her purse."

"What's he doing here?"

"He came after you to get to me."

A chill ran through Diane.

"He was a perfect gentleman with me. He left about fifteen minutes ago."

"When we hang up, call the sheriff and tell him the whole story. I'm going to call Jack to come and stay with you."

"Do you really think I'm in any danger?" Diane said.

"I don't know, but I'm not taking any chances. I'll call you back after I talk to Jack. Now, call the sheriff."

"Okay, bye," she said.

"I love you. Bye."

I called Jack. He answered on the first ring.

"Diane hasn't called yet. I'll call you when she does," he answered.

"I've already talked to her. She might be in big trouble," I said.

"What's wrong?" Jack asked, worry in his voice.

"It's Demyan Minsky. He's Bloodshot."

"What? Did he harm her?" he said.

"No. He's gone now, but he might come back."

Jack picked up his gun and stuck it in his waistband. "I'm on my way there," he said, opening the door.

"Thanks. Stay with her until this is over."

"I will. Don't worry about—"

I heard Jack yell and then the phone hit the floor.

"Jack, Jack." No answer. **"Jack."**

I could hear the phone being picked up and dropped again.

"Jack," I tried once more.

"I'm here, Cam. I've been shot in the arm," he said, a short distance from the phone.

Then I heard his door slam shut. The phone was picked up again.

"I'm back, Cam. It doesn't look bad, just a nick," he said, sounding out of breath.

"Can you call nine one one?" I asked.

"Yeah, I'm okay. I'll call them and then head over to Diane's."

"Go out the back way and be careful. I'm on the next plane from New York."

"No, don't do that. Let's think about this. He wants you out of New York because you can identify him. You need to stay there."

I thought about it for a minute. Jack was probably right. Then I remembered the bugs in my apartment.

"No, I'm on my way," I said, walking out my door.

Once outside and out of reach of the bugs I said, "You're right, Jack, but I had to say that. My apartment is bugged, and he can hear me in there. I'll give the police a description and have them watch the airports here. He's probably on his way to the airport to come back here already. Call the cops there and have them watching the airport for a six-foot-three Russian with short blond hair and blue eyes."

"Will do, and don't worry about Diane. If he wanted her, he would have already gotten her."

"Be careful," I warned.

"I will, now that I know what I'm up against. I gotta go. I've got a lot to do. Bye," he said and hung up.

I called Diane back and filled her in.

"I'll have a doctor here waiting for him," she said.

"Okay. Keep me informed."

"I love you, Cam. I'm sorry."

"You've got nothing to be sorry for. I'm sorry for getting you into this mess."

"Don't worry about us. I'm sure he's long gone by now. I think he accomplished what he came for."

"You're probably right, but keep an eye out for him and don't go out."

"Alright; I'll call you if anything happens," Diane said.

"Take care of Jack."

"I will."

We hung up, and my buzzer rang. Robin, I'd almost forgot. I let her in and met her in the hall.

"What's up?" she asked when she saw my face.

I told her about Bloodshot and Jack.

Chapter 40

We entered my apartment with a plan in mind. It was time to take advantage of the bugs planted there.

"I'll help you pack," Robin said.

"I don't need much. I hope I'm not gone long."

We packed a small bag, which I was going to take to Robin's, where I would be staying for a few days.

I placed the steaks in a plastic bowl for later. I put my gun in its holster on my belt, picked up the wine and we left, locking the door behind us.

Once in a taxi, I called McNally back and told him about my plan.

"We'll put some men on it, Cam, but honestly, it looks like a fat chance that we'll see him. He's sneaky. He won't come strolling in LaGuardia with his name on his shirt."

"Yeah, I know, but it's something."

"What about Key West? Do you have it covered? It would be a lot easier to spot him there."

"It's covered," I said.

"Okay, we'll keep an eye out," he said. "I'll call Robin, so you won't get in trouble again."

"I can hear you," Robin said.

"Oh, sorry, I didn't know you were there. You set me up, Cam," he said.

"Sorry 'bout that. Call me if you see him."

"I'll call Robin. She can call you."

"Bye," Robin said.

"Goodbye," McNally said and hung up.

We arrived at Robin's apartment in the Avalon Fort Greene building in Brooklyn and dropped off my bag.

~***~

Andrei entered his hotel room and laid his gun sack on the sofa. He made a call from his cell phone and dialed a code number. He listened for a moment and smiled. His plan had worked. Cam was coming to Key West. Now he had to get ready for his date with Julie. So many women and so little time. He knew the airports would be buzzing with FBI for the next twenty-four hours. It was better to wait a while before leaving.

~***~

FBI and local law administrations were set up at all nearby airports and bus stations. All they had to go on was an artist's rendition of my description. I was satisfied that it was a fair resemblance of Demyan.

I called Diane again. She said Jack had shown up and she was at the hospital with him now. He was fine, and there was nothing to worry about.

"Really," I said, "nothing to worry about?"

"Yeah, I know," Diane said, "there's plenty to worry about, but we're good for now.

"Find a safe place to stay for tonight and take care of Jack."

"I will," she said.

"I'll call you tomorrow."

"Love you."

"You too."

"Is everything alright?" Robin asked.

"For now. There isn't anything we can do until he shows himself."

I decided to stay put for the night and check with the police the next day. Robin would be alerted if anything turned up from the FBI.

"Shall we have our wine before we start the steaks?" I said.

"Sounds good," Robin said. "We could use the distraction."

We sat on the balcony. "So, tell me about your job offer," I said.

"I'm sorry, Cam. I know I've been a real bitch lately, but I'm stressed about what to do. This is the job offer of a lifetime."

"If it's the job offer of a lifetime, it sounds like a no-brainer to me. You have to take it. The job is there, and nowhere else, it can't move—we can."

"We?" Robin said.

"Well, kind of," I said. "I'm thinking of moving back to Key West."

"You are?"

"Yeah, this life just isn't me. I miss the Keys. Now that I know you're moving to LA, I've decided that's what I have to do. I'm even happy about it. I can fly to LA, and you can fly to Key West. It won't be the same, but we'll both be doing what we love."

Robin thought about it for a moment and said, "You're right, Cam. We will. I feel a flood of relief already. I'm going to do it."

"Good for you, Robin. It just makes sense. You can't live in Key West, and I can't live anywhere else."

I held up my wine glass, and she touched hers to it in a toast.

~***~

I went back inside and took the steaks out of the marinade. I wrapped them in handy-wrap and laid them on the cutting board. I went back out to the balcony and lit a fire in Robin's grill.

"Another wine?" I asked.

"Sure," Robin said.

I poured two glasses and took them out to her. I looked at the grill. It was already three hundred and fifty degrees, one hundred fifty to go.

"When will you leave for LA?" I asked.

"Not until I hang Bloodshot. I have to finish this one."

"I'm staying until then also," I said.

"Good. We'll have some time together."

"I have another lead for you," I said. I told her about Eric Meninx.

"And he was following you?"

"Yeah, I think so. It looks like he could be the other shooter."

"So Bloodshot has used two aliases now that we know of. Demyan Minsky, Adrian Boykov and we still don't know his real name."

The grill temperature reached five hundred. I placed the steaks on the grill and closed the lid.

191

"You want to put the potatoes in the microwave?" I said.

"I didn't know I was going to have to do everything," she teased.

"Sorry, your highness."

By the time the steaks were ready, so was the table. We ate and made small talk—movies and friends. We didn't want to speak about the case.

"I'm glad you are staying with me, but I wish the circumstances were different," Robin said.

"Me too."

"Are you finished eating?"

"Yes."

We adjourned to the bedroom where we got naked and cuddled.

"I'm sorry, but I'm not in the mood tonight," I said.

"That makes two of us."

"This is good though."

"Yeah."

Chapter 41

Julie knocked on Andrei's door** precisely at eight
thirty.

Good, he thought, *now for a little fun.* He would
rape her and then leave for Miami. He downed the glass
of vodka he had poured and answered the door.

"Julie, so glad you came to see me," he said, smiling as
he opened the door.

"Yeah, me too," Julie said and slid out of her dress,
exposing her naked body.

"I didn't come here to screw around with niceties. Get
your clothes off and fuck me," she said through gritted
teeth.

This was new to Andrei. This didn't work into his plan
to rape her, not to be raped *by* her.

He reached out and pulled her close to him as roughly
as possible. He wanted to watch her cry.

"That's it, you son of a bitch, be tough, take me here
on the floor."

Andrei was in mild shock. The roles were reversed.

She reached down and grabbed his cock through his pants.

"Give it to me now," she demanded.

Andrei lost his erection. She was beautiful, but he couldn't take her, not like this.

She felt the hardness turn soft in her hand. "Bitch," she said, and put her hands on his shoulders and, using her leverage, pushed him to the floor. She straddled him and started hunching.

Andrei didn't feel right. He felt as if he were drugged.

He pushed her off and got to his feet. Grabbing her dress from the floor, he forced her toward the door. He opened it and threw her dress into the hall and then pushed her out, closing the door behind her.

He leaned on the door breathing hard. "What just happened?" he said aloud.

Julie pounded on the door. **"Let me in, you little pussy. Fuck me."**

Andrei locked the door and yelled, **"Go away, you crazy bitch."**

He heard her yell, **"Fuck you,"** and then her footsteps fading down the hall.

He poured a tall glass of vodka from the bottle she had sent to his room. Downing it in one long drink, he breathed a sigh of relief.

It didn't feel good to be on the other side of aggression. He didn't like it. He wanted to be in charge and see the terror in the other's eyes.

Andrei packed his bag and picked up his rifle case and left the room. He was going to get as far away from that crazy bitch as he could. He would drive to Miami that night and on to New York the next day. He felt dizzy from the vodka. *Did that stupid bitch drug me?* he thought. He went to the parking garage and opened the trunk of his rental car, threw in the bags and opened the driver's door.

"**Mother fucker,**" he heard behind him.

He turned just in time to see Julie swing a roundhouse right and catch him in the nose. Before he could regain his senses, she hit him in the throat with a Taser.

He woke an hour later in the back seat of his car. He was naked and could smell the faint odor of chloroform. He knew the smell because he had used it on a few occasions himself.

His nose was tender, and he had blood caked on his face. Then he had a terrible thought. He looked down half expecting to see that his cock had been cut off. It had not, but it was bloody. He shivered. On closer examination he saw that it wasn't blood, it was lipstick.

Shit, he thought. *I've been raped.*

He looked around for his clothes, but they weren't in the car. He looked out the window and saw them lying about twenty yards away in the middle of the garage drive.

Damn, now I have to walk across the garage naked to get them. He made a mad dash for them, finding he was still dizzy and was having a hard time navigating a straight line.

Halfway to them, he heard a car start behind him. He turned to see the headlights coming toward him. He dove out of the way just as the car squealed to a stop beside him.

"Thanks for a good time, honey," Julie said; then she laughed and drove away.

Chapter 42

Andrei's cell phone rang. He recognized the number and answered.

"Where are you?" the voice said.

"I'm in Key West," he replied.

"What the fuck are you doing in Key West?"

"I'm working on a plan to get Cam out of New York and back here. I don't need him pointing me out to the FBI."

"When are you returning?"

"Tomorrow."

"It's time."

The phone went dead. Andrei smiled as he got dressed in the parking lot.

~***~

Alexis drove to her father's house early the next morning. She entered the front door and walked past the butler without saying a word.

Bill was on the terrace eating breakfast as usual when she walked out of the house and started yelling at him without even saying hello.

"Bloodshot? You killed a man and blamed it on Bloodshot."

"Good morning, sweetie," Bill said calmly. "Join me for breakfast."

"No thank you. My appetite is gone."

"It's time for you to stop yelling **and sit down**," Bill said sternly.

She sat, holding her tongue. She knew when to stop pushing.

"I did what I had to do. Osborn has been blackmailing me for years. Even though he was just as guilty as me, he'd go to the police and rat us out."

"When will it end, Dad? You promised me you wouldn't kill anymore."

"Now I can stop. Bloodshot came along at the right time, that's all."

She stared at him for a moment. He stared back. It was no use. He was never going to change.

"What is your sudden interest in protecting Bloodshot?" Bill asked.

"None," she said. "I just don't want you killing people."

"Would you rather I go to prison?"

"No, but there has to be another way."

"Why do you suppose Bloodshot shot Brady's brother in the first place?"

"It wasn't Bloodshot. It was a copycat," Alexis said.

197

"Yes. Maybe it was, but still," he said, shrugging his shoulders.

Alexis thought for a moment. Then it hit her.

"Someone knows about you and Brady," she said.

"Exactly," Bill said, slapping his open hand on the table. "Someone wanted me to have Brady killed."

Kailey stepped out onto the terrace. "Good morning, Alexis," she said and kissed her on the cheek.

"Good morning, Kailey. How do you feel today?"

"As good as new. My arm burns a little when I change the bandage, but other than that, just great."

"Good."

Then there was an uneasy silence.

"Sorry," Kailey said. "Did I interrupt something?"

"No, not at all," Alexis said.

"Join us for breakfast, darling," Bill said.

Kailey and Alexis each took a plate and walked to the buffet, half-filled their plates and took a seat at the table.

Bill looked from one to the other and said, "I am a very lucky man to have breakfast with the two women I love more than anything in the world."

The girls grinned. "We love you too," Kailey said.

"Yes, we do," Alexis said.

"Did I hear someone say something about Bloodshot when I came out?" Kailey said.

"We were just talking. Wondering if they will catch him before he shoots anyone else," Bill said.

"I sure hope so," Kailey said. "It's not very pleasant being shot."

"No, I suppose it isn't," Bill said.

"I wonder who will be next," Alexis said.

"Maybe no one," Bill said.

"Has anyone ever been shot twice?" Kailey asked.

"Not that I know of," Alexis said. "I think you are safe now."

"Are the two of you afraid? You're a part of our circle, and it seems he is trying to get us all," Kailey murmured.

"Don't worry about us, dear, we'll be okay. They'll get him soon," Bill said.

Turning to Alexis, he asked, "Are you and Chad coming to our soiree tomorrow tonight?"

"Yes, we'll be here," Alexis said.

"Oh good. We'll have a blast," Kailey said. "Be sure to bring Cam and Robin."

"We will."

Alexis finished her breakfast and stood. "I need to get a move on. Chad is expecting me to join him and Cam for lunch today. It seems like all I ever do is eat," she said and laughed.

She kissed Kailey on the cheek and then her father. When she bent down, she whispered in his ear, "I'm still mad."

~***~

Andrei's phone rang as he passed through Marathon Key.

"Yes," he answered.

"Your plan didn't work. Cam is still here in New York."

"Oh well, I guess he needs to be eliminated then."

"No. I told you he is not to be hurt."

"Okay, it's your call, but if it's him or me—it's him."

"Be here tomorrow night."

"I'm on my way," Andrei said and turned off his cell phone.

Chapter 43

I was in my office when my phone rang at seven thirty a.m. It was Jack.

"Hello, Jack. How are you feeling?"

"Not bad at all, considering."

"Any luck at the airport, finding Bloodshot?" I asked, but I knew the answer.

"No, nothing yet, but I have turned up some interesting info on Bill."

"Really? What do you have?"

"Bill and Brady Osborn know each other. As a matter of fact, they were partners along with a man named Brian Wessel. Brian was found murdered in his home twenty years ago. Bill and Brady were questioned and released. The murderer was never found."

"Where were they living at the time?" I asked.

"Right there in New York."

"Is Wessel's wife still here? I might want to talk to her."

"No, she died a year before he did. It was just him and his ten-year-old daughter. She was sent to live with some relatives in Oklahoma."

"Anything else?"

"Not yet, but I'll keep looking," Jack said.

"Thanks. How is Diane?"

"Busy being a good nurse. Being hurt does have its perks."

"Keep your hands off her."

"Don't worry, I'll behave."

"That doesn't sound like a promise to keep your hands to yourself."

"Here she comes with my lunch, gotta go. I'll call you if I get anything else. Bye."

The phone went dead. I wasn't really worried. I trust Diane, but Jack on the other hand...

Now, what do I do about Bill? He said he didn't know Brady Osborn. Did he kill him? Maybe he had him killed. I could see him doing that. Is he behind Bloodshot? No, surely he wouldn't have his own wife shot. Would he?

Next Robin called me. "Any news yet?" she asked.

I decided to keep Bill and Brady's relationship to myself for the time being.

"No. I talked to Jack, but no sign of Bloodshot."

"Nothing at the airports or bus stations either, but I really didn't expect to find him there anyway."

"You never know. He thinks we believe he is still in Key West and that I'm on my way there."

"Yeah, maybe. He's pretty clever."

"Keep me informed," I said.

"Yeah, me too. I'll talk to you later."

I knew there was no way we would find Bloodshot, but on the other hand, Eric Meninx didn't know I knew about him. If he was following me, I might be able to find him. I wanted to know what his role in this whole scheme was.

If I could locate and follow him, he might lead me to Bloodshot. He had to be the reason why Eric was there. I decided to make myself visible.

I went to Chad's office and told him I wasn't going to be able to make lunch with him and Alexis that day.

"Sorry to hear that, Cam," Chad said. "Something come up?"

"I just want to walk a little, so I can think. There has to be something connecting all the shootings. This is more than just a game."

"I'm afraid you're right. I was thinking the same thing. I'll give your regards to Alexis."

"Thanks. I'll see you this afternoon," I said and left.

I walked down Broadway to Seventy-Second Street and toward Central Park. As I passed the Dakota, I thought I saw someone duck into the hotel. I looked again and saw no one. I was being paranoid. I guess I expected to find Eric right away.

I entered Central Park and walked a path for five minutes. At the next turn was a bench. I took a seat. If someone was following me, they would turn the corner not seeing me until it was too late.

I removed my paperback novel from my inside jacket pocket and continued to read *Rum City Bar*. Sunny Ray was in trouble again, and only Wanta Mea could save him.

As I read, I kept my peripheral vision trained on the turn. After a few minutes, I was caught up in the book again and forgot to focus on my mission. I noticed a man walk by quickly. I looked up and recognized him as Eric Meninx. I don't think he even saw me.

I waited a moment and followed him. I could tell he was a man on a mission of his own. He was walking fast and kept looking in all directions, trying to find me no doubt. I stayed close enough not to lose him but also far enough not to be spotted by him.

He stopped, and I stopped. I waited anxiously for him to turn around and come back. I would have nowhere to hide other than in the bushes. If he saw me there, my cover would be blown for sure.

I waited. He started walking again. This time he was in no hurry. The path turned again. When I made the turn, he was standing in the center of the walk looking right at me.

"Hello Cam," he said.

"Eric," I said.

"We need to talk."

Chapter 44

We stood for a moment and didn't speak.
He was much larger than I first thought. I
thought I could take him if it came to that, but
not if he knew some kind of secret agent defense.

"Well," I said, "are you here to kill me or just set me
up for Bloodshot?"

"Neither. Actually, I'm here to kill Bloodshot."

I didn't know if I believed that or not. Why would he
be telling me that?

"And you thought the best way to kill Bloodshot was
to follow me?"

"In a way, yes. I was waiting for the right time to
speak with you. Without an audience, you know," he
whispered and smiled.

"Okay, speak."

"I received a message from … who knows who," he said, shrugging his shoulders, "offering me one million dollars to kill Bloodshot and maybe join the game a little."

"And you don't know who the offer came from?"

"No, although I have my suspicions, and the rest of you should too if you were any good."

"Well, you know, everyone isn't as smart as you," I said sarcastically.

"Yes, I know. Anyway, there was a time when I didn't need another million dollars, but now…" He trailed off and shrugged his shoulders again. "Bloodshot is actually kind of a friend of mine, so I'm not sure I'll accept the mission."

"As well you shouldn't. I wouldn't want to kill a friend. So, why are you telling me all this? Is your conscience heavy?"

"No."

"I didn't think so," I stated.

"I know what this is all about and I don't want to see anyone murdered," he said.

"I thought this was just a game between you and Bloodshot."

"Last time it was. This time, it's a hit, and I don't want to be any part of it. I don't want my name associated with it in any way. Because of the last game in Ontario, though, I will be."

"Why don't you just tell me who's getting hit and where to find Bloodshot, so you won't have to worry about the publicity?"

"No."

"That's it—no?"

"Yes."

"Make up your mind, yes or no?"

"It's complicated. I don't know who the target is. I'll receive a phone call and instructions when it's time," he said. "Someone is using Bloodshot, and they are planning to kill him after his work is finished."

"His work. You mean wounding innocent people?"

"Whoever hired him wants someone dead. This game is a perfect cover. Believe me when I say someone will die," Eric said.

"Someone already has," I said. "Brady Osborn."

"Yes, I know. I regret that. My instructions were to draw blood from James, his brother."

"That was you?"

"Yes."

"Eric, this is all very confusing. Are you going to help me or not?"

"I already have a little. The rest is up to you. You need to figure out who has something to gain. My research shows a lot of suspects."

"Yeah, I've thought of that. It has to be someone with a million to spend on covering up the hit," I said.

"Be careful. You could become collateral damage," he said.

"What makes you think I won't turn you in?" I said.

"Because you need help. Without it, one of your friends might die."

With that Eric turned and walked away. I could have run him down and tried to get more information or called the police while I held him down, but I had a feeling that it wouldn't do any good. No one else heard the conversation. It would be his word against mine, and he was right—one of my friends might die.

I slowly walked back to the office. My mind was reeling trying to find the clue Eric had given me. I couldn't, but I would. I hoped it was before someone was killed.

Two blocks before I reached the office a Porsche pulled to the curb and honked. It was Kailey. I stepped toward the car and bent down as the window lowered.

"Hello, Kailey."

"Hi ya, Cam. Want a ride?"

"I'm almost there now. Where were you five blocks ago?"

"Fifteen blocks back," she said and laughed.

She hit a button and the door opened. I decided to get in and see what was up.

She punched the accelerator, and the Porsche came alive.

"Where are we going?" I asked.

"I want to talk to you about something."

"Fire away," I said.

"In a minute."

She turned left on Thirty-Second and took a right on Twelfth. She pulled over to the curb and shut off the engine. We were on a secluded side street.

She turned to face me.

"I love you," she said.

"Kailey, you can't love me, you're married."

"I know. I just wanted to get that out of the way. That's not what I came to tell you."

"Proceed then."

"I overheard Bill and Alexis talking about Bloodshot this morning. I think they know who he is and might have something to do with him being here."

"Why would you tell me that? They're your family."

"I know. You see, I don't really believe what I just said. That's why I told you. If I could figure it out, someone else might too. I want you to prove that they're innocent."

"So, you think if I probe into their lives and try to prove they're guilty, I might end up showing that they aren't."

"Yeah, something like that," she said.

"What did you hear them say?"

"Bill said that Alexis was protecting Bloodshot and Alexis said that Bill killed that Brady Osborn guy."

"Did he?"

"I think so, but that doesn't have anything to do with this. It was for another reason."

I thought for a moment. This girl was certifiably crazy. I didn't know when she's being innocently blunt or when she was manifesting a story.

"Did he also have James Osborn shot?" I asked.

"Don't know."

Before I could say anything else, she leaned over and locked her lips on mine. I managed to pull away.

"That was just in case I never got another chance at you," she said matter-of-factly. She had passion in her eyes.

What could I say? I said nothing.

"Do you think Bill would have had you shot? You know there was a chance you could have been killed."

"I know. That's why I don't think he would have had anything to do with it." She looked down and frowned. "But I don't know if Alexis would care if I were killed or not."

"I don't think she would want you hurt. She knows you're making her father happy."

"Yeah, but I'm also taking some of her money. I bet she doesn't like that."

"She has plenty of money. I don't think she's trying to kill you just to have more."

"No, I don't believe so either. I don't know what the reason would be to have Bloodshot shoot people. I'm just saying that if I were gone, it wouldn't be such a loss."

"I think you're wrong about that. She speaks very highly of you. She loves you as a friend," I reassured.

"I hope so. I don't want either one of them to be the one."

"If it makes you feel better, I'll look into it," I said.

"Thank you, Cam," she said and kissed me again.

I found myself wishing neither one of us was in a relationship, but we were. And she was even married, but damn she was hot.

She drove me back to the office and pulled up to the curb.

"I'll see what I can do," I said as I opened the door.

"Thanks."

I got out and stood on the sidewalk waiting for her to pull away.

She stared at me for a moment, smiled sensually, then said, "I'll see you tonight. Toodles," and sped away.

I had forgotten I would see her that night at her house with Chad and Alexis.

Chapter 45

Instead of returning to the office, I hailed a taxi and went to the precinct to see McNally.

The building was crowded. I stood in line to talk to the officer in charge at the front desk.

I watched as police escorted a mélange of detainees through the room to various cubicles where they were cuffed to their chairs while the officers poured themselves coffee and bullshitted with one another as the prisoners waited to be booked or released.

My line wasn't moving. Everyone seemed to have to argue with the officer, who was unyielding. He turned away a black mother and her baby who wanted to see her brother who was arrested for attempted robbery. She pulled a brick from the baby's blanket, which held only a brick, no baby, and threw it at the officer. He was too slow. The brick struck him in the forehead, and he fell to the floor. Three officers immediately restrained the woman, one pulling what he thought was a baby from her to protect it.

"Motha fucka," she yelled, "you le ma brotha go."

She kicked free from the two officers who were holding her and ran through the room and down a corridor. The room emptied of police as they all chased after her.

One man, dressed in an expensive suit, who was cuffed to a chair, took the opportunity to pick it up and walk out of the building. I met him at the door and held it open for him while handing him my card.

"Just in case you don't make it," I said.

"Thank you," he said, "I'll be in contact."

Finally, the room started filling with police again. They were laughing and cracking jokes about the lady. Then one of them noticed the officer still lying on the floor with blood coming from his forehead.

"Call nine one one," he yelled.

"That's us," another said.

"An ambulance," the first said.

At that moment, the injured officer sat up straight and looked around. "Is she gone?" he asked.

"What the fuck? You ain't even hurt," the attending officer said.

"Could have been if that crazy bitch wouldn't have left."

They all laughed again and went back to their business.

The officer who lost his prisoner and his chair ran around the room in search of his man. As he passed me, I said, "He went that way," pointing out the door.

The officer flew out the door and was gone.

McNally appeared from an office at the end of the room. He saw me standing in line and motioned for me to come to him.

211

"What are you doing standing in the line of shame?" he asked, chewing on the cigar sticking out the side of his mouth.

"I wanted to see you," I said.

"Just call me and I'll meet you next time."

"Okay," I said, feeling like a scolded schoolboy.

We took a seat in his office. He offered me a shot of brandy. I accepted.

"To what do I owe the pleasure?" he asked.

"I wondered if you had any leads on the Osborn case yet," I said, trying not to be too inquisitive.

"Not much. Why you wanna know?"

"Thought it might have something to do with Bloodshot, even if it was a copycat shooting."

"You're quite involved in this case for just being a lawyer."

"My friends are in danger. Not to mention me, and I used to be a P.I. in Key West. I guess I just can't get it out of my system."

McNally looked at me for a moment, took a swig from his brandy glass and said, "What do you know that you're not telling me?"

"Nothing concrete. I don't want to start any rumors. If I put anything together, though, you'll be the first to know."

He stared at me again. I stared back. He poured us both another shot.

"Okay," he said. "James was wounded in the arm with a Black Ops tactical sniper rifle, point twenty-two caliber. Probably a four by thirty-two scope. They're easy to come by."

"Doesn't sound like Bloodshot," I said.

"No, but it was a first-class marksman."

I thought about Eric Meninx.

He went on, "Brady was killed with a Winchester point two four three. It's a deer-hunting rifle."

"You can even tell the brand of the rifle?" I asked, knowing there had to be more to it.

"Yeah, we found it a block away," he said and waited for my reaction.

I acted cool. Didn't want to look too excited.

"You mean you have the gun and didn't even tell us," I said, my voice cracking and getting louder. I could feel my face turning red. This was me being cool.

He smiled. "Okay, Cam, what do you know?"

I closed my mouth and tried to look clueless. It must have worked.

"Did you get any fingerprints?" I asked.

"Nope."

I thought for a moment while we both drank.

"So," I said, "Brady was a hit."

"Looks that way," he said.

"Do you think someone shot James so Brady would be exposed?"

"We thought of that."

"If someone knew that Brady was being hunted, they could have shot James so Brady would show himself," I said.

"That's what I think, or if someone wanted Brady dead, they could have shot James so someone else could find Brady and kill him."

"A lot of ifs," I said.

"Yep. Can you connect the dots for us?"

I thought about Bill killing Brady. If he'd wanted Brady dead but couldn't find him, then maybe someone else gave him a little help.

"No, I got nothing yet," I said.

McNally stood. I was being dismissed.

I said, "I'd like to talk to James Osborn."

213

"We already have," he said.

"It wouldn't hurt to have a second opinion," I said.

He stared at me, moving his cigar from one side of his mouth to the other.

"Okay, knock yourself out." He wrote down James's address and handed it to me. "Be careful. He's a little seedy."

I stood and downed my last swallow. "Thanks for the drink. If I figure this out, I'll call you."

"Make sure you do," he said.

I nodded and left. Now my head was swimming. I didn't know if it was the Brandy or all the speculation.

It was nine o'clock. I stopped at a coffee house long enough to drink a cup and eat a donut; then I hailed a taxi and went to see James Osborn.

~***~

The address was that of a run-down apartment building in Queens. I looked for his name on the door registry. There were only two names on it that hadn't been crossed out. His wasn't one. I tried the door and it swung open. The hallway was littered with food sacks and beer cans, a few large trash bags, which I had no interest in finding out what was in them, and a man on the floor leaning against the wall. He was staring at me, but I wasn't not sure if he could see me.

I pulled a twenty from my wallet. His eyes got bigger. He could see me. I asked him, "Which apartment is Jimmy's?"

He looked at the twenty. "Jimmy who?"

"Osborn," I said.

He looked at the twenty again and then back at me. I pulled one more from my wallet.

"Three C," he said, holding out one dirty hand.

I gave him the forty and walked up the steps. The door to Three C was ajar. I pulled my nine-millimeter from its holster on my belt and pushed the door slightly with my foot.

"James," I said.

No answer. "James," I said louder.

"What you want?" a voice answered.

"My name's Cam Derringer. I want to talk to you about your brother."

"He's dead," the ghost voice answered.

"May I come in?"

"Sure, but if you're holdin' a gun, I'll cut you down."

I holstered my gun and pushed the door open. Nothing happened, so I entered. James was sitting in a recliner reading the newspaper. He was not what I expected. He was a tall, well-built, clean-cut man. His right arm was wrapped in white gauze. He had a two-inch scar under his right eye. The apartment was also clean and very well furnished. Artwork was hanging on the wall.

"James?" I said.

"Yes. Have a seat, Mr. Derringer," he said, motioning to the sofa. "Would you like something to drink?"

"No, thank you," I said, sitting on the sofa across from him. "I'm fine."

"Are you a cop?" he asked.

"No, P.I.," I said. I thought it better not to tell him I was a lawyer.

"How may I help you?" he asked, pulling a gun from under the newspaper and placing it on the table next to him but still in reach.

"I'm investigating the murder of your brother. I just have a few questions," I said, still taking in the room.

"Not what you expected, is it?" he said.

"No, not really."

"My brother gave me money every month. He had an excellent income. I'll miss that," he said, dismissively waving his hand. "All good things. Right?"

"Yes, I'm afraid so," I said.

"Do you have any idea why anyone would want your brother dead?"

"His name is Brady," he said.

"Sorry. Do you know why anyone would want Brady dead?" I aseked.

"Yes," he said.

I stared at him for a moment. He stared back. This wasn't going to be easy.

"Who, why?" I asked.

"William Arlington," he said, "because Brady was blackmailing him."

"For what?" I asked.

"Murder."

"Who did he murder?"

"Brian Wessel. His partner," he said.

The name was the one Jack had given me.

"Any proof he's the one who killed Brady?"

"Yes, I have proof. Until I was shot by that Bloodshot guy, Brady was safe. Then when he came to the hospital to get me, his cover was blown."

"How do you think they found you?" I asked.

"That I don't know. I didn't think they would try to get to him through me again."

"Again?"

"Yeah, about five years ago they found me. They followed me for a month. I spotted them right away, so I stayed away from Brady. At first, I thought they thought I was Brady, since we are almost identical. I gave up my apartment in Manhattan and moved here. It's dirty, but I was alive, and so was Brady."

"Anyone else want him dead?" I asked.

"Not that I know of."

"Did you tell the police all of this?"

"No. I didn't want them to drag Brady's name through the mud, and I plan on picking up where he left off," he said.

"You mean you're going to blackmail William?" I asked.

"Yeah. I have all the proof. I was there. I saw him do it."

"May I say that I think that might be very foolish and dangerous?"

"Yes, you may, but that won't change my mind. I tried to stop Brady from blackmailing him, but he wouldn't listen to me. I told him he would end up dead."

"Now you'll end up dead," I said.

"One of us will," he said.

He stared at me again. "Why are you so interested in Brady?"

"Bloodshot, who, by the way, was not the one who shot you, is shooting my friends. I'm afraid one of them will be killed."

He smiled. "Yes, I know he isn't the one who shot me. It was a copycat who was sent by William to flush Brady out. Maybe William is connected to this Bloodshot person."

"I don't know about that. If he is, do you know who he might want dead, assuming that Brady was an afterthought?"

"Whose death would benefit him?" James asked.

"I don't know. There doesn't seem to be anyone," I said.

I thought for a moment.

"Do you know why William murdered Brian Wessel?" I asked.

"Brian wouldn't go along with some of William's dealings. Bill took it as a threat to his freedom."

"I guess that wasn't such a good idea," I said.

"No, it didn't turn out well for him, but the last laugh will be on William," he said, smiling.

"What do you mean?" I asked.

He just smiled even more. "Is there anything else I can help you with?"

I guess we are done here. "No, not right now," I said, standing. "Thanks for your cooperation."

"You're very welcome," he said, "and if you have any more questions, ask them now. I won't be able to be found again."

I thought for a moment. "Do you know anything about his daughter Alexis or his wife, Kailey?"

He smiled again. "Goodbye Mister Derringer. Good luck," he said.

Chapter 46

I returned to the office where my desk was starting to look like a library. I needed help.

Chad stopped at my door. "Want to go get a drink?"

I looked at my desk and pointed.

He said, "You need help."

I nodded.

"I'll get you some."

He did. Jackie Fairchild, our legal secretary, came in five minutes later and looked at my desk. I could see her turning white.

"Really?" she said.

"I've been busy," I said.

"Get up. Chad is waiting for you. I'll do the best I can."

"Thank you."

I got up, and she sat down and immediately started going through my files.

"Good luck," I said.

She didn't look up. I got my suit coat and left.

Chad and I went to a local bar, the White House, where we liked the bartender. She was worth the high prices they charged for Wild Turkey.

We found two stools at the bar, which was almost full. The tables were empty. I guess we weren't the only ones who went there for the view.

"Hiya, Cam, Chad," she said, as she pushed two Wild Turkeys toward us.

"Hiya, Ginger," we said.

"Heard your name while ago," she said, looking at me.

"Really, from who?"

"Don't know. Big guy. Wore a hat."

"Oh?"

"He was on his phone. All I caught was, 'I already talked to Cam Derringer in the park.'"

"Yeah, that was Eric. You didn't hear anything else?"

"No. He wasn't happy with whoever he was talking to though."

"Have you seen him in here before?"

"A few times, just lately though."

"Thanks. Will you let me know if he returns?" I asked and wrote my number down and handed it to her.

"Sure will. Can I call for anything else?" she asked, placing the paper in her bra.

"If you need to," I said and then wondered how I would get out of it if she did call. I enjoyed looking, but I'm a one-woman-at-a-time kind of guy.

When she left, I filled Chad in on my meeting with Eric and McNally. I left out the conversation with Kailey and James and felt guilty about doing so.

"Sounds like this thing is getting more complicated at every turn."

"It is. Now we have a hitman after a hitman that's after us. We don't know who he wants to kill, but I do know he wants me out of it bad enough to go to Key West and take my daughter out."

"At least he was a gentleman with her. I don't think he wants to hurt anyone other than his final target."

"Yeah, it looks that way."

We sat and sipped our drinks and watched Ginger bending down to get a beer from the cooler. She caught us and smiled.

"How's Robert doing in his adventure with the resort?" I asked. "Maybe it does have something to do with that."

"He got word this morning that another offer has hit the table. He's going back down there to talk with his partners."

"What if the hit is on him? Maybe the competition is trying to clean the table a bit."

"Maybe, but I don't think so. I think they would have killed him the first time instead of wounding him," Chad said.

"What about Kailey?" I said. "If she bent down just as the shot was fired, maybe he missed his target."

"Yeah, I thought of that too, but don't you think he would have taken another shot?"

"Don't know."

We watched Ginger again. We got caught again. She came to us and leaned down, placing her elbows on the bar, spilling out of her low-cut blouse. "Are you guys ready for another drink or are you just looking?"

"I'm ready for a drink," I said; then, pointing at Chad, "but I think he's just looking."

She brought us two more drinks and a very sexy smile.

"I'll order the limo for tonight," I said, "and we'll pick you and Alexis up around six."

"Sounds good. Kailey will be so happy to see you," he said and chuckled.

"I hope she doesn't do anything that could get me killed."

"I love the way you take the heat off of me," Chad said, finishing his drink and standing.

"Already?" I said.

"Yep, gotta get back to work."

"Wait for me," I said, finishing my drink and motioning for the check.

"No Cam," Chad said, moving closer and whispering.

"No?" I whispered back.

"I feel it's better if you take a few days off," Chad said.

"Why?"

"I think you're too close to this Bloodshot case. It's been consuming you. You need some time to work on it without worrying about the office. This isn't a punishment. It's for our own good."

"But what about the cases on my desk?"

"Jackie will go through them and allocate them out evenly to the interns."

I thought for a moment and realized he was right. I wasn't doing the firm any favors hanging around taking up space. I did need some time to work on the Bloodshot case. He'd made it personal.

"Alright," I conceded. "Thanks for understanding."

"Good. I'll see you tonight," Chad said and left.

I ordered one more drink and pulled a pen from my coat pocket. When Ginger brought the drink, I asked her for a piece of paper. "I gave you my last one," I said.

When she brought the paper, it had her phone number on it. "Call me," she said.

"Right."

I wrote down all the clues I had. The more I wrote the more confusing it was.

1.   Did Bill kill Brady?

2. Did someone set Brady up by finding James?
3. Who hired Bloodshot? William-Alexis-Kailey-Robert-Chad
4. Why did James smile when I asked about Alexis and Kailey?
5. What was Eric Meninx's roll in all of this? Why did he tell me he was hired to kill Bloodshot?
6. Names and players-Eric-Bill-Alexis-Kailey-Robert-Chad-James-Brady-me-Brian Wessel

The only two that had not been shot yet were Bill and Alexis. I wrote that down also.

James was a good candidate in my book. He wanted Brady to stop blackmailing Bill. What better way than to have him killed? But now he wanted him alive so *he* could blackmail him.

I picked up my drink and moved to a table for privacy. I called Jack.

"You busy?" I asked when he answered.

"Always. What ya need?"

I gave him my list slowly so he could copy it down.

"Can you try to connect any of this?" I asked.

"I'll research it all again," he said. "Do you have anyone special in mind?"

I thought then said, "Try digging deeper into the murder of Brady. It seems to have a lot of ties to Bill and Bill has ties to Bloodshot."

"Will do," he said.

I filled him in on my talk with James and gave him a description of him and his apartment.

"Thanks. I'm going to text you Brady's obituary. Call me back today if you get anything."

"Alright. Talk to ya later."

"How's Diane?" I asked.

"Sweet as ever."

"Goodbye," I said.
He laughed. "Goodbye Cam."

Chapter 47

Andrei **arrived in New York** at two fifteen, dropped his rental car off at Hertz and took a taxi to the Roxy Hotel.

He had time to shower and change clothes. He decided to grab a bite to eat at the restaurant and then went to the Roxy Bar for a drink.

A guitar player was singing a mix of classic rock songs. *Not bad*, Andrei thought. *I might have to take up the guitar after I retire.*

His drink was delivered by a beautiful and very young waitress whose breasts were spilling out of her half-unbuttoned blouse.

"Here you go," she said. "Can I get you anything else?" She batted her eyes at him.

I wish I had time for you. "No thank you. Maybe later."

"Just let me know," she said and left, turning back to look at him again. She caught him checking out her ass. She smiled.

His phone rang. "Yes," he said.

"We're on for tonight?" the voice said.

"Of course," Andrei stated.

"Only one death; *you* choose the victim."

"I will try for your number one target. If that doesn't work, I'm obliged to hit the second."

He sipped his drink and thought about his next eight hours. It was going to be an eventful night for the Arlington party. *I wish the game would last longer. I would like another chance to draw blood from Cam.*

I hate to leave a failure on the table, but my orders were to let it go. Tonight will be the grand finale. Someone is going to die.

~***~

I called Robin to see if she was going to be able to attend the party with me. It would help to keep Kailey away from me if Robin were there.

"Maybe," she said.

"I understand, but I hope you can make it."

"Me too. I need a break. I'll do my best."

"Okay. I know you will. Any leads?" I asked.

"No. Not a sign of him. He could be back in New York by now."

I thought about telling her about my meeting with Eric, Kailey, and James.

She said, "If I could just get an idea of what he's here for, it would help tremendously."

I stepped into the hall to avoid the bugs inside and told her the whole story—except for the parts where Kailey

226

told me she loved me and kissed me and got in the tub with me and kissed me some more and told me about her suspicions. I also left out James.

Robin was silent for a moment, then, "You held all of that back from me."

"I was confused as to what to do. I thought if I had some space, I could figure it out before the FBI got involved. I know how they like to rush in on hearsay."

"I'm the FBI," Robin said. "You don't trust me?"

"I trust you. I just don't trust your team. I'm sorry, but that's the way it is. If I didn't love you, I wouldn't tell you now."

More silence. "What time will you pick me up tonight?" she asked.

"Six fifteen."

"I'll be ready," she said and hung up.

Oh boy, it's going to be a really fun night.

~***~

Chad left the office at three o'clock, picked up a bottle of Tor Cabernet Sauvignon, one hundred eighty-five dollars, then met Alexis at their condo.

"Hi honey," he said as he entered. "Look what I have." He held up the bottle.

Alexis laughed and pointed at the bar.

There was an identical bottle opened and breathing.

"Great minds," she said.

They poured their wine and sat on the terrace admiring the view and each other.

"Is it going to be a big party tonight?" Chad asked.

"Looks like it. Maybe forty or fifty, it keeps growing."

"I hope Bloodshot wasn't invited. We don't need that much action," Chad said.

"Anything new on that case?" Alexis asked.

"A little. It seems there is a hitman in town to kill Bloodshot."

"Really?" Alexis said. "How do you know that?"

Chad told her what Cam had related to him.

"Sounds scary. I wish this were all over with," she said.

"It will be soon, but we don't know the outcome. That's what scares me."

"I'm sure you and I will be just fine when this is over," Alexis stated.

"I'm sure we will," Chad said, wondering if she knew for certain.

"Who do you think the target is?"

"I don't know. It worries me that Kailey was bending down when she was shot. It was like Bloodshot missed his target," Chad said.

"I don't know why anyone would want her killed."

"Who would have anything to gain?" Chad asked.

"That's a good question. If she and Dad separate, she only gets five million dollars. That's not enough to quibble over," she said.

"What would she get if your father dies?" Chad asked.

"Five million either way. She's much richer with him alive."

"Would you receive his fortune?"

Alexis looked at Chad with suspicion. "Are you trying to say I would be better off if Dad died?"

"No, no. I'm just trying to make sense out of all this. I know there is no way you would want your father dead."

They both took a drink of wine.

"Cam said something that makes me wonder though," Chad said. "He thinks the target hasn't been shot at yet. Eric told him someone would die. To make it look like an accident from the game it would have to be someone new."

228

"What about Brady Osborn? He was killed."

"That wasn't done by Bloodshot. They have the rifle he was murdered with. Not the same type Bloodshot uses."

"Maybe Senator Frasier was the target and the rest was to make it look like a game gone wrong."

"I think he would have just made the hit and left town. The rules in Canada didn't say that every target had to be related to each other. But here we're all getting hit as a group, other than the few that were actually killed."

They drank again. Alexis leaned over and kissed him.

"Now that is much better than talking about Bloodshot," he said.

"I think so," she said and removed her clothes.

Chapter 48

Chad **and Alexis picked me up in the limo** promptly at six. We picked Robin up fifteen minutes later. She was wearing a long black dress, split up the side almost to her waist, and cut down in the front almost to her waist, exposing her beautiful cleavage. The gold belt seemed to be holding everything in place. She looked good enough to eat. She wasn't in the mood for that though.

"Hello sweetie," I said as I opened the door for her and bent down to kiss her.

"Hello," she said but dodged my attempt to kiss.

She slid into the limo and kissed Alexis and Chad.

I said, "I see you're still not happy that I held back from you."

"Is there anything else I should know?"

"No. That about covers it," I said, sounding a little perturbed myself, "but if I could find out all of this, why didn't your crackerjack team come up with anything?"

"Okay you two," Alexis said, "get it out in the open and talk about it."

"He held back valuable information about the Bloodshot case," Robin said.

"Oh that," Alexis said. "Chad told me all about it. Chad even accused me of wanting my father dead, and then he made mad, passionate love to me."

"I did not," Chad said, "at least not the part about accusing you."

"Sounded like it to me."

"Okay you two," I said.

They laughed. I thought I saw a smile creep into the corners of Robin's mouth.

"Okay, Cam. I'm not mad at you. I'm just hurt a little," Robin said.

"I know I should have told you earlier, but I really don't trust your team."

"Well, I hope you can trust them tonight because they'll be at the party."

"How did you get *them* invited?" I asked.

"I didn't. They'll be outside watching."

"You're afraid Bloodshot will be there tonight?" Alexis asked.

"It would be a good opportunity for him," Robin said.

"I don't think that's necessary. He's probably still in the Keys somewhere," Alexis said.

"I don't think so," Robin said.

We arrived at the Arlington estate. It was decorated beautifully.

Lights were strung around all the pine trees, and a series of spotlights were shining up onto the house, making it look larger and even grander than it already was.

William and Kailey had gone all out. I looked at Chad and shook my head.

"Wow," Alexis said, "I've never seen it look so majestic."

"It's breathtaking," Robin said.

We were among the first to arrive. The party seemed to be taking shape on the back lawn. As soon as we stepped onto the patio, Kailey spotted us and came our way. I was worried. She looked as though she was on the hunt in her red sequined mini dress, which was also cut down the front exposing even more than Robin.

"Hello Alexis, Chad," she said and kissed them both on the cheek.

She then kissed Robin full on the lips and the same for me. "Hello, you two," she said sultrily. "So glad you could make it."

When Robin regained her composure, she said, "We wouldn't miss it for the world."

"Your house looks lovely," I said.

"Thanks. Of course, I had nothing to do with it. It's not my territory."

Awkward silence.

Kailey placed her arm in mine, nodded her head toward the bar and said, "Let's go get some drinks. It's going to be a big party."

Everyone followed me, being dragged by Kailey, to the bar.

When we stopped at the bar, Robin came up to my other side and put her arm in my other arm. Now that's an awkward moment.

"I'll have a glass of bubbly, sweetie," Robin said in the Southern accent she used on me down in the Keys.

"I'll have a soda," Kailey said in a schoolgirl's voice.

I turned and looked at Chad, who looked as though he were enjoying my predicament way too much.

He stepped beside Kailey and tried to engage her in conversation. All he got from her were one-word answers.

"Who did your decorating for you?" Chad asked.

"Veto's," Kailey said and tightened her hold on me.

"Have you used them before?" Chad asked.

"No."

I looked at Robin. She gave me a strange look. I couldn't tell if she wanted to kill me or if she wanted to fuck me. My better sense told me she wanted to kill me.

"Well, glad to see y'all arrived early," William Arlington said as he patted me on the back.

I tried to shake his hand as I said, "Hello Bill."

I couldn't get my right hand away from Kailey. That left his hand hanging in mid-air waiting.

"Kailey, for God's sake, let go of him for a minute," Bill said.

She did, but she never moved away from my side.

We shook hands. Bill didn't seem disturbed.

"Any news about Bloodshot?" Bill asked.

"Nothing yet," Robin answered. "We're still working on it."

"We have extra protection here at the party tonight," I said. "You know, all of us being together."

"Yes, it would be an excellent opportunity," Bill said. "I know about your FBI men watching us. My guys spotted them as they arrived."

"If they could spot them, I'm sure Bloodshot could too," I said, turning to Robin.

She said, "We also received word about Bill's men."

"Touché," Bill said.

"Well, at least we know we have protection," I said.

"Cam, do you mind if I borrow Kailey for a few minutes?" Bill said.

"Not at all," I said, placing my hand on her back and edging her toward Bill.

She went, reluctantly.

"I'll talk to you guys in a few minutes," he said and took Kailey by the arm and led her away.

"Alexis," Robin said, "would you mind showing me through the house?"

"Not at all," Alexis said.

"Excuse us, gentlemen," Robin said. "I think you guys need some time to yourselves."

We did.

Chapter 49

Chad and I circulated through the party. It was starting to get crowded now, and I was worried Bloodshot might be there. I realized I could be wrong. He might not be anywhere close, but this was a good chance for him to find everyone together.

~***~

Andrei's phone vibrated. He read the text. "[FBI]"

Of course they're here. I wouldn't have expected anything less of them. Not that it matters.

He moved into position. He was two streets over, far away from the FBI and Bill's guards. This spot had a perfect opening through the houses and trees through which to find his target. He opened the small sliding window on the side of his van and assembled his rifle. He then attached it to the swivel holder and adjusted the sight. He could see Kailey's nipple when she turned just right. *What a beauty. I really hated to shoot her.*

~***~

I saw Bill and Kailey standing alone on the patio. It looked like a friendly conversation. I was glad of that.

"They don't look like they're talking about you," Chad said.

"Hope not."

"She'll be back soon enough to have another go at ya."

"Yeah, I know."

Robin and Alexis returned with fresh drinks in their hands.

"What a beautiful house," Robin said.

"I know. I wouldn't mind moving in with Alexis and Chad someday."

"I bet you wouldn't," Robin said, "especially if Mommy would stay."

The three of them laughed.

"You think that's funny, but I could get killed," I said.

"Don't worry," Robin said, "it's just a schoolgirl crush."

"I'm going to get another drink," Chad said as he put his arm on Alexis's back.

"Alright," I said. "We'll meet up with you again in a while."

I walked Robin to the opposite end of the patio.

"I need to tell you one more thing," I said.

"I thought there was more."

"It's Kailey. She picked me up today as I was walking back to the office. She overheard Alexis and Bill talking about Bloodshot. It sounded to her as if one of them, if not both, are involved with him in some way. She wanted me to prove them innocent."

"Did she say what it was she heard?"

"No," I lied again. I didn't want Bill to get investigated for murder on hearsay.

"She just said if I checked into it, I might be able to prove her wrong," I said.

"Maybe I should talk to her," Robin said.

"No, don't do that. I have a line of communication with her, and if you say anything to her, I'll lose it."

"Um huh," Robin said, "you sure do. Now, is there anything else you need to tell me?"

"No," I lied once more. It was becoming a habit.

My cell phone rang. It was Jack.

"Yes," I answered.

"You might be right about James," he said.

"How so?"

"I looked at the obituary and also found a picture of Brady from ten years ago at a fundraiser in Arizona. Brady had a two-inch scar under his right eye. James doesn't."

"So, you think Brady and James swapped lives?" I asked.

"It looks that way. That's probably why he was paid monthly," Jack said.

"Thanks, Jack, will you keep looking? It could be life or death."

"I'll call you as soon as something else comes up," Jack said.

"Goodbye."

I hung up and looked at Robin.

"Okay," she said, "what else haven't you told me?"

I filled her in on James and Brady.

"You do amazing work," she said. "I should be mad again, but you're right. Why didn't my men discover any of this?"

"They're not as involved as we are. No skin off their nose."

"We need to find Bill. He might be a target for tonight," Robin said.

"Maybe, but Alexis could also be the target. Bill killed Brady's brother. An eye for an eye."

"Shit. Let's go," she said.

"You go find them, but don't tell Bill that Brady is still alive. Now that he knows where he is, he might have him killed before the night's over," I said.

"Alright, but it's going to come out sooner or later," she said. "What are you gonna do?"

"I'm going to take a look around. If Bloodshot is here, I'll recognize him."

"Be careful," Robin said and kissed me.

"Don't start that right now. The way you look tonight I might not be able to help myself," I said.

Robin went back toward the party, and I walked toward the road. The ground there was a little higher and gave me a better vantage point from which to see everyone. I took the opportunity to call McNally.

"McNally," he answered gruffly. I could tell the cigar was in his mouth.

"It's Cam. I've got something for you," I said.

"It's about time," he said.

"Really? What have you found?" I asked.

"Never mind that. What you got?"

I told him about James and Brady.

"What ya want me to do?" he asked sarcastically.

I hung up. I don't have time for the tough-guy routine.

I watched the party. Everyone seemed to be having fun. If Bloodshot was down there somewhere, he would fit in easily. Then I realized he would be a sitting duck if he fired a shot from down there. I turned and looked around the area outlining the property. I instantly spotted two of the FBI men and one of Bill's guys. They weren't any further away from the party than I was.

I began to walk up the street. Where would I hide if I were Bloodshot? I could easily hit my target from five hundred yards; the further the better.

The lots across the road were large and all contained mansions. The sawgrass grew in the areas they didn't need or want to take care of. It was also a protected area for wildlife. A perfect cover for a sniper.

Using the twilight darkness, I walked across a field and came to another street. More mansions and more sawgrass.

I turned to look back at the Arlington estate. I could see the party but not all of it. A house blocked most of my view.

I looked up and down the road. North seemed to offer the best chance of opening to a view of the whole party. I walked that way.

I came to another smaller road that curved off to the right, away from the party. I looked down the street I was on and saw nothing, so I took the smaller road.

About a hundred yards down this path, I thought I saw someone move in the tall grass. I ducked and pulled my gun from my belt holster.

I had lost sight of the movement, but another fifty yards away, parked on the street, was a black van.

Chapter 50

Robin searched for Bill and Kailey. They were nowhere to be found. She saw Chad and Alexis talking with another couple, laughing and drinking. That's what a party *is* all about.

She decided to search the house for Bill before she talked to Alexis. She found them in the kitchen going over the menu with the caterers.

"Hello, Bill, Kailey. I've been looking for you two," Robin said, being cheerful so as not to alarm them.

Kailey moved to Robin's side and placed her arm through Robin's.

"I'm glad you're here to save me," Kailey said. "I hate all this planning stuff. Bill is better at it than I am. Why don't we go get a drink and let him handle it?"

"Well," Robin said, "I really need to talk to Bill."

"Aw." Kailey pouted.

"Let me have him for a minute, and then we'll get that drink," Robin said.

Kailey perked up. "Okay," she said, lively.

Bill excused himself from the caterers and took Robin's arm, leading her to his study.

"Yes, my dear, how may I help you?" he asked.

"It may be nothing, but we're worried that Bloodshot might be here. We received word that there was a break in the case, but what it is I don't know yet."

Bill thought for a minute then said, "We have plenty of security here tonight. If he shows up, we'll get him. I can't hide at my own party."

"What if the target isn't you but Alexis?"

Bill turned white. "What do you know?"

"Nothing for sure, but the word I received was that it might be one of you," Robin said.

"I have to find Alexis," Bill said and stormed out of the room.

"Bill," Robin said sternly.

He turned.

Robin said, "Don't cause a scene. Let's get her together. We don't want to create a panic. It might set things in motion."

"Hurry," he said.

They left the study and stepped onto the patio. Kailey was waiting for them there.

"Ready for that drink?" she asked.

"Not right now Kailey," Bill said.

"Wait, Bill," Robin said, "you stay here with Kailey, and I'll get Alexis. It will be better that way."

"Bring her here," Bill said.

"What's going on?" Kailey asked.

"Just stay here by me. I'll fill you in later," Bill said.

Robin left to get Alexis.

241

~***~

I kept my position in the tall grass. I couldn't see anyone moving, but I was sure I had. I looked at the van again. It was getting dark, but I could swear there was a gun barrel sticking about six inches out of the window.

Bloodshot. If he was in the van he would have a perfect view of the party, but who was in the field?

I decided to take a chance and move closer to the van. I saw the grass move again. This time it was closer to the vehicle. Was it Bloodshot returning to the van? I crouched and approached faster, keeping an eye on the grass where I last saw the movement.

~***~

Robin spotted Alexis and Chad still standing where she last saw them. As she was nearing them, she noticed a red dot on Alexis's dress. **"NO."**

"Alexis," Robin yelled, **"get down."**

Chad grabbed Alexis and pulled her to the ground and fell on top of her. Robin ran to her side, gun drawn from a leg holster. **"Everyone, take cover."**

The crowd panicked and ran in every direction. Robin scanned the perimeter looking up the hill, the way the laser had come from. She saw nothing. The FBI men ran down the drive toward the backyard, talking on their radios and waving their guns in the air.

There was no shot. Robin looked back toward Kailey and Bill. Kailey was smiling, but Bill looked ashen. They were looking at each other. Were they too far away to see what was happening?

The red dot then appeared on Kailey's forehead. Robin shouted at her but was too far away.

Then Robin saw a red dot appear on Bill's shoulder. She yelled at him, **"Bill."** At the same time, he stepped toward Kailey, and his head exploded.

Kailey screamed and fell to the ground. Robin, Chad, and Alexis ran to them. Bill was obviously dead. Robin checked Kailey for a wound. She wasn't hit, just fainted. She was covered with Bill's blood.

~***~

I saw a muzzle flash. Instantly the figure from the grass ran toward the van. I could tell it was Eric. He had a gun in his outstretched hand.

"Eric," I said aloud.

He turned, firing immediately. I felt a sting on my shoulder.

He turned back toward the van and fired two shots inside, through a window.

I shot at Eric. At least one of my two shots hit him because he fell and didn't move.

I walked cautiously toward the van, my gun still raised. This was it, just Bloodshot and me. My nerves were on edge. I felt as if my heart was ready to tear its way out of my chest.

I approached the van from the rear. When I was five feet away, its engine roared to life. The backup lights flashed on, and the van surged toward me. I dove to the right barely clearing the rear bumper.

The van stopped and then lurched forward. I jumped to my feet and took aim at the rear right tire. My bullet found its target. The tire slowly lost air. The van sped away, but I knew it couldn't go far. I ran after it. We were at the top of the ridge. I could see ahead that the road made a one-eighty, five hundred feet down the hill. I cut right and ran across the empty lot toward the street he would be on.

I hid in the sawgrass beside the road. The van came toward me, its right rear wheel now rag-dolling the shredded tire. The van wasn't stable. I stepped into the road and raised my gun when the van was four hundred feet away.

I saw an arm reach out the driver's window and a handgun popped three times. The van turned toward me. This time I dove to the left, barely clearing the bumper again.

The van stopped, and the driver's door swung open. I was a sitting duck. I rolled into thicker grass hoping to find a little shelter.

Two more pops and the dirt a foot away from me puffed up.

Shit, I'm in a jam.

I had no choice other than to fire back, which I did. The side window of the van exploded sending glass shards flying. I took advantage of the brief pause in his firing and ran to the rear of the vehicle. We were now only ten feet away from each other using the van to hide behind.

"Bloodshot, give it up. You'll never get away alive," I said, my words sounding futile to me even as I said them.

"Cam Derringer, what brings you here? Just out for a walk?" he said in his Russian accent.

"I knew you'd be here. I wanted to say, 'Hi.' The FBI are on their way."

"They're a little busy down the hill running in circles right now. By the way, you have a lovely daughter," he said and coughed out a laugh.

Now that pissed me off.

I knew I wasn't going to get anywhere trying to talk to him and the longer we stood there the better chance that he would find a way to kill me.

I dropped to the ground to shoot him in the leg under the van.

To my surprise, he did the same. We were now on the ground facing each other. He was covered in blood. Eric's bullets must have found their target.

I fired first. Three rapid shots. I saw them hit him in the chest. He fired back in reaction. I felt another sting in the same shoulder. Damn, that hurt.

Andrei rolled onto his back and lay still.

I pushed myself up and slowly moved around the van. He still hadn't moved. I bent down and felt his neck for a pulse. There was none. It was over.

He had two bullet holes in his left shoulder in addition to the three I put in his chest. A fitting end for such a man.

Chapter 51

A couple of minutes had passed before the FBI arrived at the van. I was sitting on the ground leaning on the bumper. Three of them pointed their guns at me.

"It's me, guys, Cam Derringer," I said, raising my hands. "The other two are dead. One over there and the other a street down the hill."

They slowly walked around the van and checked the body.

"I think we got 'em," one of the agents said.

"Good work, guys," I said sarcastically. "Did anyone get hit down there?"

"Yeah, afraid so. Mr. Arlington is dead," one of them said.

I cursed beneath my breath.

"Are you okay?" one asked.

"I'll live," I said. "Help me up."

I walked back down the hill toward the party with the aid of an agent. When Robin saw me, she ran to my side. "Cam, are you okay?"

"Yeah, just a few nicks," I said. "What about Kailey and the others?"

"Only Bill was hit. He's dead."

"They radioed me and said you killed Bloodshot and another man," Robin said.

"Eric Meninx," I said.

"So, it looks like you were right, this was a hit. Down there it looked like the game went bad. The laser was on Alexis, then Kailey and then Bill's shoulder. He took a step toward Kailey just as the shot was fired and it hit him in the head," Robin said.

"Now, the question is who set all this up?" I whispered through the pain. "And which one of them was the target?"

"We need to get you an ambulance," Robin said.

"I'm all right," I said. "I need to talk to the others."

Robin pulled my suit coat off gently and ripped my shirt sleeve open, exposing my wound.

"Congratulations," she said, "this time you actually did get shot."

"Thank God," I said, "I don't think I could live through another humiliating coffee burn."

Kailey was sitting up and crying. Alexis was bent over Bill, also crying. Chad was trying to comfort her.

I went to Kailey. "Are you alright?" I asked, putting my good arm around her.

She just cried harder. When she saw the wound on my arm, her eyes widened. "Are you okay?" she asked, panic on her face.

"Don't worry about me. I'm all right," I said.

"Why? Why?" she said, bowing her head and crying more.

247

The ambulance arrived. I told them to take Kailey first. She seemed to be in shock. When they put her in the ambulance, she called my name and reached out.

I looked at Robin. She said, "Go with her. We have it covered here."

I stepped into the ambulance and took Kailey's hand.

"Good job, Cam," Robin said. "You got 'em."

I nodded to her as they closed the door.

They took Kailey to a room at the hospital and sedated her. A nurse led me to another room, and a doctor soon arrived. He cleaned and bandaged my wound. "You'll be okay," he said. "I'm going to give you some pain meds and an antibiotic."

I went to Kailey's room. She was groggy but seemed to be doing okay. The doctor came in.

"We gave her a mild sedative," he said. "We didn't want to give her much considering her condition."

"Her condition?" I said.

"Yes, her pregnancy," he said.

"Okay," I said. "Thank you, doctor."

He nodded and left the room.

"You're pregnant?" I said to Kailey.

"Yes. I told Bill seconds before he was killed," she said and started crying again.

I bent down and hugged her.

"It's my fault. He stepped toward me to hug. If I had waited, he would have only been wounded like the rest," she said and cried again.

"It's not your fault, Kailey," I said. "I think he would have been killed either way."

"Why?" she asked through her tears.

"I think Brady Osborn hired him to kill Bill."

"But Brady is dead," she said.

"No, he isn't. His brother is the one who was killed," I said.

"His brother?" she said.

"Yeah, it looks as if Brady paid him to swap lives."

"So, Bill had his brother killed?"

"Looks that way," I said.

"Have you got him yet?"

"I don't know. I called McNally when I found out."

"I hope you get him and kill him," she snapped.

"At least Bloodshot is dead."

"He is?" she asked.

"Yes, him and a man named Eric Meninx. Eric wounded Bloodshot, and I killed Eric. Then I had a shoot-out with Bloodshot."

"Good. I knew you would get him," she said and squeezed my hand.

Kailey's doctor came back in to check on her. "You can take her home now whenever you're ready," he said.

"Stay here and rest, Kailey. I'll call for the limo," I said and stepped into the hall to make the call.

The limo arrived, and I walked beside Kailey, who was being pushed in a wheelchair by a nurse.

The evening had turned chilly. I gave Kailey my jacket and held her until we got in the car.

We rode in silence back to her house. She leaned on my good shoulder the whole way.

Robin met us as we pulled into the drive. The FBI and local police were still there.

I saw McNally and excused myself, leaving Kailey with Robin.

"Hello Cam," he said. "You look like you've had a rough day."

"Yeah, a little. What's the word on Brady?" I asked.

"I sent some men over to question him. We don't have any proof he's not James," he said. "But if he is, we'll find out."

I informed him about the scar and reminded him that he told me he was going to blackmail Bill.

"Why would he kill someone he was going to blackmail?" McNally asked. "That just doesn't add up."

"Yeah, I can't figure that out either," I said thoughtfully.

"Let it go, Cam. You got Bloodshot and Meninx. They were the problem."

"Someone hired them," I said. "Don't you want to know who it was?"

"Everyone is dead that would know, thanks to you. Unless someone came to me and says, 'Hey, I had William Arlington killed,' we're not gonna catch 'em."

I looked around. The party was over. A few of the guests were still here being questioned by the FBI, but the bright lights that were on now changed the whole ambiance.

"Okay, will you let me know if something breaks?" I asked, feeling defeated.

"Sure, Cam. You do the same," he said and turned back to his business.

Chapter 52

The next few days went by slowly. I busied myself at the office. Chad was home with Alexis. Losing her father was extremely hard on her.

The funeral was set for the next day. I thought I would go check on Kailey later today. I called Robin to see if she wanted to join me for lunch.

"Yeah, I can get away for lunch, but I have to get right back for a one o'clock meeting," she said.

"How about that hot dog in the park?" I suggested. "It should be safe this time."

She laughed.

"Okay," she said, "I'll humor you this once, but those things will kill you."

"Somehow, I think they're the least of my problems as far as health goes. See ya at twelve?"

"Perfect."

I called Chad to check on Alexis.

"She's keeping busy," he said. "It's hard on her, but I think with a little time she'll be okay."

"What about Kailey?"

"She's taking it worse than I thought she would. I guess she really did love him," he said. "And now being pregnant with his child makes it harder yet."

"Yeah, I can see how it would," I said.

"I hope we can find out who did this and why," Chad said.

"Me too. If we figure out who, we'll probably know why."

"Yeah, I guess," Chad said.

"I was going to drop by and check on Kailey around one thirty if that's alright," I said.

"That'll be good. Alexis and I have to go to the funeral home at one. I was worried about leaving her here by herself," he said.

"Okay, I'll get there as soon as I can."

I left the office at eleven thirty and walked to the park. It was a beautiful day.

I had fifteen minutes to kill, so I sat on a park bench not far from the hot dog stand and watched the joggers and walkers pass by.

The wind had picked up a little causing the hot dog vendor to lower his umbrella.

To my surprise, Brady Osborn stopped at the stand and bought a dog. He looked around for a place to sit. When he looked my way, I waved him over.

He stared at me for a moment, apparently trying to decide if he wanted to join me. He decided to.

"Cam Derringer," he said. "Fancy meeting you here."

"Have a seat," I said, moving over to give him room.

He sat. "You caused me some trouble the other day. The police came to my apartment."

"I know. It's probably because you're not James. You're Brady."

"You have a wild imagination," he said.

"Do I?"

"Why would I pretend to be James?"

"So William would think you're dead," I said.

"I am," he said and laughed.

He took a bite of his frankfurter, dripping mustard on his chin. He wiped it with his napkin.

"I love these things. I really missed them when I couldn't come out in public like this," he said and took another big bite.

I waited for him to finish chewing and swallow.

"No sauerkraut?" I said.

"Too ethnic," he said.

"Maybe if you weren't blackmailing Bill, you could have been enjoying these all along," I said.

"Let it go, Cam. You'll never prove anything," he said.

"Yeah, I've been told."

"How is Kailey doing?" he asked.

"You know Kailey?" I said.

"No, just what I read in the paper."

"She's fine," I said. "Did you have Bill killed?"

"You are blunt, aren't you?" he said, smiling.

"Yep."

"The answer to that is no, I didn't. His death has cost me a considerable amount of money."

"But you know who did, don't you?" I said.

"I have my suspicions," he said and stood to take his last bite of the dog.

"It was good seeing you again, Cam. Goodbye."

He walked away as if he didn't have a care in the world.

Maybe he didn't.

Five minutes later, Robin sat down next to me.

253

"You look deeply engrossed in thought," she said.

I didn't even see her sit.

"Sorry, I am."

"Let's get some hot dogs, and you can tell me all about it," she said.

She took my hand and pulled me to my feet.

We ordered our hot dogs. She got one with mustard. I got one with chili, onion, cheese and peppers and one with mustard.

"No sauerkraut?" she said.

"Not into ethnic clichés," I said.

We sat down on the bench again.

"What brought on the cliché thing?" she said.

"I just had a talk with Brady Osborn."

"Here?"

"Yeah, he was eating a hot dog, no sauerkraut," I said.

"What did he have to say?" she said.

"He said he didn't have anything to do with Bill being killed and that it actually cost him his inheritance."

"You mean his blackmail money?" she said.

"Yeah, it does seem right," I said.

"Does he have any ideas about who did have him killed?"

"Yep, but he's not talking," I said.

We ate in silence for a while. I managed to drip chili on my shirt.

Robin gave me the look.

"Well, we're working on the case still, so why don't you take a break and enjoy life for a while?" she said.

"Yeah, you're right. I think that's what I need," I said.

"Good."

"So, what's new with you?" I said to change the subject.

She looked worried.

"What's wrong?" I asked.

"Well—" she hesitated "—I received my new assignment this morning. I'm going to LA in two weeks."

We were silent again while we pretended to enjoy our hot dogs.

"I'm happy for you," I said. "This is a good thing. It's the break you've been waiting for."

"Yes, I have, but—"

"No buts," I interrupted. "We've discussed this, and we decided it's what's best."

"Will you be going back to Key West?" she said.

"Yeah, as soon as I get caught up on my work here and make sure Chad and Alexis are alright."

"And Kailey," Robin said, "make sure she's okay too. I kind of like that girl even though she wants my man."

"Yes, Kailey too," I said. "I'm going to check on her when we leave here."

"Good."

"Are you free tonight?" I asked.

"Thought you'd never ask."

"How about a real meal then? Let's say chicken on my grill."

"I'll bring the wine," she said.

I leaned over and kissed her. We held it for a long time.

Chapter 53

I arrived at the Arlington Estate at one o'clock on the dot. The door was answered by Kailey. She was wearing black. That is, what there was of it.

"Hi Cam," she said.

"Hi, Kailey. How are you?"

"I'm doing okay, but it's kind of lonesome around here," she said.

She looked at the chili stain on my shirt and smiled.

"You've been eating a chili dog, haven't you?"

"How did you know?" I said, smiling and looking down at my shirt.

"'Cause people don't spill chili from a bowl, but it's almost impossible to eat a chili dog without spilling it," she said.

"You got me."

"Give me your shirt," she said, "I'll get it out."

"That's okay, Kailey. I'll get a new one when I get home," I said.

"I insist. Don't be shy, I've seen you naked before," she said and giggled.

I removed my jacket and laid it on the sofa. Then I removed my shirt and handed it to her.

"There, that wasn't so bad, was it?" she said.

"No, it didn't hurt at all."

"Come with me to the laundry room," she said. "I'll get this right out."

We walked to the laundry room, which was on the second floor. She rubbed some spot remover on my shirt, started the machine and dropped it in. Then she took off her dress and dropped it in. She wore nothing beneath it.

"Kailey," I said.

"Oh, don't be such a fuddy-duddy. I'm lonesome."

"We can't do this," I said.

"I can," she said. "Is there something wrong with *you*?"

"No. I mean it isn't right. Bill has only been gone for three days," I said.

She walked out of the room turning back to see if I was coming. She motioned for me to follow. I did.

Walking down the long hallway behind a naked Kailey was wrong, but it didn't stop me.

She stopped and opened the door to her bedroom. I knew what I should do. I did it.

"No Kailey," I said. "Not here, not now."

She laughed.

"That sounds to me like you mean somewhere else, some other time," she said.

"Yeah, maybe then," I said. "Will you please put some clothes on and meet me back in the living room?" I said.

"If you insist," she said.

I went back down to the living room and took a seat in a single chair. I didn't want her sitting next to me on the sofa. While I was waiting for her, the maid walked through.

"Oh, I'm sorry, sir. I didn't know anyone was here," she said.

I saw her look down at my bare chest.

"I spilled a chili dog on my shirt," I said. "It's in the laundry."

"Okay sir, I'll see to it," she said and hurried out of the room.

Well, that was embarrassing. Kailey can sure get a guy into some fixes.

"I'm back," she said, entering the room wearing a petite white dress. Not much to it but enough to cover her.

"Are we okay?" I said.

"I'm fine, but you look a little frazzled," she said and giggled again.

Changing the subject, I asked her, "How long have you known that you were pregnant?"

"Five days now," she said. "The doctor said I'm three weeks pregnant."

"Congratulations," I said. "Do you know what you're going to do now?"

"I'll get five million dollars, so I guess I can afford to find a place to live and raise my child," she said.

"Yes, I suppose you will. What about family? Do you still have any?"

"None I could rely on. It's just me. Unless you want to marry me." She smiled.

"That's very tempting, but I'm too old for you and I'm not ready," I said.

"Will you stay around here?" I asked.

"Maybe, will you?"

"No, I'm moving back to Key West. That's where I belong."

"Maybe I'll move to Key West," she said.

I just stared at her. She stared back.

"You know that someday you'll be mine, don't you?" she cooed.

The maid entered the room again carrying a shirt. It wasn't mine.

"I thought you might want a shirt until yours is dry," she said.

"He's okay," Kailey insisted.

"Yes ma'am," she said and turned to leave.

"Excuse me, but I would be more comfortable with a shirt," I said.

She looked at Kailey.

"Give him the shirt," she said reluctantly.

She handed it to me and left the room.

I stood and put it on. Kailey looked straight at my crotch while I did so.

"Kailey, aren't you sad that Bill is gone?" I asked her.

"No. I'm glad. He was an evil man," she said seriously.

"But he's the father of your baby," I said.

"I don't know if that's a good thing," she said.

I thought about that for a moment. *Yeah, that might be a good thing. His baby might inherit a mass fortune, and his baby's mother will control it.*

Her change in attitude toward Bill wasn't uncommon. I've seen it before. People sometimes get mad at someone close to them for dying.

"You might get this house and millions of dollars," I said.

"I might," she said and laughed. "Wouldn't I be the cat's meow?"

"Yes, you would," I said.

The cat's meow. I haven't heard that in a long time. Kailey is an old soul.

Chapter 54

Robin arrived at six thirty with a bottle of Spottswoode Cabernet Sauvignon. The grill was heated to five hundred degrees, and the chicken was marinating.

I kissed her and took the wine. She was wearing another low-cut dress that made it hard for me to keep my hands to myself. So I didn't.

"Alright you," Robin said, smiling. "First things first. Open the wine and let it breathe."

"Open your dress and let me breathe," I said.

She laughed and walked out on the balcony. That incident with naked Kailey earlier had left me a little more aroused than usual.

I stepped onto the balcony with two Wild Turkeys and handed her one.

"Thanks, I need this," she said.

"Hard day?"

"Yes, it was."

"The meeting?"

"Yes. We ran Bloodshot's fingerprints, his name is Andrei Gusarov by the way; we spent the day matching them with murders. His prints turned up on three. We know he made at least twenty-five hits, but most of the time there were no prints."

"He's been a busy man," I said.

"That he has, but no more, thanks to you," she said.

"You're welcome," I said.

"How did it go with Kailey today?" Robin asked.

I took a drink of my Wild Turkey.

"That bad," she said.

"Well, she's glad he's dead. She said he was an evil man."

"Really?"

"Yep, and while we were talking, we realized her and Bill's baby might be inheriting a fortune. Close to two billion I think."

"Oh my God. Now that's a reason to have him killed," Robin said.

"It sure would be, but I don't think she even realized it."

"She would have to split it with Alexis," Robin said.

"Yeah, you're right. That doesn't leave much," I said.

"Nah, only about a billion," she said. "Jeez."

"She said she would be 'the cat's meow'."

"Oh, brother."

We finished our drinks. I put the chicken on the grill and poured us each wine.

"Superb," I said, tasting the wine.

"It should be, but we're celebrating tonight. Bloodshot is all behind us," Robin said and kissed me passionately.

We set our wine down and continued our kiss.

"Wait," she said.

261

"No," I said.

"The chicken will burn."

"Me too."

We finally pulled apart. She took me by the shoulders and turned me and pushed me toward the grill.

I checked the chicken, turned it and closed the lid.

"We have two minutes," I said.

"Good," she said. "Drink your wine."

"I'm not thirsty," I panted.

She laughed. "Drink. We'll play after we eat."

I drank and checked the chicken again. It was time.

"Soup's on," I said as I laid the chicken dish on the table.

Robin sat the salads down and we dug in.

"Eat slower," Robin said, "I don't want you to choke to death. I'll need you for what I have planned."

We ate and talked. I took some deep breaths and managed to calm down a little.

Just as we finished our meal and were clearing the table Robin's cell phone rang.

"Don't you dare answer that," I said.

She looked at it. It kept ringing like a car alarm that would never stop but no one would pay any attention to it.

"I have to," she said.

"Oh no," I said.

"Hello. You're shitting me. Okay, I'll be right there," she said and hung up.

She looked at me apologetically.

"James Osborn was just murdered," she said.

"You mean Brady," I said.

"Whoever, I have to go. I'm sorry."

"I knew it was too good to be true," I said. "Would you at least get something else to wear out of the closet?"

"Good idea," she said. "Wanna watch?"

"Hell yeah," I said with vigor.

While I watched her slowly undress and then slowly dress again, I couldn't help but think about Brady getting killed. Who would want him dead now that Bill was dead?

"You mind if I go with you?" I said.

"Not at all. You're the best agent we have," she said.

I took my gun from the dresser drawer and hooked it to my belt. *You never know.*

When we arrived at Brady's apartment, there were two police cars and two black SUVs in front. There were also about fifty sightseers standing outside the crime scene tape.

Chief McNally was the first to see us. He motioned us to him.

"Good evening, chief," I said. "What have you got?"

"Cam, Robin," he said, nodding to each of us. "Looks like someone capped James from close proximity."

"You mean Brady," I said, still not giving up my belief.

He sighed. "Whoever."

"Brady," I said.

"The shooter was in his apartment long enough to have a ginger ale with him before they popped him," he said, ignoring me.

"So, it was someone he knew," Robin said.

"Maybe, or maybe a hooker or a pizza delivery guy," he said. "There was an unopened box on the table."

"Have you checked his phone for a pizza order?" I said.

"Gosh, I wish we would have thought of that," he said. "Of course we have. He didn't order one."

"So," Robin said, "someone shows up with a pizza to gain access, has a soda with him and kills him."

"That's what we think, but we didn't get to complete our investigation because the damn Feds chased us out. Now they're in there trampling over all the evidence."

"Sorry about that," Robin said. "You're welcome to come in with me."

"Thank you, but it's probably too late," McNally said.

"Let's go take a look," I said.

The three of us walked up to Brady's apartment, careful to step only on the side edges of the stairs.

When we entered, it looked like a bomb had gone off.

"What the fuck?" McNally said.

"Was there a fight in here?" I asked him.

"No, nothing was out of place when I left."

Robin shouted, **"Stop."**

The FBI men froze in their tracks. You could have heard a pin drop.

"What the hell are you doing?" she asked.

Agent Thompson stepped forward and said, "We're searching for a possible murder weapon. We have already searched the apartment for clues and dusted the glasses for prints. They've been wiped clean."

"Get out," she said, "All of you, get out—**now!**"

We looked around the apartment but couldn't tell what might have been disturbed during the murder or by the Feds.

"Not much to go on," McNally said.

Brady's body was still lying on the sofa. He'd taken one to the forehead.

I looked around again trying to remember what the apartment looked like the last time I was there. Then I noticed.

"Wait a minute," I said, "the last time I was here, there were three paintings on that wall. I don't know what they were, but they looked expensive to me."

"Would you know them if you saw them again?" Robin said.

"I think so."

She took some pictures with her camera and said, "Let's get out of here."

"That's not all," I said. "Brady had a gun in his lap when I came in. Did they find it?"

"I don't think so," McNally said. "Surely someone would have told me."

~***~

Agent Thompson made a call from his cell.

"It's done," he said. "They won't find a thing."

"Thank you," the voice on the other end said. "Your money is in the box."

265

Chapter 55

The funeral was as large as William Arlington's life had been. There were politicians, business owners and a handful of billionaires. Then there was Robin and me.

As soon as we arrived, we were instructed to get in line. We did, for an hour. Alexis and Chad greeted us at the casket. We gave our condolences quickly so as not to hold up the line. Next was Kailey. True to form, she kissed Robin and me both square on the lips.

She held my arm and asked if I would stay with her.

"I don't know what to say to all these people," she said. "Will you stay with me? Please."

I looked at Robin.

"Stay with her, Cam," she said. "She needs you."

I stood with Kailey while she had no problem handling the crowd. I repeated to the visitors, "I'm a friend of the family."

After the burial, we went to the Arlington estate with Kailey, Alexis, Chad and around fifty guests. A grand buffet was laid out in the backyard using the same tents that were erected for the party where Bill was killed.

It was a little eerie to me.

I had a chance to get Chad alone and told him about Brady being murdered.

"Yeah, I know," he said. "I thought I was safe now, but it looks like Bill can reach out from the grave."

"Seems that way," I said.

We both drank.

"Another thing I'd like to talk to you about," I said.

"Fire away."

"Have you thought of the possibility that Kailey might get this house and half the inheritance? You know, the baby and all."

"Yes, we've discussed that. Her baby is a rightful heir, and she should get it. That's not a problem for us."

"Glad you feel that way," I said.

"Maybe," Chad said, "you can live here with her."

"You're a funny guy," I said. "Not me, I'm heading back to Key West."

"I wish you would change your mind about that," he said.

"This life just isn't for me, Chad. I really appreciate the break you gave me, and I'm sorry if I'm letting you down."

"It was my pleasure. Your stay here hasn't exactly been uneventful. You know, it isn't like this all the time. Now that this is over, you'll have plenty of time to enjoy life," Chad said.

"That's what I plan on doing, only in Key West."

"Well then, I wish you all the best."

"Thank you," I said.

We drank again and watched the crowd.

"How do you think Kailey will be as a mother?" I asked.

"Hard to tell. Sometimes she seems very mature, but when you're around, she turns into a vixen."

"I do that to women."

"I noticed."

"How about Alexis, is she going to be a mother anytime soon?" I said.

"I hope so. I'd like to have a family."

"Yeah, me too, but I'm fifty-three now and no candidates to be a mother. I have Diane though. I consider her my daughter."

"Yes, and you've been a good father to her," Chad said.

"Thanks.

"Why do you think someone would kill Brady now?" I asked.

"Where'd that come from?"

"I can't get it off my mind. Now all our suspects are dead, and there is no one to answer the question, why?"

"Maybe that's why he's dead. Someone wanted to silence him," Chad said.

"Could be," I said, "or maybe Bill wasn't the only one who wanted him dead. Maybe whoever flushed him out in the first place wanted him dead. We need to find a motive. If Brady hired Bloodshot to kill Bill, he would have to have a good reason. He was living off the blackmail money."

"You have been thinking about this," Chad said.

"Yeah, a lot. There's one thing for sure. Someone is still out there who's played a significant role in the Bloodshot case."

Robin and Alexis joined us at the edge of the party.

"What are the two of you talking about so seriously?" Alexis asked.

268

"Women," I said.

"Can't live with 'em, can ya?" Robin said.

"Or without 'em," Chad said.

The gathering broke up around six o'clock. Everyone hugged Alexis and Kailey and told them if they needed anything to be sure to call.

"Thank you, I will," they said a thousand times.

When everyone had left, the five of us stood together on the patio.

"What do I do now?" Kailey asked. "I don't know what to do."

"We'll stay here with you for a while, Kailey," Alexis said, "until you're ready for bed."

"But this isn't my house anymore. When Bill dies, I get my inheritance, and you get the house. When do I have to be out?" she asked in a slightly panicked tone, a tear forming in the corner of her eye.

Chad said, "You don't have to be out, Kailey. You and your baby are welcome to stay as long as you like. I even think the courts might award you the house."

"I can't take your house," she said. "I don't need a house this big."

"For now, you stay right here. We'll figure out all the details in a few weeks," Alexis said.

"Okay, thanks," Kailey said, lowering her head a little.

We stood in silence for a moment. Kailey looked as though she wanted to say something.

"Would the four of you like to spend the night here?" she asked.

We all looked at each other. No one spoke.

"I guess we could," I finally said. "I don't have any pressing plans. How about you, Robin?"

"I'm afraid I can't. I have to go to the office at eight tonight. We're still working on the Brady-James case," she said.

Oh no, I thought. *I've committed myself to stay here without Robin.*

"I can stay," Chad said.

"Me too," Alexis said.

That was a relief.

"Well, you guys sure don't need me then," I said. "I'll take Robin home."

"Please, please stay," Kailey said. "We'll have supper and drinks and talk about Bill and the future."

I knew that Kailey couldn't have drinks in her condition. I hadn't seen her with one since she announced she was pregnant. I admired her for that.

"Robin, can you get away later?" I asked.

"Sorry, not tonight. You stay and help here. I'm fine. I'll have the limo take me to the office and see you in the morning for breakfast," she said.

"Great," Kailey said, "we'll have breakfast set up on the patio when you get here."

"Sounds good to me," Robin said.

She hugged Kailey, Chad, and Alexis before I walked her to the limo.

"I'm sorry," I said. "I wouldn't have committed if I knew you had to leave."

"Don't worry about it, Cam," she said. "She buried her husband today. I think the shock is starting to set in. She needs friends around her."

"Okay," I said. "I love you."

"I love you too," she said and got into the limo.

Chapter 56

The evening went smoothly. Kailey kept her hands to herself, other than a few hip bumps while I was helping her in the kitchen.

Around nine thirty we all retired to our bedrooms. I had an elegant suite on the second floor three doors down from the master, where Kailey was sleeping.

She provided me with a toothbrush, and there were towels for the shower.

I showered and slipped into a soft, comfy bed. Then I slipped into a very sound sleep.

The wine woke me around two a.m. to use the bathroom. When I turned over, I rolled right onto naked Kailey.

"Hi," she said.

I tried to roll off her, but she held tight. I couldn't get away. She had her legs wrapped around me.

"Kailey, what do you think you're doing?"

"I think I'm about to have an orgasm," she said, lightly grinding her hips on me.

Before I could get her legs loose, she did. She arched her back and cried and humped more. Then she fell limp and released me.

Her breathing was heavy. I waited for her to calm down.

"How long have you been in here?" I asked her.

"Ever since you went to sleep. You sleep soundly," she said, still breathing heavily.

"I was tired."

"I pulled the sheets back and fooled around for a while, and you didn't even wake up," she said, giggling.

"Well, I'm awake now, and I think you should go."

"Please don't make me go. I just want to lie beside you," she pleaded in her schoolgirl voice.

"If you stay here, I won't be able to go to sleep."

"Better yet," she whispered, "we could fuck all night and no one would ever know."

"Kailey, you buried your husband today. You should be mourning," I said sternly.

"I told you, he was an evil man. He killed people. I didn't love him. Hell, I didn't even like him."

"But you are carrying his baby," I said a little more softly.

"I can't help that," she said. "But maybe that's my reward for putting up with him. Now I'll have half his money, not just the five million he was going to leave me."

She was really starting to make me wonder if she could have had something to do with his death.

She looked at me for a moment.

"I know what you're thinking," she said, "and no, I didn't have anything to do with him getting killed."

"I don't think that," I lied.

"If you don't, you're not a very good detective. I'm the only one who gained from his death."

"Well, that's so," I said, "but to tell you the truth, I think it was an accident. I believe he was supposed to get wounded like the rest and he stepped forward at the wrong minute."

"Then it was my fault. He was stepping toward me," she said.

"Did you know that Bloodshot's sight was on Alexis first?" I said.

"No," she said wide-eyed and sat up. "You mean Bloodshot was going to shoot Alexis?"

"It sure looked that way," I said. "Then his sights were on you."

She thought for a moment.

"If this was a game, then they were the last two. Everyone else had been shot," she said. "But why was it on me again?"

"That I don't know."

"He already shot me once."

"I know," I said, "everyone but Robin. I figure she didn't get shot because of being the FBI."

"What if she was the final target? What if someone wanted her dead?" Kailey said.

"Why?"

"Maybe she arrested someone or killed someone's friend or kin."

I had to think about that. What if she was the target? She sure had made some enemies. If so, whoever hired bloodshot was still out there, and he could hire someone else.

273

That's when I realized that, sometime during our conversation, Kailey had put her hand around me under the cover, and I had responded.

I looked down. She giggled and released me.

"Just something to think about," she said, getting out of bed.

I didn't know if she meant the hit being on Robin or the erection she had created under the cover.

"I sure have some good conversations with you while we're naked," she said.

"Yes, you do seem to open up," I said.

"Toodles," she said and left the room naked.

I guessed that was the way she arrived.

Chapter 57

We were sitting on the patio when Robin arrived at seven thirty the next morning. She was dressed in her FBI clothes.

"Good morning, sweetie," I said.

"Good morning everyone," she said. "How did you sleep?"

"I slept great," Kailey said and smiled at me.

Don't start that this early, Kailey.

"So did I," I said. "How about you?"

"Well, the three hours I got were great," Robin said.

"Three hours? You didn't have to come here. You should have gotten some sleep," I said.

"Don't have time. I have to get back to work," she said.

The food was delivered to the tables, and the smell was making us all hungry.

"I would rather come here and not miss this breakfast than sleep," she said.

"I know what you mean," Alexis said, "I've been eating these meals since I was ten years old."

"I'll miss them too," Kailey said.

"Why is that?" Chad said. "Are you going somewhere?"

"I think so," Kailey said. "I don't belong here. This is your house, and you deserve it. I have plenty of money to live somewhere else."

"You're not going anywhere until after you have the baby," Alexis said. "Then we'll see what's best for you. Okay?"

Kailey just nodded her head slightly in a thoughtful manner.

"Did you solve any problems last night?" I asked Robin.

"Maybe," she said. "I think we've eliminated Brady as the one who hired Bloodshot."

"Brady?" I said.

"Yes, you were right. It was James who was killed first. Brady didn't have a million to spend on a hit. You said Eric told you he was offered a million to kill Bloodshot."

"Yeah, that's right. That's what he said," I said.

"Well, according to his bank account, he didn't have more than six hundred thousand," Robin said.

"If he didn't have another account somewhere, that would surely eliminate him," I said.

"We also found a witness, for fifty dollars, who said he saw a hooker with a pizza go into Brady's apartment. McNally says they sometimes pose as pizza deliveries to keep the heat off them," Robin said.

"How did the guy know she was a hooker?" I said.

"Long blonde hair, short skirt, tall boots, and too much make-up," Robin said. "He said he thought he had seen her around. Anyway, she left carrying some pictures."

"Coincidence?" I said.

"Maybe."

"Does that leave you with no suspects?" I asked.

"Right now, we don't have any. We're going to keep an eye out for the pictures."

"Cam and I think it's possible that you might be the next target," Kailey said.

Robin looked at me inquisitively.

"I don't think that, Robin," I said. "We were just talking different scenarios last night."

"When was that?" Alexis said.

"In the kitchen," Kailey said. "I guess we were both hungry and found each other getting something to eat."

Thank God. I had expected her to say, "In bed."

"Why would that be a scenario?" Robin said.

"It was just that everyone else had been shot. We thought maybe you might have made some enemies in the Fed business."

Robin thought. We were all quiet.

"Maybe," she said, "but I don't think so."

"You know," Kailey said, "whoever hired him is still out there."

"Yes, I realize that," Robin said, a little short.

Kailey looked down.

"I'm sorry," Robin said, "I'm just too tired to talk about Bloodshot." Here he's dead and we're still trying to find out who hired him."

"Can I say one more thing?" Kailey asked.

"Sure," Robin said. "Every bit helps."

"Did you look at any of Bill's business partners? Maybe one of them would benefit from his death."

"Do you have access to his office and books?" Robin asked.

"No, but Alexis does," Kailey said.

"Not so fast," Alexis said. "Without a warrant, I would like to go over them first. I'll let you know if anything looks suspicious."

"Sure," Robin said. "But if I need a warrant, I can get one."

"You won't need one," Alexis said. "Some things aren't relevant and it might be in our best interest to keep them private."

"Okay," Robin said. "Will you have time to go over them this afternoon?"

"Not a problem," Alexis said.

"Chad," I said, "how do you think the Patriots are going to do this year?"

"Good job changing the subject," he said. "They'll win the Super Bowl."

~***~

I rode with Robin back to town. She dropped me off at my condo.

"Can you get away tonight?" I asked her.

"I hope so, but if I do, I'm just going to take a long bath and get in bed."

"I don't blame you," I said. "Maybe we'll have some time tomorrow."

"Maybe," she said and kissed me. "I'll try to call you later."

"Bye," I said and got out.

She drove away. I could tell she had a lot on her mind, and we were kind of winding down our relationship. After all, in another week we wouldn't see each other for quite a while. If ever.

Chapter 58

Alexis spent the afternoon going over her father's books, which he kept in his office. She had the key to the file cabinets and his desk since she often kept the books for him and regularly made entries.

Kailey stuck her head in the office door. "Can I help you in any way," she asked Alexis.

"I don't think so, Kailey. I know the books pretty well. It shouldn't take me long. Thanks though," Alexis said.

"Okay. I don't know much about business, but if you need something ring me and I'll get it," Kailey said and closed the door as she left.

"Thank again," Alexis said to an empty room.

Two hours into the inspection and Alexis found something, although it wasn't what she was looking for. The books showed that she had withdrawn ten million dollars from the trust fund last June to November. That was impossible, but that's what she had been on trial for.

This didn't show up in the trial. No wonder her father thought she was guilty. There must be a second set of books somewhere, she reasoned.

She thought of where he could be hiding them. She went to the bookshelf and slid a trim piece to the left. The case released and slid open.

She walked into the secret room and checked the locked file cabinet in there.

She found them. The second set of books. At least two of them, but they were the ones that showed she had not embezzled the money.

Someone had managed to change the books and make her look guilty. Her father must have produced the second set for the trial so it wouldn't show up. *Even if he thought I was guilty, he didn't want me prosecuted.*

She replaced the books in the cabinet and left the secret room. She started going over the books again.

There was nothing more to be found in them. Next, she began going through the files.

There were a few deals he had going that would definitely be beneficial to his partners if he were dead. But his associates were multi-millionaires and these advantages would only be from one to five million dollars. Not worth killing him for. Then she saw one that caused the blood to drain from her face.

She locked the books back in the file cabinet and left the room. She needed to talk to Chad.

~***~

Alexis met him at the door when he came home from work that afternoon. He could tell by the look on her face that something was bothering her.

He kissed her and asked, "How was your day?"

"Not so good," she said. "I went over the books and the files."

"Yes, I know. What did you find?" Chad asked cautiously.

"First, I found a second set of books hidden away. I expected as much, but I didn't expect to find what I saw there. One set showed that I did embezzle ten million dollars. Of course that's not true, but someone made it look that way."

"The books we had for the trial didn't show any such thing," Chad said.

"I know. I think Father sent you the second set. The implication wasn't in them."

"Well, that's over now. No need to worry," Chad said.

"Yes, but someone tried to set me up," Alexis said. "We send our books to Dillard and Shanks every quarter to have them inspected and revised. I think someone there modified them."

"Why would they do that?"

"I think someone there actually embezzled the money. If Father was on to them, maybe they had him killed."

"It's certainly worth looking into," Chad said.

Alexis went to the bar and fixed them both a potent cocktail.

She handed Chad his and drank hers halfway down.

Chad watched her and decided he had better do the same. Something else was about to come.

"That's not all," she said.

"I didn't think so."

"When I went over the business files, I found a few cases where people would benefit in the event of Father's death but none worth killing him over. These men didn't need the money," she said.

"And?" Chad said.

"I found the file showing the business meeting with Father and Robert."

"Oh," Chad said. "What was in it?"

Alexis finished her drink. Chad did the same.

"Father didn't want to be involved in the gay resort deal. He cited 'Moral reasons.' He did, however, believe in Robert and gave him the five million dollars he asked for. The terms of the loan were strict but fair. Father stated that, since Robert was going to be family, if Father died, the loan would be forgiven. He wanted Robert to make the best of his life, and if this is what he wanted, he would have it."

Chad listened to the details of the loan and the repayment. It was strict and would be awfully hard to repay if anything went wrong. One bad move on Robert's part and he would lose everything.

"So, you think Robert would have your father killed?" Chad asked in disbelief.

"No, I don't think so because I know him," Alexis said. "He's a good man, and he would never do that, but if these records get into the hands of the Feds, it would be a different story."

Chad thought again for a moment.

"Could we destroy the contract?" he said.

"No, we've already had it recorded. We're not the only ones with a copy."

"I need to talk to Robert," Chad said.

Chapter 59

I called Robin at six o'clock to see if she made it home okay. She answered on the second ring.

"Hey, Robin. Just checking on you," I said. "Are you home safely?"

"Yeah, about fifteen minutes ago. I was just running a bath," she said.

"Good, I hope you sleep like a baby," I said.

"You know, I think I could use a little workout before bed," she said. "Wanna come over for about an hour?"

"Really, a whole hour?"

"If you think you can take it," she said.

"I'm on my way."

"I'll be in the tub. The door will be unlocked."

"Don't do that," I said. "Remember, I have a key."

"Oh yeah, well, come on in then."

"Bye," I said as I was locking my door.

~***~

I arrived at Robins at six thirty. I made excellent time. I opened the door and entered, locking the door behind me.

I could hear her singing in the tub. When I stepped into the bathroom, she had her eyes closed and earbuds in, listening to music and still singing.

I paused to look at her. She was beautiful lying there. I could see myself spending the rest of my life with her, but that wasn't possible. For now, I'd just take what time I could get.

I undressed and stepped into the tub. She started and gave a little "Yeek."

Seeing it was me she laughed and took out her earbuds.

"How long have you been here?" she asked.

"Long enough to hear how great you sing and how great you look," I said.

We had our bath session and then we took to the bedroom. I could tell when we were finished that Robin was spent. I thought she would sleep like a baby.

"Don't get up," I said. "I'll see myself out and maybe see you tomorrow."

"I hope so," she said. "One more thing I need to tell you. Eric had cancer. He was going to die anyway, and soon, so don't feel bad about killing him. There was a deposit of one million dollars made in his wife's banking account. I guess he did it for her."

"Where did the deposit come from?" I asked.

"Offshore banking account. No way to trace it. We're leaving it in her account. He did us a favor," she said.

"Good," I said. "He told me he didn't have the money he once had. Now his family will be okay."

"Goodnight," Robin said in a faint voice.

285

"Goodnight," I said and kissed her on the forehead.

~***~

My cell rang on the way home, it was Chad.

"Hey Cam," he said. "Got a minute?"

"Sure, I just left Robin's. I'm on my way home."

"I need to go to Florida and see Robert. I was wondering if I could get you to go to the office tomorrow and handle the Turner case."

"I thought you didn't want me in the office," I teased.

"Yeah, but now it's to my advantage," Chad said.

"Okay, for you I will."

"See Janice, she has the information and the file. I know you're familiar with it," he said.

"Okay. Is Robert alright?" I asked.

"Yeah, just a little business."

"When will you be back?"

"Couple of days. Is that okay?" he asked.

"Fine, see you then," I said and disconnected.

Robin only had one more week here, and I had a few weeks. I hoped this case wouldn't interfere with our getting together.

I wasn't ready for bed when I got home, so I called Jack.

"Cam, why don't you just come to Key West so you can check on Diane yourself?" he answered.

"That's what I've got *you* for," I said.

"She told me you haven't called her for a week."

"I know. A lot has happened. Where are you?"

"At Diane's," he said.

"Really? It's nine o'clock there."

"Don't get your panties in a bunch. We're watching some movies—PG," he said.

"Okay, I guess. I'll talk to her after I'm finished with you," I said.

"Yes, sir."

"Did anything else come up on any of those names?"

"Nothing yet," he said. "Anything new there?"

"Yeah, Bloodshot is dead and so is Eric," I said.

"When did all this happen?"

"Three nights ago—Bloodshot killed William Arlington. Eric Meninx wounded Bloodshot, and I killed them both."

"Shit Cam," he said. "Are you okay?"

"Yeah, just a slight wound to the arm."

I could hear Diane in the background trying to get the phone away from Jack.

"Put her on," I said.

"Cam, what happened? Are you okay?" Diane asked.

"Yep, I'm fine. What about you? Is Jack keeping his hands off you?"

"Don't worry about that. He's too afraid of you," she said.

"I love you, and I'll be home in about two weeks. For good," I said.

"That sounds fantastic. Your boat should be ready by then," she said.

"Great. Okay, put Jack back on, and I'll call you in a few days."

"Okay, love you too," she said and handed Jack the phone.

"Will you check on Brian Wessel's daughter?" I asked. "You told me she was sent to Oklahoma to live with her aunt and uncle when her father was killed. I want to stop and see her on my way home. I think she would like to know that her father's murderer has been dealt with."

"I will. I think I have the address. I'll text it to you. Anything else?"

"Not for now, unless you have a theory about who hired Bloodshot."

"Sorry," he said.

"Okay, I'll be home in a couple of weeks. Don't keep Diane up late," I said.

"Not to worry."

"Yeah," I said and hung up.

Chapter 60

The next morning, I went for a jog through Central Park. It was a little chilly, but the run warmed me up.

I woke up that morning with an epiphany. It must have come from talking to Jack the night before. What if someone in Brian Wessel's family had Bill killed? Sure, it's been a long time, and the charges were dropped, but it wasn't impossible.

I was going to call Jack and have him trace the whole family. His daughter went to live with the aunt and uncle. Was it Brian's sister or brother? It was a long shot, but I was just spinning my wheels.

As if on cue, my cell toned that I had a text.

I stopped to check it. It was from Jack. Brian's daughter Elizabeth, age ten, went to live with his sister Sharan and her husband Dennis McBride in Lawton, Oklahoma. The address was written below.

Like I said, a long shot, but what did I have to lose?

I stopped and bought my usual donut at my favorite shop and sat on a park bench with a cup of coffee to partake.

The park and the coeds were a stunning sight, but I didn't think I would miss it—much.

Key West was calling my name. All my favorite bars, the beach, all my old friends, and Diane. I would be a P.I. again. That meant truly little paperwork, no significant scheduling and the best chocolate cinnamon honey buns in the world. Life would be good again.

I finished my donut and was downing the last of my coffee when I felt a burning pain in my shoulder and a blunt force drove me to the ground.

I couldn't move. I could hear someone screaming and could see people running. I tried to get up, but someone gently pushed me back down and told me to lie still.

"What happened?" I asked.

"You've been shot," a man's voice said. "It looks like it went through your shoulder. I'm calling nine one one. You'll be fine."

Great, I thought. *It's not over yet.* Then everything went dark.

I woke in the hospital with Robin and two of her agents standing over me.

"Cam, wake up," Robin said.

"I'm awake," I said, but it came out, "I wake."

It took me a few minutes to regain any intellect. I asked, "What the hell happened?"

"You were shot in the park," Robin said.

"In my park?"

"No, in the arm," she said. "You were *in* the park."

"Oh yeah. Did you get my doughnut?"

"No, your doughnut didn't make it," she said and giggled.

"Who shot me?" I asked, my world becoming a little clearer.

"We don't know. Whoever it was they were hiding in the bushes and shot you with a forty-five. All the would-be witnesses ran for cover, so no one saw him."

"Why would someone want to kill me now?" I asked.

"I don't know, Cam, but this thing isn't over yet," Robin said.

"Mister Derringer," one of the agents said, I thought I recognized him as Agent Thomas from Brady's apartment, "did you see anyone following you in the park or anyone who looked suspicious?"

"No. I was just jogging and enjoying a doughnut. I do it almost every day," I said.

"Same routine every day, huh?" he said. "You know, that isn't wise."

"Yeah, I figured as much," I said.

"Get some rest," Robin said, "I'll take you home in a few hours."

"Do you think whoever did this was trying to kill me?" I said.

"Could be. Difficult to tell. It's hard to hit a target with a pistol," she said.

She kissed me on the forehead, and they left.

The doctor came in and checked me.

"You're a lucky man," he said. "The bullet didn't hit any vital organs or arteries. I couldn't have placed it better if I had tried. You'll be sore a few weeks, but you'll have a full recovery. I'm going to put a sling on you. In two days, I want you to start taking it off for a few minutes at a time and move your arm around."

"Thanks, doc," I said.

I lay there and thought, *Why would someone shoot me now?* Bloodshot was dead as was Eric. We didn't have any leads other than Brian Wessel's family, but no one knew I was going to see them. Was Bill just an accident? Was the real target still out there and was it me?

Robin and Alexis picked me up at noon and took me home. On the way, I remembered Chad.

"Oh no," I said. "Chad needed me in the office this morning."

"I called the office," Alexis said. "Janice canceled the appointment. I have talked to Chad. Everything is alright. He said for you to just rest and he would dock your pay."

"Really? Nice guy," I said.

After I was settled in my recliner and had my pain pills, the girls left. They stationed an agent outside my door. Robin said it would just be for a couple of days until I was able to fight for myself.

"Are they gone?" Kailey asked, walking out of the bedroom naked, towel over her shoulder.

"Kailey, what the hell? How did you get in here?" I asked.

She just looked at me.

"Never mind," I said.

"I thought you would need to talk, so I dressed for it," she said, smiling.

I just looked at her.

"Come on now," she said, "doesn't this cheer you up a little?"

"Yeah sure," I said. "Have a seat."

It really did cheer me up.

She placed the towel in the chair and sat.

Chapter 61

Kailey asked. **"How are you feeling?"**
"Not bad considering," I replied.
"I'm sorry you were shot. I got here as quickly as I could. I was hiding under the sink when the FBI searched the place.

"Really? That makes me feel safer. Did they pilfer anything?" I said.

"Yeah, one of them took the pot of gold."

"What would you have done if Robin would have stayed here with me?" I said.

"I knew she wouldn't. She has to find all the bad guys. You need a woman who will stand by you and love you," she said.

"Oh," I said, "and I guess that woman is you."

"Yep," she said. "You would never have to work again. We could travel all over the world together."

"And how long do you think it would be before you got bored with a fifty-three-year-old man slowing you down?"

"You wouldn't slow me down. I would speed you up," she said.

I laughed. I hoped it was the pills because I had a somewhat serious problem here.

"Would you like to get dressed?" I asked.

"No."

"Okay," I relented.

"We talk better naked, and I have something to say," she said.

"Okay, fire away."

"I want you to quit trying to find the person who hired Bloodshot. Let the FBI do it. You're going to wind up dead," she said.

"But it's personal now," I said.

"I know, it's really personal to me too, but you don't see me out there asking questions, do ya?" she said.

"It's kind of my job," I said.

"No, it isn't. You're a lawyer. Your job is to help people with legal matters," she said with a little anger in her tone.

I knew she was right. I probably should let the FBI handle it, but so far, I'd come up with a lot more than any of them had. It was like they had a leak or something.

"Yeah, I know, but—"

"No buts," she interrupted. "You quit it right now," she said with tears in her eyes.

She came to me and knelt in front of the chair and put her arms around me.

"Please," she said.

"I'll think about it, Kailey. Right now, I'm too groggy from the pills. I just want to rest," I said.

"Okay, you rest. I'll be right over here if you need anything," she said, standing and moving back to her chair.

This was still awkward. Watching her walk around naked was not easy. She was so beautiful and loving. I hoped she would be a good mother.

We were watching an old detective movie on TV. The P.I. placed a hearing device in the suspect's apartment. Kailey and I looked at each other.

I held my finger to my lips. She came over and whispered in my ear.

"Did you get all the bugs out of here?" she said.

"No," I whispered back. "Be careful what you say."

"Okay."

I couldn't believe I had forgotten about the bug. With Bloodshot dead, though, who would be listening?

Kailey stood in front of me with her hands on her hips. She was giving me a dirty look.

"Sorry," I mouthed.

She moved toward me and placed a leg on each side of mine. She was now in the recliner and straddling me. She leaned forward and whispered again.

"Did you say anything that might have given someone a clue as to who you might be investigating?"

I thought. The only person I had talked to was Jack. I asked him to check on that list of people and to get Brian's family's information.

"Maybe," I said.

"You should get that bug out of here or use it to your advantage," she said.

I nodded my head.

She hugged me. Her breasts were pressed to my face. I imagined Robin walking in.

She released me and moved back to the chair.

"Have you thought about giving up on the investigation yet?" she said aloud, for the benefit of the bug.

"Yes," I said, "you're right. I'm done with it. It's not really my problem. I just hope they find the guy who shot me."

"Good," Kailey said and smiled. "Now we just need to get you feeling better."

"I already do," I said. "You may leave. I don't think I'll be up much longer."

"I can't go," she said. "How do you think I'd get out of here?"

I forgot. The FBI was outside the door. If she left, they would have to tell Robin she was here. They might even arrest her.

There was a knock at the door. Kailey jumped up and ran to the bedroom.

"Yes," I said to the door.

It opened, and an FBI agent stuck his head in.

"Do you need anything, Cam?" he asked.

"No thank you," I said, "I'm fine. I'll be going to bed in a few minutes."

"Alright," he said. "Someone will be out here all night. Just let us know if you need us."

"I will. Thank you," I said.

Kailey came back into the room and kissed me as she walked by.

"That was a close one," she said.

Chapter 62

Robert met **Chad at the Fort Meyers** airport baggage claim.

"Have a good trip?" Robert asked.

"Not bad, other than a quite huge man sitting next to me spilling into my space. I've decided to fly first class going home," Chad said.

"Good choice," Robert said.

"I got a message while I was on the plane. Cam was shot this morning," Chad said.

"Who shot him?"

"We don't know."

"Do you think it had anything to do with Bloodshot?" Robert asked.

"Probably."

"Is he okay?"

"Yeah, sounds like it."

Chad waited while Robert got the car and picked him up. They rode in silence until they maneuvered out of the airport.

"How's the bid on the resort going?" Chad asked.

"It was going good, but the new bidders want it pretty bad. I think we'll have to up the ante," he said.

"Don't get caught in a bidding war. You'll end up overpaying and never make your money back."

"Yeah, I know. I don't think it really matters anyway. Now with William Arlington dead, I don't have the money," Robert said.

"You don't have the money?"

"No, we never signed the final papers. Bad timing."

"Alexis was going through the file and found yours. It said the money had been deposited into your account and if Bill died, the loan would be forgiven," Chad said.

"Really? I guess that's why you're here then. To ask me if I killed Bill."

"No. I know you didn't kill anyone, but if the FBI sees that contract, they'll have some questions," Chad said.

"It will be easy enough to prove," Robert said. "Just check my accounts. You won't find more than three hundred thousand in there."

"When was the last time you looked?" Chad asked.

"Couple of days ago."

"We had better check again," Chad said.

Robert looked at him and smiled.

"That *is* why you came. You need to see for yourself," Robert said.

"I came to warn you. You might be in trouble if that money is in there. It would be a little hard to explain," Chad said.

Robert pulled the car over at a Marathon station and retrieved his cell phone from his pocket.

He flipped through it for a minute typing in passwords and came up with his bank account.

"Here you go," he said, handing Chad his phone. "Take a look."

"You don't need to do that," Chad said.

"Yes, I do. It's alright, just check them."

Chad took the phone and opened the accounts. There was three hundred forty-five thousand in one account and five million and fifty thousand in the other.

Chad looked at Robert.

"Well?" Robert said.

"I think you had better look for yourself," Chad said, handing Robert the phone.

Robert thumbed through his accounts. His face turned white.

"What the hell?" he said.

"You had no idea Bill was going to deposit that money in your account?" Chad said.

"No. We never came to an agreement. I don't think he wanted to be involved in the gay resort," Robert said.

He looked at his phone again. "It's been in there for two weeks," he said. "It wasn't in there two days ago when I checked."

"Sometimes it takes a while to show up," Chad said.

"It doesn't make sense," Robert said.

"We need to go to the bank and get records on the deposit," Chad said. "We'll see how long it has really been on the books."

~***~

I must have slept soundly because when I awoke, I was alone, in bed. I remembered Kailey and got up to see where she was. She was gone. I looked under the sink. Not there either. How in the hell did she get out of there?

I called her cell.

"Good morning, sleepyhead," she said.

"Where are you?"

"I'm at home," she said.

"How did you get out of here?" I asked her.

"I looked through the peephole, and the agent was asleep, so I snuck out, but he woke up after I closed the door," she said.

"Oh no," I said.

"I told him I wanted to see you and asked him if he'd had a good sleep. He said he wasn't asleep, that he had watched me walk down the hall to your room. He wouldn't even let me in to see you," she said.

"I should tell Robin about that," I said.

"Well, it was two o'clock in the morning," she said.

"That's why he wouldn't let you in, but he shouldn't have been asleep."

"Yeah, I know, but let it go," she said. "There would be too many questions."

"Okay," I said. "Thanks for last night. You were good company."

"Anytime, or all the time. Your choice," she said.

"I'll think about it," I said. "Talk to you later."

"Toodles," she said.

I took a shower and dressed. My shoulder was sore but not as bad as I had anticipated. I decided I would go for a walk and maybe a doughnut. I opened the door and was met by an FBI agent. He stood and said, "Can I help you, sir?"

"I'm just going for a walk," I said.

"No sir," he said. "My orders are not to allow you to leave before Agent Anderson arrives."

"Robin? When will she be here?"

"About fifteen minutes, sir. Would you please step back into your apartment?" he said.

"Yeah, I guess, but I don't like being held captive."

"It's for your own protection," the agent said.

I acquiesced, closing my door behind me.

Kailey was free to come and go, but I was a prisoner.

Five minutes later, Robin knocked on my door. I opened it.

"Are you alone?" she asked.

"Of course. I am being held captive. I can neither leave nor have company," I said.

"You'll be free to go in a few minutes," she said. "I need to talk to you first."

No kiss yet.

"What's up?" I asked.

"We found Bloodshot's apartment," she said. "He was staying at the Roxy Hotel. There wasn't much there, but we did find his recording device. We listened to it to try to find who might have hired him. He didn't record that conversation. We did, however, hear everything you and Kailey said last night and another time in your bathtub. You can imagine how embarrassing that was for me in the room with my agents."

"Yes, it probably was, but I could do nothing about it. I'm not about to physically toss her out," I said.

Robin just stared at me. I could feel her daggers piercing my heart.

"Is that all you have to say?"

"No, but I have a feeling it wouldn't matter what I say. You know I love you and you know I didn't invite Kailey in, but it is what it is. You're the one who has to decide what you can do."

She stared at me again.

"You know she wants you," Robin said.

"Yes, and she wants you too," I said. "She wants everyone."

301

"On the phone with her you said, 'I'll think about it,'" Robin said.

"I know. I was tired of arguing about it."

She just looked at me again.

"How did your man outside my door explain her being here?" I asked.

"I haven't talked to him yet," she said.

"She left and then asked him if she could come in to see me. He wouldn't let her. He said he saw her walking down the hallway, when, in fact, she had just stepped from my room. She said he was asleep."

I thought if I gave her something else to think about it would take a little of the heat off me.

"I'll take care of him. You take care of Kailey," Robin said.

She turned and left. I followed her to the door.

"Take Agent Van Winkle with you," I said.

That got a dirty look from the agent.

I closed the door.

Chapter 63

C had and Robert arrived at the **Fifth-Third Bank** in Lehigh Acres the next morning as soon as it opened. They asked for the bank manager and were shown to her office.

She pulled the records and verified that the deposit was made on the fifth, which was two weeks before. It took some time to clear since it was such a significant amount.

They asked where the money had come from and were told it was sent from William Arlington's business account by Mister Arlington himself.

They thanked her and left.

"Well, Robert, if this isn't a red flag to the FBI you just came into five million dollars free and clear," Chad said.

"It's not right," Robert said. "We didn't do the deal."

"From a legal standpoint, though, the money is yours, and the transaction looks legitimate."

"Is someone trying to set me up for the murder of Bill?" Robert said.

"Either that or Bill had a change of heart," Chad said.

"What do we do now?" Robert asked.

"I'm going back to New York to try to figure this out. You go on about your business. The money is yours. Spend it wisely."

"Aren't you going to stay for a few days?" Robert said.

"No reason to now. I'd be more help to you in New York," Chad said.

"Okay."

~***~

I filled my morning with a walk and a badly needed doughnut. I couldn't wait to get out of that city. While I was wondering what my next move would be, I was mugged by two knife-wielding Hispanic gangbangers. I handed over my doughnut first then pulled my nine-millimeter from my waistband and told them to lie face down on the sidewalk. One of them took a bite of my doughnut and called me a mother fucker. They turned and walked away.

Now I had to go buy another doughnut.

I was going to leave as soon as Chad returned. I decided to go to the office and get my affairs in order.

Jackie was in my office when I arrived.

"Cam, what are you doing here? You were shot yesterday," Jackie said, surprised to see me.

"Yes, I know. I was there," I said.

"You should go home and rest," she said like a mother.

"I'll be okay. I just came in to see how you were doing with my files. I see you almost have my desk emptied."

"Yes. Everything is good here. You don't need to worry yourself," she said.

I could tell I was being kicked out of my own office.

I held my good hand up in surrender and said, "Okay, okay, I'm going."

"Before I do, though," I said, "is there anything I might need to sign?"

"Why? Won't you be coming back?" she asked.

"Maybe not," I said. "I think it's time to go to Key West."

She laid out a few papers and I signed them.

"Thank you. We'll miss you around here. You were always good for a laugh," she said, smiling.

I hugged her and told her I would miss her too.

I stepped out of the office building and Kailey pulled to the curb in her Porsche.

"Need a ride?" she asked.

I didn't know whether to get in or not. She was dangerous.

"Are you dressed?" I asked.

"Yeah, but I can take it off if you want me to." She giggled.

What the hell? I thought. *How much worse can it get?*

I opened the door and got in.

"Were you following me?" I asked.

"Maybe. I just want to make sure you're safe. I almost shot those thugs that mugged you a while ago," she said. "Then I saw you had everything under control."

"You saw that, huh?"

"Yep."

"Check out the sack on the floor," she said.

I saw a white paper bag on the floor by my feet. I opened it. Inside there were two chocolate-covered cinnamon honey buns.

"They're from Key West," she said.

"How did you manage to do that?" I asked.

"Diane," she said. "I called her and asked what would be something nice I could do for you, for all the help you've been to me."

"And you got them?"

"Voilà," she said.

"I'll be damned. That is incredible," I said, and I meant it.

I leaned over and kissed her on the cheek.

"What's our next move?" she said.

"*Our* next move?" I said.

"Yeah, I've decided you need help. You seem to always be getting in trouble."

"Have you considered the fact that some of that trouble is because of you?" I asked.

"Maybe, but this way we can keep an eye on each other," she said, smiling at me as if it were an excellent idea.

"I'm afraid I work alone," I said.

"Not anymore," she said.

"Robin heard everything we said last night and the night in my bathtub. They found Bloodshot's recording device last night," I said.

"You should have gotten rid of that bug. If I were there to work with you, I would have made you get rid of it."

"Yes, in hindsight that would have been wise. I didn't really fool anyone with it," I said.

"So, I guess Robin is mad at me," Kailey said.

"She's mad at both of us," I said.

"I'm sorry for that, but I'm not sorry for the time I've spent with you," she said.

"Yeah, I'm not sorry for our time together either," I said.

Kailey smiled bigger and drove on.

I had her drop me at my apartment. She wanted to come in, but I told her that I needed to rest my arm for a while.

"When will I see you again?" she asked.

"You never know, Kailey. I'm sure it won't be long."

"Oh, you're messing with me because I keep showing up," she said.

"Yeah, I am."

"Enjoy your doughnuts," she said.

"I will. I'm going to eat them slowly. I'll try to ration them out," I said.

"I love you," Kailey said.

I looked at her for a moment. How could you not love this woman?

"I love you too, Kailey, just not in a romantic way," I said.

"I know," she said, "but you will."

I closed the car door. She said, "Toodles," and drove away.

Chapter 64

Robin called me ten minutes after I returned **home.** I was just fixing a Wild Turkey on the rocks.

"Are you busy?" she asked.

"No," I said. "I was just about to have a drink."

"Already?"

"It's been a hard day," I said.

"I hope it's not your arm. Is it okay?"

"A little sore, but I'll live."

"Can we get together tonight?" she asked.

"I don't know. Are you going to shoot me?"

She laughed. "No. I'm sorry for the way I acted this morning. Jealousy will do that."

"I don't blame you a bit," I said.

"Have you talked to Chad or Alexis today?" she asked.

"No, is something wrong?"

"I've been getting some pressure to check Bill's files. I think I'll call Alexis."

"Will you try to put that off for as long as you can? Give them a chance to go over everything," I said.

"I'll try, but I need to touch base with them anyway," she said.

"Okay. Give her my love. I'll see you around six?"

"That will be perfect. I'll bring food and booze to your place," she said.

"Sounds great," I said.

I called Chad's cell phone as soon as we hung up.

"Hey Cam," he answered.

"Where are you?" I asked him.

"Getting in the limo at the airport. I just got back," he said.

"How's Robert?" I asked.

"Same ol' guy," he said.

I gave him a heads-up on my conversation with Robin.

"I hate to hear that," he said.

"Something wrong?"

"Can you meet me at the White House for a drink or is your arm keeping you down?" he asked.

"I'll be there. I have a lot to tell you too. You'll get a kick out of it at my expense," I said.

"Okay, I'm on my way," he said.

The taxi dropped me off in front of the White House. When I entered Chad, was at the bar talking to Ginger. She noticed the sling and asked what happened.

"Too many doughnuts," I said.

"Those things will kill ya," she said.

She left to get me a Wild Turkey.

"What's up?" I said.

"You first," he said, "I can't wait to hear what trouble you've been in since I left."

Ginger returned with my drink.

309

"Can I listen too?" she asked.

"Why not," I said. "First of all, I was shot in the park while eating a doughnut. After Robin dropped me off at home and got me settled in and left, Kailey walked into my living room naked."

This got a big laugh from Chad.

"Who's Kailey?" Ginger asked.

"My mother-in-law," Chad said.

"Eew," Ginger said.

"She's only thirty," Chad said.

"Oh?" Ginger said, smiling.

"Anyway," I continued, "she couldn't leave because the FBI was stationed outside my door. So we watched TV and talked all night."

"Was she still naked?" Ginger said.

"Yep, the whole night."

"Robin would kill you," Chad said.

"It gets better," I said. "Kailey sneaks out in the middle of the night. Robin comes over the next morning and tells me she heard everything we said plus the conversation that Kailey and I had in my bathtub a few weeks ago. She had Bloodshot's listening device."

I thought Chad was going to fall off his stool. Ginger laughed out loud.

"This morning, I was mugged walking down the sidewalk. They took my doughnut before I could pull my gun. Then they called me a mother fucker and left."

"Oh shit, Cam," Chad said between laughs, "how the hell do you do it?"

"I don't know," I replied.

Ginger had to leave for another customer, but I could see her still laughing at the other end of the bar.

"And that," I said, "was my last two days. How were yours?"

"Let's move to a table," Chad said, still laughing.

When he regained his composure, he said, "I went to see Robert because of a file Alexis found on him."

He proceeded to tell me the whole story.

"That does sound bad," I said. "And now Robin is in a tough spot. She doesn't have any choice other than to review the files."

"Yeah, I know. It makes Robert look guilty," Chad said.

I thought about it.

"He couldn't be," I said. "The Bloodshot thing started more than two weeks ago. Robert wouldn't have known about the death clause in time to get Andrei here and set all this up."

"You're right. I didn't think about that," Chad said.

"See when that contract was signed," I said.

"Yeah, I'll do that," he said.

We drank in silence for a minute, and Chad started laughing again.

"Sorry," he said. "So, I guess Robin, and you are kaput?"

"No. We have a date tonight. She's bringing food and booze over."

"You should get a personal taster," he said.

"I don't think she'll try to kill me," I said.

"Hope not. I'd miss all the funny stories."

"Yeah," I sighed. "Another thing, I stopped by the office a while ago and signed everything I need to in order to leave."

"I can't believe you're going. You've had so much fun here," he said.

"I know. What a fun town."

Chapter 65

Robin knocked on my door at six o'clock, and when I opened the door, she was standing there naked with a grocery sack and a bottle of wine in her hands.

I took her arm and hurried her in.

"What the heck?" I said and started laughing.

"I just thought we needed to talk," Robin said, "so I dressed for it."

I took the wine and the sack and placed them on the table and hugged her.

"You're crazy," I said. "Where are your clothes?"

"In the sack," she said.

"Where did you walk from naked?"

"I took them off in the taxi," she said.

I knew better than that, but just the thought really turned me on.

Instead of giving her clothes to her, I took mine off.

"Now we can talk," I said.

"Open the wine," she said.

"I have some breathing. I'll pour."

I poured two glasses of wine and handed her one. I opened her bottle to let *it* breathe.

"Thank you," she said and walked out onto the balcony.

I joined her.

"I see why Kailey does this," she said. "It feels good."

"You know, it's still daylight, and the neighbors have an excellent view," I said.

"Yeah, I know, but we'll both be gone in a few days, so what the hell?" she said.

"You're right."

We took a seat on the chaise. The sun felt good. Robin leaned against my chest.

I thought about the first time we made love. In a fit of wild passion, she pulled my shirt off and threw it out the window. We laughed hard. Thinking about it now made me laugh again.

"What's so funny?" she asked.

I told her, and she started to laugh too.

"We have had some fun and some real adventures, haven't we?" she said.

"That we have. It's a wonder we've survived," I said.

"Do you mean physically or romantically?" she asked.

"Yes," I said.

"I don't know about you," Robin said, "but I'm horny as hell."

"Me too," I said, "Shall we go in for a few minutes?"

"What's wrong with right here?" she said.

"Not a thing."

Afterward, we lay there panting. It was a very wild two minutes. Making love outside knowing there's a chance of being discovered and the fact that I only had one arm to maneuver with made the experience that much more exciting. I heard someone applaud but couldn't tell where it came from. I waved my good hand in the air.

We laughed again.

"More wine?" I said.

"Might as well," Robin said.

We went inside, deciding to let the neighborhood calm down a little, and poured more wine.

"Where should we go next to make love?" I asked.

"How about Central Park?" Robin said.

"Too dangerous. If we get busted, it won't bode well with the FBI," I said.

"True," Robin said.

"I know, the next time we're in the Arlington estate," Robin said, "let's make love in Kailey's bed. We could sneak up there and no one would know."

"How do you think she would react if we were caught?" I said.

"I think she would join in on the fun," Robin said.

"Way to go," I said. "Now I'm horny again."

"Me too."

The kitchen island took the brunt of our next encounter. We ended up on the floor.

We lay on the kitchen rug for a few minutes.

"If we're going to keep this up," I said, "I'm going to need some nourishment."

"I brought pork chops for the grill, but I think you should put on an apron," she said.

"Good idea."

We stood on the balcony, still naked except for my apron, while I grilled and talked about the Arlington files.

"I spoke with Alexis today," Robin said. "I'm going over there tomorrow morning to go through the records with her. She said there was something there I should see, but she couldn't explain. Any idea what that is?"

"Maybe," I said. "But if you don't mind I would rather you and Alexis discuss it."

"Okay," she said. "Would you like to go with me?"

"I'll see what tomorrow brings," I said.

"You know, we'll be in the Arlington estate," Robin said slyly.

"Oh yeah, I think I will go with you."

Chapter 66

We arrived at the Arlington estate at seven thirty the next morning. Chad answered the door.

"Alexis is waiting in the office. Can I bring you two some breakfast? The buffet is still set up," Chad said.

"I'll have a coffee please," Robin said.

"I'll walk with you to the buffet," I said to Chad. "We'll give the girls some time alone."

We walked to the office and dropped Robin off. I stuck my head in and said, "Hi," to Alexis. I told Robin her coffee would be there soon.

When we reached the back patio, Kailey was filling her plate.

"Join me, please," she said to us.

"It does smell good," I said, getting a plate.

"How are you feeling today?" she asked.

"Just fine. I start taking off the sling to exercise my arm today."

"Good. Hope it heals quickly."

"I think it will," I said.

Chad just watched us. I knew what he was thinking. I thought I saw him stifle a laugh.

"Are you going to come to the reading of the will today?" she asked.

"I wasn't aware it was happening today," I said.

"Yes, at five o'clock, here. I wish you would come," she pleaded.

"Well, I don't think it's my place, but if you really want me there, I'll come," I said.

"Thank you," she said.

"You might as well stay here for the day, Cam," Chad said. "Maybe we can get in a round of golf."

I pointed to my sling.

"Oh yeah, I forgot," Chad said.

"I like to golf," Kailey said. "I never get to play anymore."

"I wasn't aware you were a golfer."

"Used to be. It's pure freedom out there. Like walking in a manicured forest," she said, smiling and looking past us as if remembering something in the past.

"I'm going to check on Robin and Alexis," she said, standing.

We stood also.

"Well, aren't you gentlemen," she said.

"Kailey, would you mind taking Robin a cup of coffee?" I said.

"She won't throw it on me, will she?"

"No, she's fine with you," I said. "You've inspired her."

When she left, I told Chad what she said about golf didn't seem right.

"That doesn't fit in with the childhood she described to me," I said.

"Nor me," Chad said. "Maybe she embellished a little, hoping to spend some time with you."

"Probably so," I said.

We finished breakfast and joined the girls in the office. Robin was going over Robert's file.

"I know it looks bad," Kailey said, "but Robert would never do anything like that."

"Yes, I know," Alexis said.

"I'll have to make a copy of all the records," Robin said. "Maybe someone in here needed the money just enough."

"None of this answers the question of who shot Cam," Kailey said.

"Maybe it was just dumb luck," Chad said. "Wrong place at the wrong time."

"Could be, but I don't feel it," I said. "My apartment is still bugged, and maybe someone else has a receiver. I gave Jack a list of people to check on. Maybe one of them is involved."

"Could I have that list?" Robin said.

"Sure, it's all yours. I'm bowing out," I said.

"I don't blame you," Kailey said.

"I feel I've done my fair share in this case," I said. "I'll let the FBI and McNally handle it from here. It's time for me to go home."

"I agree," Robin said.

Chad and I walked to the pool and sat in the lounge chairs.

"That's bullshit," Chad said.

"What?"

"You giving up. You're just trying to get them off your back."

"I need room to work," I said.

"What are you going to do?" Chad said.

318

"First, I'm going to leave. I'll go to Oklahoma to inform Brian Wessel's family that his killers are dead. I think they need to hear it. It will also give me a chance to eliminate them from my list."

"What then?"

"I'll come back for a little while. Try to keep a low profile. Probably talk to McNally," I said.

"Who do you suspect?" Chad said.

"Right now. One of Bill's business partners would be my first choice. Even if the deal they're working on now isn't that lucrative, it might be to their advantage in the future not to have him around."

"Makes sense," Chad said.

"Can you get me a copy of those files?" I asked.

"I'll do my best. I think Alexis would be glad to turn them over to you."

"Thanks," I said.

The girls finished, and Robin told me she needed to go work on the files with her staff.

I walked her to the car.

"I'm going to spend the day with Chad," I said. "Kailey wants me to be at the reading of the will tonight."

"Good. Will you fill me in on it?"

"Sure," I said. "Why?"

"I found a few small areas in the records that would make it awful beneficial to Alexis if her father died."

"Alexis?" I said.

"Yes. I know my staff will see it too. I need to get ahead of it," she said.

"What about Robert?" I said.

"If it wasn't for the timing, I'd already have him in cuffs," she said.

I opened the door for her. "What about our little plan to go upstairs here for a while?" I said.

"Rain check?" she said.

319

"Okay, but I was all jacked up for it."

"You're always all jacked up for it," Robin said and kissed me goodbye.

.

Chapter 67

Chad and I went to Per Se for lunch and drinks.
Looking around I wondered if I *would* miss this
just a little.

There was quite a lunch crowd. I found myself a little
edgy. I could imagine a sniper somewhere in the crowd.
This city was taking a toll on me. I surveyed the crowd. I
was surprised to see Chief McNally sitting at a table with
NYPD Commissioner Patton.

Chad saw the look on my face.

"Yeah, I saw them when we came in," he said.

"I guess they have to eat too," I said.

"Do you need to talk to 'em?"

"Not right now," I said. "I'd rather talk to McNally
alone."

Our drinks arrived, and we ordered our lunch, steaks
and potatoes.

The waitress came to our table again and said, "Chief McNally and Commissioner Patton would like for you gentlemen to join them at their table."

I looked in their direction. McNally waved.

"I guess we don't really have a choice," I said to Chad.

"There goes our peaceful lunch," he said.

We stood and the waitress took our drinks following us to their table.

"Chief," I said, extending my hand.

He shook it and introduced Chad and me to the commissioner.

"Have a seat," Patton said.

"Thank you," I said, and we sat.

"The commissioner and I were just talking about the Bloodshot case when I looked up and who did I see," McNally said.

I smiled.

Patton said, "I wanted to personally thank you for the excellent work you did, assisting the NYPD on this case."

Assisting? I thought.

"You're welcome, commissioner, although I didn't have much of a choice considering he was trying to kill my friends and me."

"Still," he said, "you were quite some help."

"Thank you," I said.

"So," he said, "now we need to find out who shot you. Do you have any idea why someone would feel threatened by you?"

"I'm working on a few court cases that might trigger a reaction," I said.

"Anyone particular?" Patton said.

"Well, I reported a death threat from Emanuel Barona to Chief McNally," I said.

"I followed up on that," McNally said defensively.

"You don't think it has anything to do with Bloodshot?" Patton asked.

"I doubt it, although, whoever hired him is still out there. They made sure there were no loose ends by having them both killed."

"So, you think someone made sure you would be there to kill Eric Meninx after he killed Bloodshot?" he said.

"Don't know, but it sure turned out to their advantage," I said.

"It sounds like maybe that person is still threatened by you. You might know something and not realize it."

Our food came. I removed my sling so I could cut my steak.

"Need help?" McNally asked.

"No," I said. "It's therapy."

Chad and I ate while the four of us made small talk. They had already finished their meal before we arrived.

When we finished our meal, the commissioner picked up where he left off.

"I wonder if you might allow the chief here to take a look at those cases you're working on," Patton said.

"I doubt it," I said. "Client confidentiality."

He stared at me.

"Alright," he said, "I can understand that, but would you at least review them and let us know if you come up with anything?"

I looked at Chad.

"It's your call," I said. "I resigned yesterday."

"I'll take a look," Chad said.

"You resigned?" Patton said.

"Yes, I'm moving back to Key West."

"I'd prefer you stay here until this is solved," he said.

"No," I said bluntly. "If it weren't for me the Bloodshot case wouldn't be this far along. If I have to wait around for the NYPD to solve the rest of it, I might be here for the rest of my life."

McNally gave me a dirty look, and the commissioner leaned back in his chair.

"That's a little harsh, isn't it?" Patton said.

"It's just the truth," I said, shrugging my shoulders. "If it sounds harsh, then..."

"Listen here, you son of a bitch," McNally said.

"Chief!" Patton said.

They both looked at me.

"I can understand your frustration," Patton said, "but the NYPD has to work within guidelines. We can't be the vigilantes that the rest of you can."

He paused. "That being said, however, we still appreciate your help, and I hope your present lack of cooperation doesn't come back to bite you in the ass."

It was my turn to stare at them.

"If you'll excuse us," the commissioner said, "we have other cases to solve."

We stood as they did and extended our hands. We all shook.

"It was a pleasure meeting you men," Patton said. "Thanks again for the assistance."

"You're welcome, commissioner," I said.

When they were gone, Chad said, "Shit Cam, that was enjoyable."

I laughed.

"I hope that doesn't put any pressure on you since you have to stay here and work."

"I'll probably lose my license," Chad said.

"I don't think you'll have a problem. Besides, you're a billionaire."

"Yeah, that's right."

We ordered two more drinks. "Make 'em stiff," I told the waitress.

Chapter 68

At five o'clock I entered **William's office** where the will was about to be read. Alexis and Kailey were seated and talking at the conference table. Chad was at the bar fixing a drink. At the head of the table was Alexander Benton, the family lawyer. A sheriff's deputy was standing behind him.

I kissed Alexis and Kailey on the cheek and joined Chad at the bar.

The mood was sedate. It reminded me of a funeral. I guess in a way it was. It was the final disbandment of Bill's belongings.

I fixed a drink.

"This is quite unusual to have a will reading nowadays, isn't it?" I said to Chad.

"Yes, but we requested it because of Kailey. We wanted to make sure there was a provision in there for her and her child. They would be entitled to the same portion as Alexis," he said.

"I see. That's big of you," I said.

"We all received copies of the will two days ago. This is just a reading of the final revision."

Alexander stood and cleared his throat.

"I guess everyone is here if you would like to proceed," he said.

There was a general agreement.

"Alright, as you know, I am the executor of the will, so I will read the changes made. We must all agree with the changes before the will is considered closed."

He put on his glasses, sat down and picked up his copy.

"The sole beneficiaries are Alexis Diane Arlington Kendall and Kailey Marie Arlington. I'll speak freely now if you don't mind," he said.

"That's fine," Alexis said.

"Thank you," he said. "As you know, the will reads that the assets of two billion three hundred million would go to Alexis, his only child. On Alexis's wishes, the estate would be split equally among her and Kailey. Kailey has set up a trust fund with her being the grantor and her child being the beneficiary. JP Morgan Chase will be named the trustee."

He paused and took a drink of water.

"Here's the unusual part," he said. "Kailey doesn't want the estate to be liquidized. She wants only three hundred million dollars. The houses and business will all go to Alexis."

There was a slight murmur in the room. I found myself even making a low-pitched sound.

"Kailey," Alexis said, "you're entitled to that money."

"I don't want it. I'll live fine on three hundred million. Anything more I would find prolific," she said. "My child will have plenty. I don't want to divide a conglomerate that so many people depend on for their living."

"If that's what you want, Kailey," Alexis said, "then a lot of people owe you. Your child has a great mother. I hope you'll let us be in his or her life."

"You're entitled to be close to your sibling," Kailey said, "and you will be."

"Alright," Alexander said, "I'll finalize the will and make the arrangements. We'll get together again in a few days and sign the papers. Now, do you think I could have one of those drinks?"

Kailey and Alexis stood and hugged.

I told Kailey that was quite a sacrifice on her part so many other families didn't have to suffer.

"Cam, did you miss the part where I took three hundred million?" she said.

"No, I still remember that part," I said.

"Would you walk with me for a minute?" she asked.

"Sure."

We excused ourselves and walked down the hallway toward the staircase.

"Where are we going?" I asked.

"To my room," she said.

"And why is that?"

"I feel like celebrating," she said.

"I can't do that," I said.

"You could call Robin. She could join us."

"Tempting," I said. "Very tempting, but it just isn't going to happen."

"We'll see," she said and started up the stairs. "If you'll excuse me for a while, I'm going up to celebrate alone. You know where you can find me. Toodles."

I went back to the office.

"Where's Kailey?" Alexis asked.

"She went to her room to rest for a while. I think this was a little stressful," I said.

Chad smiled at me and took a drink. I rolled my eyes.

"We'll let her sleep for a few hours and then wake her for supper," Alexis said.

"That would be good," I said.

Her batteries can't last much longer than that.

I stayed and had a few drinks with everyone, and we talked about the future. Where would Kailey go? How would she be as a mother?

"I hope she stays here until the baby is born," Alexis said.

"I don't see why she wouldn't," Chad said. "I don't think she has anywhere else to go."

At seven o'clock I excused myself and called for my limo.

"I guess the two of you will be staying here from now on," I said.

"That's the plan," Chad said, "but we're keeping my condo in the city. There will be times when it will be more convenient."

"Has it sunk in yet, Chad? You're a billionaire."

"No, I don't think it has. I wouldn't be standing here talking to you. I'd be lying on the floor receiving CPR."

I laughed. "You probably would. I'm close to it just knowing a billionaire."

"Yeah, me too," Chad said.

"Will Alexis be able to pay Kailey three hundred million without liquidating any of the assets?" I said.

"Yeah, there is about five hundred million in cash."

"I wonder how she knew that," I said.

"Maybe Bill told her," Chad said.

Alexander came to the bar where we were standing.

"Crazy day," he said. "Thought I'd fix a second."

"Have all you want," Chad said.

Alexander fixed another drink.

"May I ask who set up the living trust for Kailey?" I asked Alexander.

"She did it herself," he said. "I went over it afterward, but everything was in order."

"Good for her. I'm glad to see she knows how to handle money."

"She knows very well," he said. "That's quite a complicated ordeal."

"Yes, I know," I said.

We chatted for a few minutes then my cell phone buzzed. The limo had arrived.

Chapter 69

I called Robin from the limo.

"Where are you?" I asked her.

"Actually, only about two blocks from your place. Are you home?"

"I'm on the way. Go on in and wait for me."

"Will do. I'll stop at the corner market and get some snacks," she said.

"Great, there's wine in the cooler. Pick one out," I said.

"Okay, bye."

I walked into the apartment to find her standing naked in the kitchen.

"Oh, it's gonna be like that, huh?" I said.

"Join me?" she asked.

I did.

"Kailey has been a lot of trouble," Robin said, "but I have to hand it to her, she sure spiced up our lives."

"Yes indeed. What kind of snacks did you get?"

"Really," Robin said, "I'm standing here naked and you want to know what kind of snacks I brought."

"Yep, I'm hungry," I said.

She opened the sack on the counter and poured the contents on the tabletop.

"M and M's, cheese popcorn, pretzels, and bagels," she said. "But the bagels are for breakfast."

"Oh good, you're staying for breakfast," I said.

"Wouldn't miss it," she said.

Even though she was naked also, I still felt strange walking around the apartment this way. I fixed a Wild Turkey.

"No wine?" she said.

"This first."

The oven timer went off.

"Pizza's ready," she said.

"Thank God you brought pizza. I thought I was going to have to fill up on junk food," I said.

"I wouldn't do that. We're having good ol' sausage pizza," she said.

We sat out on the balcony and ate. At least it was getting dark now, and we weren't as exposed as the last time.

"So how did the reading of the will go?" she asked

"It was a little strange," I said. "Kailey turned down a billion dollars. She took three hundred million. She didn't want to liquidate any of the businesses. She said it would cause hardship for the employees."

"I hope she has someone to advise her on the money," Robin said.

"It sounds as if she doesn't need any help. She set up a living trust by herself, her as the grantor and her child as the beneficiary. JP Morgan Chase will be the trustee."

"Really? I didn't think she had it in her," Robin said.

"One never knows."

We ate and drank for a few minutes.

"How did the investigation into the files go?" I said.

"Robert's in the clear, but someone tried to set him up. The files have unquestionably been altered, but we can't tell how."

"It doesn't have to be someone on the inside either," I suggested, "Alexis said they send their records to Dillard and Shanks. Someone there could have embezzled the money and now they're trying to throw the blame somewhere else."

We paused to eat more pizza, and I refilled our drinks.

"We only have a couple of days left together," I said.

"I know. I try not to think about it. It depresses me," Robin said.

"Yeah, me too," I said, "but we're both going to where we belong. You have a dream and a goal coming true, and I have my home back."

"It's a hollow victory," Robin said.

"We'll work it out. Enjoy your promotion," I said.

"You're right, let's enjoy," Robin said and reached for my cock.

~***~

The next morning, Robin was up early.

"I have to get to the office. I've been thinking about the case all night. I have an idea of who might be behind all this," she said.

"Care to share?" I asked.

"No, not yet. I have to connect some dots first."

"Well, don't forget your bagel," I said.

"It's in the toaster."

She was dressed, and I was still in my robe.

She looked at me.

"Are you practicing for Key West?" she asked.

"We don't need robes there. It's au naturel."

"Okay, Mister Au Naturel, drop the robe," she said.

By the time we came back from the bedroom, her bagel was cold.

"You can have mine," I said.

"No, that's for you."

"I'm going for a run in the park. I'll get one there," I said.

"Okay," she said and put the other bagel in the toaster.

She put cream cheese on her bagel and kissed me goodbye.

"See you tonight," I said.

"Okay, I'll call you when I can get away."

When the door closed, I went to the cabinet and pulled out my white sack.

"Chocolate honey buns," I said to myself.

Chapter 70

I received a phone call from Chief McNally around noon. He wasn't in a good mood.

"Derringer?" he said.

I could tell he had been chewing on his cigar for a while. I could imagine the slobber running down his chin.

I knew who it was, so I said, "Yes, this is Mister Derringer."

"Mister huh," he puffed.

"Yep."

"What the hell was that at Per Se yesterday?" he said.

"It was a T-bone," I said.

"You know what I mean. Givin' the commissioner a hard time in front of *me*."

"Oh that," I said. "He rubbed me the wrong way. I was there to enjoy my meal not get the third degree from someone who hasn't contributed a damn thing to the case."

"He's pissed. You might not want to go speeding or anything."

"I'll drive carefully," I said. "Have you come up with anything new?"

"I wouldn't tell you if I had," he said.

"To bad. I was hoping we could exchange stories," I said.

"What do ya know?" he asked.

"Whadda *you* know?" I asked.

"You first," he said.

"Okay, I'll go first, or we'll play this stupid game forever," I said.

"Go," he said.

"Eric Meninx had cancer, and a million dollars was transferred to his family's bank account from an offshore account," I said.

"I already knew that," he said.

"Your turn," I said.

"Okay," he said, "Brady Osborn and William Arlington were investigated for murder ten years ago."

"I already knew that," I said.

"Then why didn't you tell *me*?"

"I know so much that if I had to take the time to tell you everything, I wouldn't have time for myself," I said. "And why didn't you already know they had been investigated?"

There was a brief silence on the phone.

"Look, I just called you to say don't get me in trouble with the commisssioner," he said.

"Why didn't you say so then?" I said. "I won't."

"Call me if you get anything," he said.

"You too," I said.

We disconnected.

I called Chad to see if he wanted to get in a round of golf.

"Sounds good to me," he said. "But what about your arm?"

"I think it would do it good."

"You're on then."

"When can you get away?" I asked him.

"About one thirty. I'll call the club and get a tee time."

"Alright, see you there," I said.

I dug my clubs and shoes out of the closet. They were both dusty. It had been a while. I hadn't played since I was in Key West.

I walked in the bar at the golf club at one thirty. We had a two-fifteen tee time. Chad wasn't there yet, but Kailey was.

"Hiya Cam," she said.

"Hi, Kailey. What are you doing here?"

"I came hoping to get in a round of golf. Talking about it the other day made me miss it," she said. "What about you?"

"I'm waiting for Chad. We're playing at two fifteen."

"Have you got room for me?"

"I don't see why not," I said.

No matter how hard I tried, I couldn't see why not.

"Cool."

Chad walked in the door and saw us.

He kissed Kailey and asked her why she was there.

"She's playing with us if you don't mind," I said.

"Fine by me," he said.

We teed off. My drive was a little left. I blamed it on my shoulder. Chad hit a bomb right down the center of the fairway.

"Nice shot," Kailey said.

"Shall we move to the ladies' tee box?" I asked.

"If that's what you want," she said.

Kailey hit a screamer about twenty yards past Chad. It was a thing of beauty.

"Where did you learn to hit like that?" I asked.

"An old boyfriend," she said. "He played the circuit."

She proceeded to beat us all day. She was a natural.

Afterward, we sat at the bar and had a drink. Chad and I licked our wounds.

"You missed your calling, Kailey," I said. "I've never played with anyone of your caliber."

"Me neither," Chad said. "You must have played a lot."

"I got around for a while," she said.

Chapter 71

Robin came over around six. We had a drink and talked for a while.

"I'm going to Oklahoma tomorrow to see the McBrides. I'll be going to Key West from there," I said.

"Yeah," she said. "I'll be leaving for LA tomorrow evening."

"I have reservations for eight o'clock at Per Se for old times' sake," I said. "Do you want me to cancel them?"

"No," she said. "Let's go out. It's our last night on the town. We'll come back here afterward."

"Alright, it's a date," I said.

I fixed us another drink.

"Did your theory turn out to be right?" I asked.

"I'm not sure yet," she said. "I hope not."

"Why's that?"

"Well, my suspect is Kailey," she said.

"Kailey? No way," I said. "She couldn't orchestrate anything this complicated."

"I don't know, but I won't move on it unless I'm sure."

"Yeah, you have to walk on eggs with this case. Everyone is a suspect," I said.

"Did you see Kailey today? It was your last chance, you know," she said.

"Yes, unfortunately for Chad's ego and mine, we did see her."

"What happened now?" Robin said.

"Chad and I played golf at the club and guess who was waiting at the bar for us?"

"No, Kailey?"

"Yep, she wanted to play, so we humored her and let her join us," I said.

"I bet that was ugly," she said.

"It was. She beat us both. She's a great golfer."

"Really?"

"Really," I said.

"She comes off as credulous, but I think she's hiding a brilliant mind," Robin said.

I laughed. "I don't believe so, but she was hiding a boyfriend who taught her to golf."

"Maybe, but—"

"What else makes you suspect her?" I asked.

"She had the most to gain," she said.

"She would only get five million if he died—until the baby came along. The game had already started by then," I said. "And she was also shot."

"Yeah, I thought about that," she said. "I'm just kind of grasping at straws."

"Well don't feel bad," I said. "I've suspected Kailey on and off through this whole thing, but I could never come up with any evidence. I just don't think she could pull it off."

"Neither do I really."

"I guess Alexis isn't a suspect."

"No," Robin said, "that was cleared up. It turns out she was in line for the money either way and her father wasn't holding anything back. She had total access to the whole fortune. Bill had been mentoring her to take over the company for years."

"Well, it will be up to your replacement after tomorrow. So why don't we just forget about it and have a romantic evening?" I said.

She smiled. "Works for me."

~***~

We arrived at Per Se at eight on the dot.

"Hello Cam," the hostess said. "Will you be joining the Kendalls?"

"I didn't know they were here," I said.

"Yes, last-minute reservation."

"We'll stop by their table to say hi," I said, "but we'll keep our table."

Chad saw us and stood.

We all shook hands and hugged.

"How about joining us?" Chad said.

"We don't want to impose," I said.

"Nonsense, unless the two of you want to be alone. It is your last night here."

We decided to join them.

"Chad tells me Kailey kicked your asses today in golf," Alexis said.

"Yes, it wasn't pretty," I said.

"She hasn't come home since the game," Chad said.

"Really? Is that unusual for her?" Robin said.

"Yeah, a little. I would think she would come back and take a shower if she were going out," Alexis said.

"Well, maybe she ran into a friend and got tied up," I said.

The waitress took our drink order.

We ordered our food when she returned with the drinks.

"Have you decided to stay here and get rich?" Chad asked me.

"I'm rich enough," I said. "More money would just be a burden."

"Has your boat been repaired yet?" Alexis asked.

"Diane said it should be ready in a few days. I'll stay with her till then."

"Have you settled in yet, Robin?" Alexis said.

"They have a temporary condo for me. I'll start home hunting when I get there."

We finished our meal and talked about the events of the last six months. Mostly about Bloodshot. Robin said Robert was cleared and there weren't any other suspects.

It was getting late. We decided to call it a night.

"I'll pick you up at seven a.m.," Chad said.

"Alright," I said. "That's going to come early."

"Do you need a ride tomorrow, Robin?" Alexis said.

"No thanks, the Feds are picking me up," she said and laughed.

We said our goodbyes and took the company limo back to my place.

"I'm going to miss this place," I said. "We've had a lot of good times here."

"Yes, we have," she said.

"I wonder what the future holds for us," I said.

"No way to tell," she said. "But I think we should take it one day at a time. If there is someone you would like to go out with, then I think you should, and me likewise."

"You're right, I guess. Our visits will be few and far between no matter what we say we're going to do."

"For now, though, I think I have a good idea," she said.

We went into the bedroom for the last time, there.

Chapter 72

I landed at **Fort Sill Regional Airport** in Lawton Oklahoma at ten twenty a.m.

The airport was small but charming. I picked up my luggage and rented a car. The drive to the McBride house took me through a picturesque landscape and into the city. I passed the Cameron A&M College, County Hospital and the edge of the Fort Sills Military Reservation. It was marked as a national historic landmark. I thought about how it would be to grow up in a town like this. It would definitely have its advantages.

I found Dennis McBride's house. It was a modest brick house with an American flag flying in the front yard.

An attractive lady in her mid-fifties answered the door.

"Hello," I said, "my name is Cam Derringer. Are you Sharon McBride?"

"Hello, Mister Derringer. We were expecting you," she said.

"You were?" I said.

"Yes, won't you come in?"

"Thank you," I said and entered a small but immaculate living room.

The house had a faint smell of baked cookies.

"Have a seat," she said, motioning to a chair, "I'll get Dennis."

I sat. Sharon returned with a plate of cookies and three glasses of tea.

She handed me one glass and set the cookies on the coffee table in front of me.

"Thank you," I said.

"I hope these will satisfy your sweet tooth for a while," she said.

Dennis McBride entered the room. He was a tall man and well built. I could tell he worked out.

I stood and shook hands.

"How was your trip?" he asked.

"Great," I said, wondering why they acted as if they knew me.

"Do you know why I'm here?" I asked.

"Yes, Mister Derringer, we do. You killed those sons of bitches who murdered my brother," Sharon said.

"Well..." I said. "They died in the process of our investigation."

"Without you, they would still be alive," Dennis said.

"Maybe so," I said, "I'm not sure."

I ate a cookie and took a drink of the tea.

"Very good," I said, and they were.

"Is your niece here?" I asked. "I would like to meet her."

"You just missed her, Cam," Sharon said. "She was here yesterday. She was thrilled that the men paid for killing her father were dead."

"So, she knows?" I said.

344

"Yes, she knows. I'll tell you a little about her life since that day," Sharon said.

"I'd like to hear it," I said.

"She saw Brady Osborn and William Arlington kill her father. When they came to the door, Brian told her to hide in the closet. From there she saw Brady hold Brian while William cut his throat with a knife. She was in shock when some friends found her the next day, still in the closet."

"That had to be very hard," I said.

"The police interviewed her at the hospital," she continued. "She told them what she saw, but they didn't follow up on the investigation. We later realized that William had the police in his pocket."

"That was it?" I said. "No one filed charges?"

"None. They questioned both men but never charged them," Dennis said.

"I'm sorry to hear that, Mrs. McBride," I said.

"It's Sharon," she said. "Lizzy came to live with us, and we raised her as our own. She was withdrawn for a couple of years, but one day she said she was ready to live her life to the fullest, and she did. After graduating high school with honors, she went to the University of Oklahoma on a golf scholarship of all things. There she made law her major and graduated top of her class at the university law school. She passed the bar three months later."

"That's a great story," I said. "I'm happy for her."

"So are we," Sharon said.

"Where does she work now?" I asked.

"She was here for a year; then she went to New York. She would send us money every month. She said it was for raising and loving her. We told her she didn't need to pay us for the honor, but the money kept coming."

"Do you know what law firm she worked for there? I might have run across her," I said. "I have been practicing law there the last year."

"No," Sharon said. "I think she told us once, but it was a strange name and I forgot it over the years."

"That doesn't matter," I said. "I'm just glad she is doing well."

I stood. "I won't take up any more of your time," I said. "I just wanted to tell you personally that the men who killed your brother are dead."

"Thank you for coming and for all you've done," Sharon said.

"You're welcome," I said. "How did you know William and Brady were dead? Was it in the paper here?"

"No, Lizzy told us yesterday when she visited. She was ecstatic," Sharon said.

"I'm sorry I missed her. She sounds like a fascinating young lady."

"You didn't miss her, Cam," Sharon said. "You just didn't see her."

"What do you mean by that?"

Sharon went to the fireplace, removed a picture, and handed it to me.

"Here's her graduation picture," she said.

I took the picture and stared for what seemed an eternity.

"This is Lizzy?" I finally said.

"Yes," Sharon said. "Elizabeth Kailey Wessel."

Chapter 73

I was looking at a slightly younger version of **Kailey**. She'd hired Bloodshot to avenge her father. She even married William just to get close enough to make him pay. She had all of us shot and even herself. She embezzled money and put the blame on Alexis. She worked me as well. I thought she was just a loving little girl. Now Bill was dead, and she had three hundred million dollars. Now the golf made more sense also. No wonder she clobbered us. It was ingenious.

"She told me her name was Kailey Parker from Biloxi, Mississippi," I said.

"That's her mother's maiden name. She was from Biloxi."

"Where did Kailey go?" I said.

"I don't know," Sharon said. "She said it would be better if we didn't know. When she came yesterday, she deposited five million dollars into our account. She said she earned that money."

I thought for a moment. That was the money promised to her when she married Bill.

"Yes," I said, "she did earn that."

I replaced the picture on the mantel. I saw a few more pictures of her there. In one she was standing holding a trophy that read, "Marksmanship, Department of Health and Physical Education, Lawton, Oklahoma."

"She was a marksman?" I said.

"Yes, she started that when she was fifteen. It was a passion and a stress release for her. She was quite active in the NRA."

"She was a very busy young lady," I said.

"We don't know all of what she did in New York, and we don't want to know. She seems quite happy now, and we're happy for her. She said she would contact us from time to time, but she had to go away for a while."

I was in shock. I stood there staring at her picture again and then a big smile came over me. I couldn't help it.

"She'll be fine," I told them. "Kailey will be just fine."

"Thank you for coming by, Cam. Kailey spoke very highly of you. I think she has a crush on you," she said, smiling.

"And I her," I said.

I walked to the door.

"Oh. Wait a minute," Sharon said. "I almost forgot."

She went to the kitchen and returned with a white sack.

"Kailey said this was for you."

It would be a good flight home.

~***~

My cell phone rang on the way back to the airport. It was Robin.

"Did you have a good flight?" she asked.

"It was good," I said.

"Well, I wanted to call you before you got to the McBrides'. Did I get you in time?"

"No, I just left them," I said.

I guessed her theory was right. Somehow, she must have figured out that Kailey was Elizabeth.

"We know who hired Bloodshot," Robin said. "We think it was Kailey. She's gone."

"That doesn't prove anything, does it?" I said.

"When I started to connect the dots, I called the hospital and asked for Doctor Bishop."

I remembered him from the ER. He was the one who treated Kailey after Bill was killed. He told me she was pregnant.

"They don't have a doctor on staff by that name," she said.

"I talked to him myself," I said.

"You talked to someone," she said, "but it wasn't a doctor."

Now that was starting to make sense too. She faked her pregnancy to gain three hundred million dollars. An amount that could be transferred to her immediately.

"I guess we were duped," I said.

"Kailey signed the papers transferring the cash to her yesterday morning. The living trust was closed before the transfer, and the money went to an offshore account," Robin said. "She left town right after your golf game."

Kailey was a genius. She got revenge and money and got away with it.

"We'll probably never see her again," I said.

"No, we probably won't," she said. "I'll fill you in on the rest when you get to Key West. I'm leaving for LA in about an hour."

"Have a good trip," I said. "I love you."

"I love you too," she said. "Oh, how was your visit with the McBrides?"

"Fascinating. They are nice people. I didn't get to meet the niece though. She was away," I said.

"Too bad," she said. "I hope they can live in peace now."

"I think they can," I said.

I stopped at the restaurant in the airport and bought a glass of milk. I sat at a table where I could watch the few people pass by and opened the white sack.

I kissed the chocolate honey bun before taking a bite.

"Are you in love with that doughnut?" a voice from behind me said.

I would have recognized that voice anywhere.

"Hello Kailey," I said without turning. "Or should I say Lizzy?"

"Kailey will do. I won't be either one for long," she said, walking around to face me.

"Why are you here?" I asked. "It could be dangerous."

"I knew if anyone would understand it would be you," she said. "You went to great lengths to bring down the man who killed your wife."

I thought back. Yes, I did. I wouldn't stop until I had my revenge.

"How did you know about that?"

"I do my homework," she said.

"May I?" she asked, pointing at an empty chair.

"Please do. Sorry I don't have a doughnut for you, but I only have one," I said.

"That's fine," she said, "I'm watching my figure."

"Yeah, me too. My doctor says I need to give these up," I said.

"What doesn't kill you makes you stronger."

"True, but I think these might kill me."

"Chose your battles wisely."

"Speaking of which, one thing bothers me," I said.

"What's that?"

"Who shot me?"

"It was Emanuel Barona," she said. "I saw him do it."

"I should warn Chad then," I said. "He might be after him too."

"I don't think so," Kailey said. "I heard Emanuel was killed shortly after he shot you."

"I didn't hear anything about that," I said.

"Maybe they haven't found the body yet," she said. "Anyway, Chad's safe."

"That reminds me," I said, "I saw your trophy for marksmanship."

"I use it as an escape," she said.

"Yeah, I bet you do."

"Only when necessary," she said.

"Why did you have everyone shot?" I said. "Why didn't you just kill Bill?"

"It was supposed to look like the game in Ontario, but Eric told you about the arrangement I had with him. After that, I did my best to make people think it was still a game, but I guess it didn't work."

"Someone could have gotten killed," I said.

"Andrei was an expert marksman. He promised that no one would die," she said.

"Robin called me a while ago. They know it was you," I said.

"They *think* it was me," she said. "I wish I could tell them why, but then my aunt and uncle would be investigated. They might even lose their five million. I guess you and I knowing why I did it is good enough for me."

"You're not pregnant, are you?" I said.

"The doctor said I was."

"That wasn't a real doctor," I said.

"Really? I feel violated," she said in her little girl accent.

"But you told Bill you were pregnant just before he was killed," I said.

"No. What I really told him was the truth. I told him who I was and that I watched him kill my father and that he had only about five seconds left to live," she said. "That's why I was laughing."

"And when he stepped forward and reached for you then…"

"Yes, he wanted to kill me," she said.

I pondered that for a while. This girl wasn't only a genius, but she was dangerous.

"What will you do now? I asked.

"That depends."

"On what?"

"On you," she said.

"Why me?"

"I want you to come away with me. I honestly love you, Cam," she said sincerely.

"Kailey, like I told you before, I love you too. Just not that way. Besides, you'll have a better chance of staying free without me."

"I already have our new identities set up. All you have to do is say yes," she said.

"I have family and friends. Diane for one, I can't leave her," I said.

"That's too bad," she said. "It won't be the same without you."

"I'll miss you too," I said.

"I guess you don't need me now that Robin walks around naked," she said.

"How did you know we walk around naked?" I said.

She took a recorder out of her purse and handed it to me.

352

"When I put the bug in for Bloodshot, I tuned it into two recorders. That's how I knew you would be here."

"Listening to me, huh?"

"Are you going to turn me in?"

I stared at her for a few seconds. I thought I could see the little girl hiding in the closet in her eyes. I wanted to hold her and tell her everything was going to be okay.

"No, I'm not," I said.

"Good, then I'll see you from time to time in Key West," she said.

"If you think it's safe, I'll be glad to show you the town, but no shooting," I said.

"Okay, I promise," she said.

I took another bite of my doughnut and a swig of milk.

"I guess this is it for a while then," she said. "I owe you a lot. I have a present for you, but I won't give it to you just yet."

"That's not necessary."

"Yes, it is," she said. "Besides, I can afford presents now."

"Be safe, Kailey," I said, standing.

"Practice your golf game," she said.

I laughed. She put her arms around me and kissed me. It was a long, soft kiss that made my knees weak. When we broke it off, she turned and walked away. "Toodles," she said over her shoulder.

Chapter 74

I **landed in Key West at five forty-six p.m**. As soon as I stepped off the plane, I could feel the salt air. Diane was there to greet me. She jumped into my arms and kissed me.

"Are you really home for good?" she asked.

"You better believe it," I said.

"Are you going to miss being a lawyer?"

"It really wasn't that much fun," I said.

We laughed.

"Before I take you home, we're going to have a piña colada," she said.

"Fine by me," I said.

She pulled into a parking spot beside Sloppy Joe's. We took a table in the front by the street.

"This is the life," I said. "I missed all these quirky people."

"They missed you too."

Tanya was our waitress. We had a history. Not sexual, but legal. I helped her out of a marijuana bust one time.

"CAM," she said and threw her arms around me.

"Tanya, great to see you again."

"Are you back for good?" she asked.

"Yep."

"Wanna go out tonight?"

"Not tonight. It's been a long day, and I haven't even been home yet. We just stopped in to have a piña colada and to see you."

"Comin' right up," she said.

When she left, Diane giggled. "You haven't changed a bit."

"Don't want to."

Our drinks came, and I told Tanya I'd see her in a few days.

We took a few swallows of our drinks. I got a brain freeze.

"Oh," I said. "I forgot about that."

After a minute, I was okay again.

"Drink it slow, Cam," Diane said.

"I thought I was."

"Did you get your chocolate doughnuts from Kailey?" she said.

"Yes, I did. What a pleasant surprise that was."

"She seemed like a really nice person," she said.

I laughed. "You don't know the half of it," I said.

"Tell me."

I did. The whole thing.

Diane thought a minute.

"Well, good for her," she finally said. "She deserved his money, and he deserved to die."

"Right and right as far as I'm concerned," I said. "But the rest of us didn't deserve to get shot, and you were put in grave danger."

"He was nothing but a gentleman with me," she said.

"I'm glad."

"Are you going to tell Robin the truth about Kailey?"

"No, that stays between you and me," I said.

"I won't tell."

We finished our drinks.

"Can you run me past my boat before we go to your house?" I asked. "I'd like to see how far along it is."

"Sure, it's almost finished," she said.

We drove to my boat dock. I couldn't believe I'd ever left this place, but I didn't have much choice. My houseboat was blown to smithereens and sunk right at my dock. Going to New York gave me a chance to get my law license back and to be with Robin. Now I'd lost both again.

From the parking lot, I could see the boat still had a lot of work to be done. I opened the gate at the top of the dock. It squeaked as it always did. That was our security alarm.

A head popped out of the first boat.

"CAM," Stacy said.

"Hey, Stacy."

"Are you coming home?"

"When the boat's finished," I said.

"You can stay here with me. Barbie's gone for a month."

"Thanks, but Diane already called soups on me," I said.

Stacy and Barbie are two gorgeous twenty-something girls who live in a houseboat on my dock. We've been through a lot together. I put them in danger when some terrorist was after me. Thanks in part to Robin, that is over with.

There was no one working on my boat.

"Where are the workers?" I asked Diane.

"Don't know," she said. "I'll call them."

She took out her cell phone and pressed the speed dial.

"Jimmy, this is Diane," she said into the phone. "I thought you guys were about to wrap up Cam's boat. There's no one here, and it looks like there's plenty to be done."

She listened for a moment.

"By who?" she asked.

She listened again.

"Do you have their number?"

She wrote down a number.

"Thanks, I'll get back to you," she said and hung up.

She looked around the dock and then at me.

"Jimmy said he received a stop-work order from his company. They told him the boat didn't need to be finished."

"What?" I said. "That's crazy. Can you call the company?"

"They're closed until Monday," she said.

"So, I have to stew over this for two days," I said.

"Guess so. We'll get it straightened out," she said.

This wasn't a good start to my coming home. We drove to Diane's house, and I settled into the second bedroom.

"Thanks," I said. "I'll try to find a condo to rent until the boat is finished."

"No, you won't," she said. "You'll stay right here. You can start working on getting your name back out there for the P.I. work. You have plenty to do so you won't be in my way."

"Thanks again. We'll take it one day at a time," I said.

My cell phone rang. It was Robin.

"Miss me already?" I answered.

"Yes, I do," she said. "I just got to my apartment. It's lovely."

"Great," I said. "I'm at Diane's."

"Is your boat ready?"

"Not quite," I said.

"Well, I received a phone call as soon as I landed," she said. "They found Emanuel Barona dead in the park this afternoon. His body was under some bushes and covered with rocks. It looks like he's been there three or four days. They think he's the one who shot you. His gun matches. He also had a card in his pocket. Any guesses as to what it said?"

"'Bloodshot' would be my guess," I said.

"Give the man a cigar," she said. "On the back, it read, 'Robin–arm–twenty-five thousand. We're quite sure he's the one who hired Bloodshot. It looks as if William *was* an accident. The game evidently wasn't over yet. I was next."

"Wow," I said. "That's shocking. I wonder who the other shooter was."

"Maybe Eric, we'll probably never know that, but it takes the heat off Kailey for it," she said. "Now we need to find her to recover the money."

"What if she is pregnant?" I said.

"I don't think so. She diverted the money to offshore."

"True," I said. "So, she's still wanted?"

"Yeah, there is the problem of her stealing three hundred million dollars."

"She could have another reason for wanting to get away," I said. "What if she's pregnant but doesn't want the kid growing up around all the violence and controversy that surrounds the Arlington family?"

"Then she needs to call us and straighten it out," she said.

"That would certainly help," I said. "What's your next move?"

"We'll put out a warrant for her."

"No, I mean there. When will you report to work?" I asked.

"Oh that. Tomorrow I check in and then I have a week to get settled and find a condo."

"That's not long," I said.

"They're a lot of bad guys out there that need to be caught," she said.

"A woman's work is never done," I said.

"I'll talk to you in a few days," she said, "but I guess it'll be a long time before we're together again."

"Yes, I guess it will. We'll work it out if it is meant to be."

"Love you," she said.

"I love you too," I said and hung up.

It didn't feel right loving someone you know you can't see for a long time.

"Everything okay?" Diane asked.

"A big break in the Bloodshot case," I said. "They think Emanuel Barona hired Bloodshot."

I told her the rest.

"You think Kailey put that card in his pocket?" she asked.

"Yep," I said. "But I don't know if she killed him because he shot me or if she killed him first and then shot me to make it look as if he did. She knew he was dead before they even found the body."

"Do you think she would have shot you?"

"The doctor said it was perfectly placed so it wouldn't do any damage," I said. "I would like to think she wouldn't, but…"

"I hope her escapades are over now. She can't go on living like that," Diane said.

"I think they are," I said. "I can't prove it, but I think she'll just kick back now and enjoy life. I wouldn't be surprised if we didn't see her again someday and not even recognize her."

Epilogue

We spent the weekend catching up and partying. We went out bar hopping to all the places I'd been dreaming about. Jack joined us on Sunday afternoon.

"It sounds like you had an exciting spring, Cam," he said.

"It sounds like you did too," I said, looking at him and Diane.

"We behaved ourselves, Cam," he said. "Even though I would marry her in a heartbeat, I would never touch her without your consent."

"Sure," I said.

"Have you talked to Chad since you've been back?" Jack asked, changing the subject.

"Not yet, I'm trying to give him some time to miss me."

As if on cue, my cell rang.

"It's Chad," I said, looking at the caller ID.

"Hey Chad," I said, answering the phone.

"Hey, yourself. How's life in the real world?"

"I'll let you know if I ever find it."

"I've got some news that might cheer you up," he said.

"Good, I could use it," I said.

"I received a call from the FBI. They said due to the outstanding job you've done helping them, they have decided to reinstate your law license permanently."

"Really?"

"Yes, sir. Congratulations."

"That is good news. It gives me more options for a way to make a living," I said.

"There is one more thing, and it's a done deal, so don't argue," he said.

"Sounds serious," I said.

"It is," he said. "I've deposited one million dollars into your account. You've helped this family more than you know. We owe it and more to you."

"I can't take that," I said.

"Cam, I've made that much while we were having this conversation and Alexis insists. You can't fight that."

"Thank you then," I said. "I wouldn't want to get you into trouble."

"You're welcome. If you ever need more, call me."

My heart was beating so fast I thought I was going to pass out. There were so many things I wanted to say but couldn't find the words. I wondered if they would have been so generous if they knew about Kailey and me.

"Have you heard from Kailey yet?" I asked.

"Yes, this morning," he said. "She called from somewhere in Europe. She said she had to get away for a while. It just came over her, and she acted on impulse. She invested the money with another company so no one could trace her whereabouts. She also said that when the baby was born, she would return to visit."

Now my head was spinning. I never knew what to believe when it came to Kailey. Was she listening to the conversation I had with Robin?

"Well, I know that's a hard pill to swallow for Alexis," I said, "the baby being her sibling, but maybe it's for the best for Kailey right now to step away from all the past."

"I agree," he said. "Tell Diane hello and give her our love. I'll talk to you in a few days."

"Thanks again for all the great news."

"Oh, one more thing," Chad said. "Robert's deal went through."

"I hope it works out for him."

"I think it will," Chad said.

"Talk to you later."

I hung up and looked at Diane and Jack.

"You're not going to believe what all just happened."

~***~

Monday morning I was at the gym working out when Diane came in.

"I couldn't wait for you to finish," she said. "I got a call from Lower Keys Marina. They said your boat's ready."

"That's impossible."

"Yeah, that's what I thought, so I called Stacy. She said it sure looked ready to her."

"They must have put a big crew on it all weekend," I said.

"You wanna go look?" she asked.

"Sure, I guess it's worth a look."

We drove to the docks. What we saw when we arrived was not a finished boat. As a matter of fact, my boat wasn't even there. In its place, sitting in my slip and part of the next, was a new ninety-foot yacht.

363

We walked cautiously toward the boat as if it would jump up and attack us.

"It's a beauty," Stacy said as we passed her boat.

"Where did it come from?" I asked.

"A crew came this morning," she said, "and took your old boat away and parked this one there. I asked them if you moved and they said no, this boat was ordered to replace yours."

"To replace mine," I said.

"That's what they said," Stacy said. "If you don't want it, I'll take it."

"Let me check it out first," I said.

Diane and I walked to the boat. It was a beauty. Two stories plus a flybridge. It was at least twice the size of my old boat.

"This thing would cost a few million dollars," Diane said.

"Five million anyway," I said.

"Do you think Chad sent this to you?" Diane said.

"He must have, but he didn't say anything about it."

We stepped on board. The shell was a beautiful white, and the deck wood was a gorgeous teak. There was a sliding door to the cabin. I slid it open. The interior was plush. It had beautiful walnut built-ins. We took the grand tour.

The first floor had a state-of-the-art kitchen, a huge dining room and a large living room with a sixty-five-inch TV. In the rear were the master bedroom and full bath. Both were as exquisite as any custom home I had ever been in.

Another full bath and laundry room finished the first floor.

The second floor held three more bedrooms and two bathrooms. The flybridge was state of the art also with all the navigation devices.

"This is unbelievable," I said.

"I think I'll sell my house and live here with you," Diane said.

We went back to the first floor and discovered another side door off the living room. We slid it open and revealed a large hot tub. In the tub was naked Kailey.

"Hiya, Cam," she said. "This must be Diane."

Kailey stood to shake Diane's hand.

"Hello Kailey," she said. "Nice to meet you. I've heard a lot about you."

"Kailey, is this boat from you?" I asked, puzzled.

"Yeah, I told you I had a present for you."

"I don't think I can accept this," I said, confused. "I can't afford the taxes."

"Everything is taken care of, including the slip fees for the next five years. That should give you time to make a little money," she said.

"Kailey, would you mind sitting back down?" I said.

"Oh, sorry," she said and sat.

Diane said, "I'll think I'll run along and let the two of you catch up."

"Bye," Kailey said. "Will you join us for supper tonight? We have steaks in the fridge."

We? Did she say we?

"Please do," I said. "Help us break in the boat."

It was more a desperate plea than an invitation.

"Sure," she said, giggling. "I'll bring Jack. He'll *love* to see *this*."

"Toodles," Kailey said as Diane was leaving.

"Toodles," Diane said.

When she left, Kailey said, "Join me?"

"I'm afraid I don't have a suit," I said lamely.

"Really?" she said, smiling.

What the hell, I'd had a hard six months. I removed my clothes and joined her.

I slid closer to her and held her.

"Can I stay with you for a while?" Kailey asked.

"I guess for a while, but you might be in danger of getting caught."

"I don't care. It'll be worth it," she said.

"Kailey, did you shoot me?"

"Why would I shoot the man I love?"

I thought about that for a second. Why indeed?

She kissed me. This time I didn't break it off.

"Someone will be here Wednesday to go over the boat with you," she said between soft breaths.

"I'll need a crew," I said.

"Aye, aye, captain," she whispered.

"You?"

"I'll learn," she said.

"Yes, I bet you will."

She leaned in and kissed me again.

"Have you seen the master bedroom yet?" she cooed.

"Yes, I have."

"Wanna show me?"

Toodles

Please leave a review for me. As an author reviews are particularly important. They enable us to advertise our books on promotional book sites. Thanks for your help. You can leave a review at https://www.amazon.com/dp/1546900624 Then you can return to this page to get your free novella.

About Mac Fortner

Mac grew up on the Ohio River in Evansville, Indiana. He lived in the Philippines and Vietnam for two and a half years while serving his country as a helicopter crew chief.

Writing songs in his spare time, he got the idea for his first book—RUM CITY BAR. By adding suspense and humor to his songs—along with an intriguing plot—he has managed to write books you can sing along with.

Don't miss these books

IN THE SUNNY RAY SERIES

RUM CITY BAR–BOOK ONE

BATTLE FOR RUMORA–BOOK TWO

CAM DERRINGER SERIES

KNEE DEEP–BOOK 1

BLOODSHOT–BOOK 2

KEY WEST: TWO BIRDS ONE STONE–BOOK 3

MURDER FEST KEY WEST–BOOK 4

HEMINGWAY'S TREASURE–BOOK 5

SAME OLD SONG–BOOK 6

FREE NOVELLA- THE PREQUEL TO THE CAM DERRINGER SERIES

You can get it at macofortner.com

Made in the USA
Middletown, DE
16 September 2020